D0500293

# THE
# FINE ART
## OF MURDER

# THE
# FINE ART
## OF MURDER

## Anthony Quogan

St. Martin's Press
New York

To Johann Quogan
For whom there ought to be a more
fitting memorial

THE FINE ART OF MURDER. Copyright © 1988 by Anthony
Quogan. All rights reserved. Printed in the United States
of America. No part of this book may be used or
reproduced in any manner whatsoever without written
permission except in the case of brief quotations
embodied in critical articles or reviews. For information,
address St. Martin's Press, 175 Fifth Avenue, New York,
N.Y. 10010.

Library of Congress Cataloging-in-Publication Data

Quogan, Anthony.
The fine art of murder.

I. Title.
PR9199.3.Q66F56 1988     813'.54     88-11578
ISBN 0-312-02210-7

First published in Great Britain by Macmillan London
Limited.
First U.S. Edition
10 9 8 7 6 5 4 3 2 1

# Chapter One

Henrietta threw Matthew out on Christmas Eve. As in a Victorian melodrama, it was snowing heavily – and on top of that the car wouldn't start. But Bryn, his fifteen-year-old son, was sorry enough for him to help carry his bags to the nearest underground station, Belsize Park. Bryn stood frowning at him near the ticket machines.

'I don't know why you keep coming back,' he said. 'I think people who get divorced should stay divorced.'

'That's a very modern point of view,' said Matthew, blinking as some melted snow trickled from his hair into his eye. 'I suppose I keep coming back because your mother keeps taking me back.'

'After six years you should both know better.'

Matthew sighed. Bryn was wearing a leather jacket, distressed jeans, and a T-shirt that said: 'Excuse me, but I think you've mistaken me for somebody who gives a shit'. Matthew had bought it for him in Los Angeles when he had been there 'taking meetings' about a projected film version of his play *Drummer Toole*. The film was never made because they couldn't get Jeremy Irons or Mel Gibson, or even Malcolm McDowell.

'Bryn,' Matthew said finally, 'you're still young enough to believe that age brings wisdom. But in fact all you'll get as you grow older is more of what you were to begin with.'

Bryn whistled in mock amazement. 'You mean I'll keep on getting sexier?'

'Only up to the point where the law of diminishing returns kicks in.'

Bryn sniggered, though as sniggers go it was quite an attractive one.

'Anyway, old dad, where do you go from here? Sarah Heartburn or the strong arms of the law?'

Sarah Heartburn was Bryn's name for Nell Finnigan who was currently playing in *A Chaste Maid in Cheapside* at the National Theatre, and 'the strong arms of the law' referred to Dorothy Bedlington, a senior policewoman at Scotland Yard. Both of them were, intermittently, having affairs with Matthew.

'Wherever a door is opened for me and a table spread' was Matthew's answer.

It was on the tip of Bryn's tongue to say 'and a bed unmade' but he knew how far to go with his father.

They stood awkwardly for a moment, in silence, not quite able to find the right way of saying good-bye, but at last Bryn shrugged and thrust out his right hand clumsily. Matthew ignored the hand and hugged the boy instead. Matthew's eyes moistened, and Bryn sniffed valiantly then was gone with a clack of steel-capped boots into a swirl of snow. Till he was completely out of sight, Matthew gazed after him and when all he could see was the dim glow of streetlamps down Haverstock Hill, he lifted his bags and headed for the public telephones. Nell's answering machine apologised to him for not being a living, breathing person and suggested that he leave his name and number after the beep. He declined huffily, hung up and dialled Dorothy's number. His luck was better this time.

'Dorothy Bedlington speaking.'

'Dorothy, it's Matt.'

'Oh, is it?'

'Well of course it is! Look, could I drop by? I'm in a bit of a bind.'

'I have the Assistant Commissioner and his wife here. We're having dinner.'

'What about after they've gone?'

'We're all going out to a party at Hendon Police College.'

Matthew groaned. There were some seconds of silence.

'Are you all right?' Dorothy asked finally.

'No, I'm not all right. It's Christmas Eve and I'm homeless.'

'You've sold Down Hall?'

'Of course I haven't sold Down Hall. But it's in Dorset; it's hours away by train, and besides the last possible one left at 7:35.'

'What's the matter with your car?'

'It's suffering from nervous prostration. Look, can I come by?'

There was another silence on the line as Dorothy pondered.

'All right,' she said finally, 'if you can get here in twenty minutes, you can join us for coffee and dessert.'

It was actually twenty-two minutes later that he presented himself on the rubber welcome mat outside Dorothy's flat in Torrington Mansions, Bloomsbury. He was panting and dishevelled after lugging two suitcases all the way from Goodge Street station.

'Hello, Matthew,' said Dorothy, standing in the doorway looking very unpolicewomanly in a clinging jersey-wool dinner-gown in pale coral that might have been designed by Edith Head for Gene Tierney.

'Hello, darling,' said Matthew.

Dorothy's eyes grew a little icier. 'You're looking skinnier than ever,' she said, 'and what in heaven's name are you doing with those bags?'

'They're mine.'

7

'I didn't suppose you'd turned into a suitcase-snatcher; I meant why did you bring them here?'

'They contain all my worldly goods; I couldn't very well abandon them in the middle of Tottenham Court Road.'

Dorothy gritted her teeth. 'Get them into the small bedroom before the Assistant Commissioner sees them; he'll think I'm a fallen woman.'

'Aren't you?'

'I can't be. Mrs Thatcher put me on the New Year's Honours List.'

'Oh, not as a Dame of the British Empire I hope. That's almost worse than being a fallen woman.'

'Come on, dolt: get those bags hidden and get tidied up and then come and meet the others.'

Matthew took his time washing his face and straightening up his clothes. He was not eager to greet Tuppy Claverhouse and his wife, Bib, which was understandable given their last encounter. It had been during the Peter Parley murder investigation and Matthew had almost killed Tuppy — accidentally, of course. Neither the Assistant Commissioner nor his wife had forgotten the incident.

'Good evening, Mr Prior,' said Bib, as Matthew entered.

Tuppy merely grunted and glowered.

'Happy Christmas,' Matthew said. 'I haven't held up the plum pudding flaming in brandy, I hope.'

'The plum pudding flaming in brandy is a kiwi-fruit flan with whipped cream,' Dorothy answered sweetly. '*Do* have some.'

'Oh, Lord, I forgot it was the year of the kiwi fruit. What was everyone eating last year? Was it goat cheese or spinach fettucini? I can't remember.'

As soon as he had seated himself with them at the table, Matthew grinned amiably at the Assistant Commissioner who looked daggers back at him from under lowering eyebrows. The season of goodwill had clearly failed to soften his attitude. Bib, however, who was a very social creature and hated awkward silences, asked Matthew about his new play. Matthew, like many writers, hated to talk about work in progress. He had a superstitious dread that to let his creative impulse escape through the spoken word would dissipate it for ever. In such cases, he would make up something to satisfy the curiosity of his questioner. He did so on this occasion.

'Ah,' he said, 'I'm trying something new. It's a history of the world told in terms of the adventures of a theatrical troupe.'

'It sounds fascinating,' said Bib. 'Is it – experimental?'

She whispered the last world almost as if it were an obscenity. Matthew's face became a mask of seriousness, a sure sign to those who knew him well that he was about to lie outrageously.

'It's quite unlike anything I've ever done before. I'm using a Brechtian epic structure but with overtones of existential expressionism. The whole thing ends in a Beckett-like post-nuclear void.'

Bib glowed earnestly. 'Marvellous,' she said. 'I'm so glad that you're tackling something really serious. If you'll forgive me for saying so, I thought your last thing – what was it? – *Swine Fever*? – was, well, a trifle frivolous.'

He would never forgive her for saying so but he managed to conceal the fact.

'And does it have a title?' continued Bib.

Matthew's mind scrambled to find the most unlikely and nonsensical one possible. 'Hm, er, well, just a working title, you know,' he temporised. 'It's, er, *The Armageddon Excuse-Me Fox-Trot*.'

Tuppy Claverhouse snorted, and Dorothy kicked Matthew delicately under the table with the toe of her pointed court shoe. The conversation then turned to the forthcoming joys of the Hendon Police College Christmas Ball, about which Matthew had little to say.

After coffee, the ladies huddled into their fur coats and Tuppy into his double-breasted alpaca.

'I suppose you want a lift somewhere,' Tuppy said grudgingly to Matthew.

'No, I'm staying . . .' Matthew began, but caught Dorothy's furious look of denial and concluded, 'I'm staying just around the corner – with some friends.'

He then had to go through the charade of leaving with them, having the door-key pressed furtively into his hand by Dorothy, waving at the Claverhouses, and walking briskly away in the direction of Gower Street. The snow was no longer falling, but the wind was keen and the going treacherous underfoot. However, Matthew felt restored by the two large slices of kiwi-fruit flan he had eaten and the cup of hot coffee that had washed them down. He decided, therefore, not to return to the flat immediately but to head off in the direction of Fitzroy Square. There was a pub there which had once in the late sixties been almost his second home and earlier in the forties had played host to Dylan Thomas, Julian Maclaren-Ross, Gully Jimson, and other members of war-time Bohemia. It was called *The Prince of Denmark*, and its landlord, whose name – oddly enough – was Hamblett, had known Matthew since he was an undergraduate at Cambridge.

A warm feeling came over him when he saw through the gloom its etched-glass windows cheerfully lighted and artfully decorated with cotton-wool snow and cardboard cut-outs of silver bells and reindeer. He pushed open the familiar brass-handled doors and entered the saloon bar where he was immediately engulfed in the heat and noise of a crowded Christmas Eve revel. The mingled aromas

10

of beer, whisky, hot sausages, wet wool and tobacco were given an added pungency by the occasional wafts of Old Spice, old sweat, L'Air du Temps and Lifebuoy soap. Battling his way to the bar, shoulder-first, he glimpsed several vaguely familiar faces: a BBC-TV announcer, an assistant editor of the *Times Literary Supplement*, a retired musical comedy actress and a middle-aged thug who had once had his ear nailed to the floor by one of the notorious Kray brothers. More familiar than any of them was the swarthy and improbably gleeful face of his agent, Meredith Llewis ('Hchluh-wiss – not Loo-wiss').

'Good God, man, there you are! I've been trying to reach you for days, now.'

'Right,' said Matthew, 'but first things first. I need a drink.'

'You shall have one; you shall have one.'

'Horatio,' he called to the sweating Mr Hamblett behind the bar. 'Set up a double cherry brandy for my friend here – and a double whisky for myself.'

'Happy Christmas, Mr Prior,' yelled Mr Hamblett over the din. 'Good to see you again. That'll be two pounds eighty pee.'

'Well, Matthew,' said Meredith as they clinked glasses, 'caught any murderers lately?'

Matthew grinned feebly. 'What was it you wanted to see me about?' he asked.

'Oh, right . . . Before I go into that, tell me something: how is *Battersea Bridge* coming along?'

*Battersea Bridge* was the working title of the play Matthew was writing and which he had lied so unscrupulously about to Bib Claverhouse. It was about a street musician who attempts suicide by jumping into the Thames, only to find after he has been rescued that his musical talent has been mysteriously augmented with the result that he goes on to

11

fame and fortune on the international concert circuit. It was not going at all well.

'It's coming very slowly,' said Matthew.

'God save us, Matt, why don't you try a thriller – like your brother? *Cadaver* must have put him in the top tax bracket, and now *Suspect* has been running for nearly a year!'

'Being put into the top tax bracket hardly seems an incentive. Anyway I don't want to talk about Paul. Get to the point, Meredith; what were you trying to reach me for?'

Meredith smiled broadly and tapped his nose. 'An offer; and it smells like a good one.'

'The boys in Hollywood aren't re-activating the *Drummer Toole* project?'

If that were true, Matthew felt, he might really get into the Christmas spirit. But Meredith shook his head.

'Dead as a doornail – or as Dickens would have said: a coffin-nail. No, it's something quite different. You remember Roger Mold?'

Exasperated, Matthew drained his cherry brandy and called for another round. Then he turned back to Meredith.

'Meredith, will you for heaven's sake get to the point. Yes. I remember Roger Mold. We were all on the same goddamned staircase at the Hall.'

'Good days, eh, Matt? Drinking beer on the terrace overlooking the Cam . . . dodging the proctors in Senate House Passage . . .'

Matthew raised his hand. 'Stop. No more Cambridge auld lang syne. Why are you stalling? It's because it's a lousy offer, isn't it?'

Meredith put on a great show of being wounded and misjudged. 'Certainly not! A lousy offer! Would I consider a lousy offer? It's a prestigious position that's being offered you, boyo. A visiting professorship in theatre at Wacousta University.'

'Last orders,' bellowed Mr Hamblett. 'Come along, ladies and gents. Last orders, please.'

Back at Dorothy's flat, warm and woozy under Dorothy's duvet in Dorothy's bed, waiting for Dorothy to come home from the ball, Matthew considered what Meredith had told him. Their old Cambridge friend, Roger Mold, now chairman of the Theatre Department of Wacousta University in Canada, had invited him to come for the winter semester to direct one of his own plays and to teach play-writing. The university was prepared to pay him twenty thousand Canadian dollars (about ten thousand pounds) for what was no more than three months' work. It sounded very attractive. On the other hand, he had never heard of Wacousta University. He gathered from Meredith that it was of recent foundation and that its location was a small town called Mapleville some forty miles west of Toronto, Ontario. This did not sound so attractive. Matthew had been in Canada once before, to attend a production of his first play, *Flocks by Moonlight*, at the Citadel Theatre, Edmonton, and had almost died of boredom.

Besides, he wondered, what play could he direct? Roger had expressed some wish that it should be a new play, a work-in-progress; but *Battersea Bridge* was not progressing and, in any case, scarcely seemed suitable for a bunch of late-adolescent acting students with Canadian accents. If he stayed in England, though, the prospects were not enticing. He could go back to Dorset and sit and brood in Down Hall, or he could try to set up some ménage with Nell or Dorothy. The more he thought about this latter possibility the less likely it seemed: Dorothy was clearly not about to smirch the good name of Scotland Yard by openly cohabiting with anyone, and Nell was impossible to pin down, always flitting off on location, or casually going off with people after the evening performance and not coming

13

home until the milkman started rattling his crates up the street. Of course, he could stay at the Garrick for a while or check into a hotel or sublet a flat. Each one of these prospects produced in him a feeling of dull despondency; and furthermore, would he make ten thousand pounds if he stayed in London for the next three months? The answer was a regretful 'No'.

When Dorothy returned at around two in the morning, he was still awake. He watched as she removed her shoes, the jersey-wool dress, her stockings, jewellery and underwear and came towards the bed naked, an Olympian figure radiating health and strength. Soon, under the duvet, a warm and mutually satisfying conjunction was taking place.

'Happy Christmas,' said Dorothy afterwards.

'I think "Compliments of the Season" says it better. But what I'm worried about is "Happy New Year".'

Dorothy got out of bed and put on a plum-coloured velour dressing-gown.

'I'm going to make some cocoa,' she said. 'Want some?'

He got up, wrapped the duvet around his skinny naked body and followed her into the kitchen.

'The thing is,' he said, 'I seem to be in the middle of a mid-life crisis. I can't finish my play. You won't let me live with you. Henrietta can't live with me. I don't quite know which way to turn. So maybe Canada is the answer.'

'Canada?' Dorothy murmured in faint surprise.

'Yes, it's that place at the top of North America where the Eskimos and the Mounties live.'

'Nanook of the North,' said Dorothy irrelevantly.

'Her, too,' said Matthew. 'Anyway Roger Mold's there, running some kind of university theatre department. He wants me to go there and direct one of my own plays and teach play-writing.'

14

'For how long?'

'Three months. Ten thousand pounds.'

'Sounds perfect. What's holding you back?'

'It's a long time to be away from you.'

Dorothy laughed and handed him a steaming mug of cocoa. 'Here, drink up,' she said. 'And don't worry about missing me. They're sending me to Hong Kong for two months to start a new training scheme for senior officers.'

'You didn't tell me,' said Matthew with some resentment.

'I thought you were safely ensconced in Belsize Park with Henrietta. Anyway, with me gone and Henrietta being hostile, what's to stop you?'

'I haven't got anything to direct there. *Battersea Bridge* is still under construction – and in any case it just wouldn't do.'

Dorothy sipped thoughtfully at her cocoa, found it too hot and blew gently into the mug.

'Well, what about the play you were telling Bib about? She went on and on about it at the dance.'

'*The Armageddon Excuse-Me Fox-Trot*? That was a joke.'

'Still . . . it didn't sound like a bad idea. You've had worse.'

Matthew stared at her in disbelief. 'Are you serious?'

'It doesn't sound any dottier than *Hopper's Ashpit* and the *Sunday Times* loved that.'

Matthew drained his cocoa and rinsed the mug in the sink. Dorothy knew nothing about theatre, but on the other hand, he told himself, she was no fool.

'You know,' he said thoughtfully, 'you may have something there. It's a flexible enough concept to accommodate all kinds of characters. It could be an ensemble piece that wouldn't put too much of a burden on any one performer. And where better to try an experiment like that than at a

15

university nobody's ever heard of? If it's a flop, who would know?'

'Absolutely,' said Dorothy. 'Nobody will – unless you get involved in another newsworthy murder case.'

'In Mapleville, Ontario? Most unlikely, my dear.'

Dorothy ushered him out of the kitchen and switched off the light. 'That's settled then. Now you'd better get to bed or Santa won't come down the chimney.'

'You know something, Dorothy?'

'No, what?'

'Sometimes you remind me painfully of my old nanny.'

Dorothy threw off her robe and sprawled seductively on the bed.

'But only sometimes,' he amended and climbed in beside her, drawing the duvet up over both of them.

# Chapter Two

To the students returning from their winter vacation, everything seemed boringly normal on the campus of Wacousta U. The great expanse of snowy tundra, interrupted at irregular intervals with angular buildings of red brick and glass, was a kind of outward image of their collective unconscious. Nothing exciting had happened last semester; nothing exciting was likely to happen this semester. They trooped from dining-hall to lecture hall, from seminar room to library, from student pub to student residence, muffled in sweaters, windbreakers, earmuffs, scarves and gloves. The cold seeped through their boots and numbed their feet. The wind hurled itself at them around corners, stinging tears into their eyes. They sniffed and coughed their way through classes.

Even in the Faculty of Fine Arts, where colour, brio and creative zest might be expected to reign, there was a pall of greyness. In the sculpture gallery an exhibition of what looked like fungus-covered cooking-pots chilled the heart. In the dance studio, a group of neophyte dancers were lugubriously rehearsing a work based on the Dead March from *Saul*. The film students, meanwhile, were beginning an in-depth study of the work of Antonioni and, having watched a screening of *La Notte*, were drifting out of the viewing room in a trance of misery. From the music department, the sound of someone playing Stockhausen's *Piano*

*Piece IX* created an intensification of ennui that was almost unbearable.

Nor was the theatre department any livelier. The first-year students were dozing through a lecture on the structure of the Roman playhouse; the second-years were in the middle of a practical exercise in flat-building and were hammering their own thumbs and dropping hammers on their own toes; the third-years were rehearsing a scene from *The Lower Depths*, and the fourth-years were worrying about the future.

Five of them, if they could have foreseen it, had more reason to worry about the future than the others. Someone had plans for them that were far from pleasant and that someone was sitting in a room not far away working out the details and glancing up every now and then at a photograph on the wall: a group photograph of five smiling people standing in front of a wall on which part of a sign could be seen. Someone's hand reached out, unstuck the photograph from the wall, and laid it on the desk-top. The other hand reached for a pin and, after making several circling movements in the air, swooped down and jabbed the pin into one member of the group. The hand then dropped the pin and reached for a ball-point. The ball-point wrote a name on a sheet of paper and underlined it. The hand then put down the ball-point – and someone began to weep helplessly.

The wind slammed against the windows as the temperature sank to −5° Celsius.

At that very moment, Matthew Prior was clearing customs at Pearson International Airport outside Toronto. There had been a bomb threat that day and airport security was so tight that the disembarking travellers had been backed up, five deep, all the way down the stairs from passport control to the baggage pick-up area below. Matthew was tired and frazzled after the six-hour flight across the Atlantic and afflicted with heartburn from airplane food and too much free liquor. His bags, of course, were among the last to come down the chute and he had lost the battle over the one remaining luggage cart. So it was in a mood of irritation and disgust that he eventually passed through the automatic doors into the arrival lobby.

The telegram that had come the day before indicated that Roger Mold would meet his flight, but as he stood there, among noisily reunited families and warmly embracing lovers, he saw no sign of the slight, bespectacled figure of his friend. There were a number of people holding up pieces of cardboard with names amateurishly lettered on them and, among them, he finally spotted a young man with cropped dark hair and a moustache, flourishing a sign that read 'Mr Prior from London'.

'Hello, I'm Matthew Prior,' he said, approaching him.

'Oh, Mr Prior. Am I glad to see you! I thought I must have missed you.'

'Where's Roger?'

'Professor Mold is awful sorry, Mr Prior. He got called into the Dean's committee at short notice. And if you knew Dean Ripper, you'd know that's not the sort of call you can turn a deaf ear to.'

'I knew a soprano at Covent Garden like that,' said Matthew. 'Well, never mind. Maybe you can take one of these bags for me.'

The young man agreed eagerly, stuffed his cardboard sign into the nearest waste receptacle and grabbed the largest of Matthew's bags.

'I'm Calvin Knox,' he said as they set off. 'Professor Mold assigned me to you as assistant director on your play.'

Matthew paused and looked at Calvin sideways. It was a bad moment to stop moving. Someone ran into him from behind with a luggage cart and propelled him forward into

19

a large woman who was festooned with duty-free packages. She glared at him and he was forced to mutter an apology. Calvin gave her a gleaming smile and offered to relieve her of some of her burdens. Mollified, she refused and went on her way, while Matthew massaged his bruised heel and reflected that Calvin seemed to have considerable charm.

'So you're my assistant director,' he said. 'Have you done much in that line before?'

As he spoke, they were passing through the main doors of the terminal building and out into the cold Ontario afternoon. A dozen or more people were lined up, shivering, at the limousine rank.

'Sorry about this,' said Calvin. 'It would have been easier if I could have picked you up in a car – but I don't drive, unfortunately. Oh, excuse me – you asked me a question?'

'Have you done much directing?'

Calvin laughed. 'Sure,' he said. 'You ever hear of Thimble Theatre?'

Matthew confessed that he hadn't.

'No big deal, really. A kid's company. I started it when I was fifteen and we'd do stuff like *The Emperor's New Clothes* in the parks during the summer. But it did get my picture in *Time* magazine once.'

'Impressive,' said Matthew. 'What's your connection with Wacousta University?'

'I'm doing my grad work there. It's one of the few places in Canada where you can get an MFA in theatre.'

'MFA?'

'Master of Fine Arts.'

They had finally reached the front of the line and they boarded the next limousine that drew up.

'Good Lord, this is luxurious,' said Matthew as he sank into the softly cushioned back seat. 'I hope I've got enough Canadian dollars to pay for it.'

'Don't worry,' said Calvin. 'It's on the theatre department.'

The smartly uniformed East Indian driver steered them smoothly through the confusion of traffic around the terminal and soon they were speeding down a six-lane highway, through a bleak snow-covered landscape flatter than Norfolk, which was punctuated here and there with tall featureless buildings with names like the Skyport Hotel and the Empyrean Inn. The horizon seemed alarmingly distant.

'It's funny,' Matthew said. 'When I'm in England I always forget how vast this country is.'

'Second biggest in the world. In terms of land-mass, that is. This isn't your first visit then?'

'No. I've been to Edmonton.'

'Talk about vast. All those wide open spaces in Alberta. I guess you already know, then, that if you don't have a car in Canada you're in trouble.'

'It does seem to be one of life's necessities. But you got to the airport without one.'

Calvin groaned and rolled his eyes. 'I had to come by public transport. The department wouldn't pay for both ways in the limousine. It took me all of an hour and a half.'

'I think you've made your point. Where do I get a car?'

Calvin leaned forward to the driver. 'Drop us off at Budget Rent-a-Car in Mapleville, OK?'

The driver made the faintest motion of assent with his head.

'We'll get you an Aries,' said Calvin. 'It's the *Motor Trend* Compact of the Year.'

Late that afternoon, Matthew – dizzy with jetlag – finally managed to rest. In the meantime, he had picked up his rental car, driven it very nervously on what was to him the wrong side of the road all the way to the university, with Calvin navigating, allowed Calvin to escort him to his guest quarters, given Calvin a tot of duty-free Scotch before saying good-bye to him, and made a phone-call to Roger's wife, Alison, to say he had arrived. After that, weariness descended on him like a lead blanket.

It was about five o'clock when he threw his lean frame down on the narrow, unyielding bed and prepared to sleep. Immediately his mind became as active as a rat on a treadmill. Images of Henrietta, Dorothy and Nell intruded on his consciousness: Henrietta at the door of the Belsize Park house, red-eyed and furious; Dorothy languorous on a bed in Torrington Mansions; Nell raising a wine glass to him across a table at Annabel's. Some day he would have to sort it all out. At last, sleep seemed about to shroud him. Then, with an exclamation of annoyance, he sat up again and reached for his travel alarm-clock. It wouldn't be a nice long nap after all, he grumbled to himself. He had an engagement that evening.

'Come to dinner,' Alison had said. 'You won't find anything worth eating on campus.' So, at six-thirty, Matthew got into his rented Dodge Aries and set off in the gathering dusk for the Molds' house. Mapleville was a curious mixture of English Victorian suburb and American Mid-West small town. There were redbrick villas with turrets, but without the privet hedges and dripping laurel bushes that would have surrounded them in England; there were ranch-style bungalows with picture windows and pink flamingos on their lawns; there were steakhouses built to look like Gold Rush saloons, banks that looked like Georgian churches, and horrible little shopping malls that looked like nothing in the history of civilisation. Built round two sides of a parking lot, a jumble of buildings (supermarkets, hairdressing salons, Chinese restaurants, pizza parlours, laundromats and dry-cleaners) presented a striking object lesson in anti-architecture. At that time of day, though several businesses were still open, the malls were almost deserted; one of the few signs of life was a group of bored teenagers sitting in a pick-up truck outside the BiggaBurger, eating french fries and drinking Coke. Everywhere there was snow.

The Molds' house was in Glenside, a small suburb of Mapleville – though what was suburb and what was town was hard to determine in that centreless community. In the early twentieth century, Glenside had been the home of well-to-do factory owners, railway executives, insurance vice-presidents and sales directors of farm-implement companies. It had declined into a near-slum in the forties and fifties when the big draughty residences had been turned into rooming-houses for a population of students at Wacousta U. and workers at the local branch-plant of a US tire manufacturer. Beginning in the late seventies, the area had been reclaimed by the middle class, who were moving away from the uniformity of early fifties suburbia in their search for houses with character, fireplaces and high ceilings. Roger and Alison had bought a solid three-storey with lancet windows and a Regency Gothic porch, which reminded Alison of the vicarage in the North Riding of Yorkshire where she had grown up. They had done up the interior with Laura Ashley fabrics and wallpaper and re-upholstered antiques picked up at auctions. The walls were covered with Roger's collection of theatrical prints and paintings (Charles Kean as Macbeth; Master Betty as Young Norval; Fanny Kemble as Lady Teazle) and with Alison's experiments in acrylic abstractions. It was as if the Museum of Modern Art had joined forces with the Garrick Club to invade Haworth Parsonage.

Alison greeted Matthew at the door, kissed him warmly on his cold cheek, and helped him out of his overcoat.

'Galoshes go in the corner over there,' she said, pointing at a heap of rubber overshoes by the umbrella stand.

'I'm not wearing any.'

'Oh, but you must. You'll ruin your shoes in this climate if you don't. Not to mention my carpets. Take your shoes off and I'll get you a pair of Roger's slippers.'

Roger came out of the sitting-room as Matthew stood awkwardly on one leg unlacing his black Oxfords.

'There you are, old man,' he said, slapping Matthew on the back and almost precipitating him into the umbrellas.

'Here I am,' admitted Matthew, kicking his shoes out of the way. 'Good to see you again after . . . How long is it?'

'Years! The last time we were together was Sofia and Bryn's ninth birthday. We all went to see *The Rocky Horror Picture Show* at some dingy cinema in Dalston and people threw things at the screen.'

'Ah, yes. Bryn went around for weeks after that being Tim Curry. Henrietta and I were quite worried about him for a while.'

'Here: I want you to meet some people.'

Roger led Matthew into the living-room, where there was a comforting fire, roaring and crackling in the tiled Victorian fireplace.

'You've already met Calvin, of course.'

Calvin and Matthew exchanged smiles and nods.

'And this is Marie-Ange Sabatier. She'll be your stage-manager.'

Matthew shook hands with a slender, plain girl whose most striking feature was a mane of shining chestnut-brown hair.

'And these are two of our faculty members: Julia Dean who teaches movement, and Bob Pfaff who's our voice coach.'

Julia Dean was what Matthew thought of as an archetypal New England college girl. She was tall and bony with good features and expensive clothes. Bob Pfaff, on the other

24

hand, was short, fiery, and had a bristling red moustache.

'We didn't think you'd want to be plunged into a big faculty party on your first night,' said Alison, who had returned with a bowl of avocado dip, 'so we just invited a few people in for dinner.'

'You get plunged tomorrow night,' added Roger. 'That's when we're having the big official "welcome-to-Wacousta" bash with all the heavy guns and panjandrums.'

Julia Dean's handsome brow crinkled. 'Is that to be taken as meaning that neither Bob nor I are to be considered heavy guns and panjandrums?'

Roger looked alarmed. 'Oh, g-g-g-goodness, no!' he stuttered. 'But we wanted Matthew to be with nice relaxing people on his first night.'

It was Bob Pfaff's turn to look offended. Clearly he felt that to be categorised as nice and relaxing was not quite in accordance with his self-image.

'Oh, shut up, Roger,' Alison said. 'Your foot is about to become permanently lodged in your mouth. Matthew, here are your slippers.'

Feeling self-conscious, Matthew slipped his feet into a pair of brown-and-white checked slippers that had the appearance of an unsuccessful Christmas gift.

'I understand you're writing something for us,' said Julia Dean when Matthew had settled himself on the sofa. 'It'll be a thrill for the department to première a new play.'

'It won't be the first time, Julia,' Bob Pfaff protested. 'Don't you remember *The Lost Harvest*?'

'*The Lost Harvest*! How *could* I have forgotten that? All that anguish in the wheat belt – and by one of our *leading* Canadian playwrights.'

'Oh, who?' asked Matthew politely. He was uneasily aware that the ironic tone of Julia's speech had not gone down well with Bob Pfaff. Roger, however, leapt in before Julia could reply.

'A very good chap called Wilf Albertson,' he said. 'Actually, he was born on the Isle of Wight.'

'That's classic for our great Canadian literary stars,' Julia went on relentlessly. 'They're mostly from somewhere else originally – and they mostly wind up somewhere else finally. Take Brian Moore – and Malcolm Lowry. Stay here for three months, Matthew, and *you'll* be claimed as a great Canadian writer.'

Bob Pfaff's fiery little moustache seemed about to incandesce and he was just opening his mouth to answer her, when Roger hastily changed the subject.

'Marie-Ange!' he exclaimed. 'How is everything in the production wing?'

Marie-Ange brushed back some stray locks from her brow, gave Bob Pfaff a sympathetic glance, and began to talk about problems in the props shop.

'And on top of that,' offered Calvin, 'there've been more thefts lately from the costume department. Skirts, blouses, wigs . . . '

'More thefts!' said Roger. 'Well, what the devil is Ted Campbell doing about it?'

'He's changed all the locks. But that's the third time he's had to do that in the last couple of years.'

'The locks on the dressing-rooms too,' said Marie-Ange. 'Several of the girls have complained about some strange guy hanging around backstage – and money missing from their purses, even when they've been super-careful to lock the dressing-room doors behind them.'

'A lot of strange things have been happening on campus lately,' Calvin said. 'It's not just the theatre department. There was that hockey player who was kidnapped. And the photographs stolen from the art gallery.'

Bob Pfaff snorted. 'There was nothing strange about either of those incidents,' he said. 'The hockey player was kidnapped by the team from Trent because the Wacousta

26

team stole their mascot. He was only gone overnight. And the photographs were removed – not stolen – from the art gallery by the Christian Action Group because they were pornographic. Or, at least, *they* thought they were.'

'Actually, I got the impression that things have been extraordinarily dull on campus this semester,' said Julia Dean. 'The students seem to be in a positive quagmire of boredom.'

'It's always like that when the weather's bad. They all retreat into their little cosy cocoons until Reading Week. Then off they go to Florida and riot along the beaches,' Marie-Ange observed.

Roger clapped his hands together and waved exuberantly towards Matthew. 'Well, Matthew's going to wake us all up, aren't you, Matthew? Meanwhile I'll have a word with campus security and get this theft business sorted out.'

'Don't drag me into the investigation,' said Matthew. 'I handle nothing less than homicide.'

Julia Dean cocked her head questioningly.

'Matthew is not just your ordinary dramatist,' Alison explained to her. 'He's also a super-sleuth. A play-writing Poirot. A Shaftesbury Avenue Sherlock. A . . . '

'Alison, my dear,' Roger interrupted gently, 'I think I smell your *boeuf en daube* burning.'

# Chapter Three

Matthew had faced icy first-night audiences, unpleasant television hosts, and Cypriot bullets, but entering his first play-writing class at Wacousta U., he felt his palms moisten with the sweat of panic. The small windowless basement classroom contained a number of trestle tables set out in a hollow square, a dozen or so tubular steel chairs arranged around the tables, a black-board, a folding projection screen, and a No Smoking sign. The walls were painted mustard yellow and the floor was covered with mud-grey industrial carpeting, blotched with coffee stains. On the tubular steel chairs slumped a collection of dough-faced, dull-eyed late adolescents in their uniform of blue jeans and sweat-shirts. Some of them were male, some female, but at first glance they gave an impression of glum homogeneity.

'Good morning,' said Matthew bravely.

'Grrrmmmmmmm,' mumbled the class.

Matthew sat down, opened his brief-case and took out a sheaf of papers. Then, with a deep breath, he began.

'I'm Matthew Prior and I've been invited to take over this course in play-writing while I'm visiting here. As you may already know, I'm from England. I've had a few of my plays done in the theatre over there – as well as on television. I'm directing my new play while I'm here, as a project for the fourth-year performance students. Now you know something about me, and I'd like to know something about you – so as I read your name from the class-list perhaps you'd identify yourself and tell us all something about your background and what makes you want to write plays.'

The doughiness immediately metamorphosed into defensiveness and Matthew hastily continued.

'Alithea Birnbaum. Which one is Alithea?'

'It's Trudy. Trudy Birnbaum,' said a dark-haired girl with heavily outlined eyes. 'I go by my middle name. I've told them over and over again at Student Records to put A. Trudy on the list and not Alithea T.'

'Sorry, er, Trudy. Tell me something about yourself.'

'Like what?'

'Well, where do you come from? What plays do you like? What do you want to write about?'

'I come from right here in Mapleville. I like rock musicals. And I haven't really done much writing up to now – except for essays and junk like that.'

'I see,' said Matthew desperately, 'and how about Walter Dunn? Where's Walter?'

'Walt,' said an angular, pale-haired boy with constantly blinking eyes.

'Well, Walt,' Matthew sighed, 'tell me about you.'

As he went down the list, the students began to emerge as individuals. They were by no means as dull, recalcitrant and indistinguishable as Matthew had, in that first panicky moment, assumed. There was a light-skinned black girl called Meriel Kitt, who was sly and witty, a freckled Huck Finn-ish boy called Ken Meldrum, who was bright and excitable, a quiet thoughtful Latin called Tiberio Turchino, and a pretty blonde with a spiky punk hair-do, whose name was Celia Isaacs. When the session was well under way, after he had covered some of the general principles of dramaturgy and told some anecdotes about well-known theatrical personalities, Matthew realised that

29

he was beginning to enjoy himself, and that the students had loosened up and were actually laughing at some of his jokes. This isn't so bad, he thought; not much worse than being interviewed on television, really.

After the class was over, Ken, the freckled boy, caught up with him in the corridor. 'I enjoyed that,' he said, almost dancing along beside Matthew. 'I want to get on to that first assignment right away. Can it be about anything?'

'Anything you think will make dramatic sense,' Matthew answered, and then, feeling that this was not explicit enough, 'Try to imagine an audience watching and listening. What would interest them about the situation you're dealing with?'

The boy nodded, grinned and danced away, yelling 'Thanks, prof!' over his shoulder as he disappeared.

Matthew was still riding on a wave of good humour when he met the fourth-year performance students that afternoon. Had he seen them first, he would have been overwhelmed with depression at the idea of having to mould fourteen sceptical and sullen young adults into a successful acting ensemble. Fortunately the morning session had convinced him that resistance was the normal first response of students at Wacousta to someone or something unfamiliar; though, God knows, an actor without a free, flexible and open attitude to experience was unlikely to make much headway in the profession.

He began as he had before by introducing himself and then asking them for their names and some background information about themselves. That out of the way, he started to tell them something about the play.

'The working title is *The Armageddon Excuse-Me Fox-Trot*, and what it tries to do is to parallel the history of the theatre with the history of the world from the creation to the day of judgement. There are fourteen characters: seven men and seven women. They are members of a theatrical troupe – and between them they portray all the stock characters to be found in drama: the old man, the young hero, the hero's friend, the villain, the villain's henchman, the low comedy man and the utility man who plays all the messengers and extra roles; then there are the matron, the heroine, the heroine's confidante, the villainess, the maid, the character-comedy woman, and the utility woman. The concept behind it is the struggle between the hero and the villain on stage and between good and evil in the world. Your actor-characters will each play a variety of rôles both from world drama and from world history: Thespis, Everyman, Lady Macbeth, Queen Elizabeth I, Abraham Lincoln, Eva Peron, etc. etc. . . .'

He paused and looked round at their so-far-unyielding faces.

'Can I ask a question?' a small handsome boy said, idly plucking at the single dangling earring that hung from the lobe of his right ear.

'Certainly.'

'Are there any Canadian characters in this play?'

Dear Lord, thought Matthew, I'd forgotten: Roger warned me about this touchy nationalism I'd run into.

Aloud, he answered: 'Well, no – I'm ashamed to say that I'm fairly ignorant about Canada. Apart from Robert W. Service, Lester Pearson, Mordecai Richler and Pierre and Margaret Trudeau – oh, and, of course, Stephen Leacock – I'm not very up on celebrated Canadians.'

A look of grim and triumphant confirmation spread across the faces of the assembled students. The boy with the earring gave a faint sigh and closed his eyes.

'But,' said Matthew determinedly, 'remember, it's a work in progress and I'd welcome any suggestions as to who you think might be included. Let's be realistic, though. The play is dealing with archetypal figures, and

31

instantly recognisable historical and theatrical characters. Queen Elizabeth and Oedipus will be familiar to most audiences both here in Canada and anywhere else the play might be done. Can you think of any Canadian characters who would have that kind of recognition internationally?'

There was a moment's silence, and then a mousy-looking girl with beautiful brown eyes broke it.

'Rose Marie,' she said.

Suddenly, the wall of resistance crumbled, shaken by some internal fission.

'Anne of Green Gables,' someone else yelled over an avalanche of laughter.

'Anne Murray,' shrieked another.

'Wayne Gretzky.'

'Dan Aykroyd.'

'Billy Bishop.'

'Mary Pickford.'

'Laura Secord.'

'Honest Ed.'

Gradually they subsided but obviously some kind of catharsis had been achieved. Slightly bewildered, Matthew grinned at them and, not being able to think of anything to say, asked his stage-manager, Marie-Ange, to hand out copies of the script. The first read-through then proceeded with only an occasional interruption, and the cast seemed absorbed in the text. Matthew began to feel that perhaps his task would not be quite as burdensome as he had feared, but several times, glancing up at the faces before him, he caught the boy with the earring eyeing him with faint derision.

'How did the first day go?'

Matthew was standing in Roger and Alison's sitting-room, feeling desperately in need of a drink.

'Anxiously,' said Matthew, 'but I think I'll get on top of it.'

'Oh, they're not a bad bunch once you get used to them. What'll you have to drink?'

'How about a Suze?'

'A what?' Roger squeaked.

'The favourite drink of French commercial travellers, an alcoholic distillation of gentian roots. I love it with a dash of yellow chartreuse and lots of ice.'

Roger raised his eyebrows. 'The Liquor Control Board of Ontario isn't likely to stock that – at least not in Mapleville.'

'Oh, well – Pernod and water, then.'

Roger sighed. 'There's scotch, vodka, rye, gin, white wine and beer . . . Oh, yes – and I think we have a drain or two of rather sweet sherry.'

'That'll be perfect – I have a very sweet tooth. It's not South African, is it?'

'Canadian.'

'Hmm – at least it's politically inoffensive. I'll try some.'

Roger went off to find the sherry and Alison ushered two newcomers into the sitting-room.

'Matthew, I'd like you to meet Ted and Vera Campbell. Ted's the technical whiz in the theatre department and Vera designs costumes. They're looking forward to working on your show.'

Looking at the three of them, Matthew thought again how much like a marmoset Alison looked. Ted and Vera on the other hand were brown bears – Papa Bear and Mama Bear. Ted enveloped Matthew's hand in his big, furry paw and Vera beamed like a grizzly about to attack.

'We saw *Swine Fever* in London last summer,' she said. 'Wonderful show. Pity the designer used all those ugly mauves and greys.'

33

'Yes,' agreed Ted, tugging at his beard. 'It was a first-rate piece of writing. Mind you, I wouldn't have liked to be the technical director. He must have gone out of his mind with so many blackouts and cross-fades.'

Matthew responded with all the grace he could muster. By that time more people were arriving and a large sherry had been thrust into his hand. Alison then led him away from the Campbells and began to introduce him to some of the other guests. They were mostly faculty members from the theatre department but the Dean of Fine Arts was there, as were the chairman of the dance department, two or three English professors and their wives and a handful of non-academics, the most prominent of whom was a youthful-looking middle-aged man in a dinner-jacket and kilt. His name, Matthew gathered, was Fraser McCullough, and Roger later whispered to him that Fraser was 'an indefatigable patron of the arts and a very big noise on Bay Street', adding, when Matthew looked blank, that Bay Street was Toronto's equivalent of Wall Street. In other words, he was rich, influential and worth cultivating, as Matthew could have surmised from the fact that the Dean and the chairman of the dance department were performing an obsequious pas de deux around him in the clear hope of raising funds for some essential improvement to the dance studios.

Eventually as more guests arrived and the room became crowded, Matthew and Fraser McCullough found themselves squeezed together in a corner.

'So you're Matthew Prior,' said Fraser, arching his fine sandy eyebrows. 'I was very impressed with *The Harmonious Blacksmith*. So impressed that I invested in the Broadway production. Very heavily. Lost every cent.'

Matthew mumbled some expression of regret to the eyebrows.

'Don't worry. I won't lose in the long run, you know. Tax lawyers are clever about that sort of thing. Anyway it wasn't your fault; it was that damned John Simon. Poisonous critic. He should be boiled in his own ink – like a squid.'

'John's hated me ever since prep school,' said Matthew. 'I put a dead frog in his pyjamas.'

McCullough frowned. 'Really? I thought he grew up in Yugoslavia? And surely he's a good twenty years older than you?'

'Ah,' said Matthew, improvising furiously. 'He did – and he is. But he spent a term teaching at my prep school in England after he graduated from Harvard.'

'Hmm,' said Fraser dubiously. 'Anyway, good luck with the new show. How's it going so far?'

'Hard to say, really. We've just had the first read-through.'

McCullough arched his eyebrows at Matthew again as he began to turn away. 'Well, ride them hard. Canadian actors need fire-crackers up their backsides to get them going. Too much goddam restraint.' The eyebrows returned to their normal position and he was gone. Matthew exhaled and looked frantically around for another sherry. Fortunately, Roger was now at hand with the bottle.

'McCullough chatting you up?'

'Drowning me in his personality.'

'He's on the Board of Governors of the University. Not a bad chap, though. Had a sad domestic life.'

'Oh?'

'Yes. He lost his daughter, and his wife and son left him and moved away to Winnipeg.'

'One of those lonely tycoons?'

'In a way – though he seems to find compensations. Look over there.'

Matthew turned his head in the direction Roger had indicated and saw Fraser McCullough doing his eyebrow routine for the benefit of a slight young woman in a pale green dress.

35

'She's pretty,' he said.

Roger nodded. 'Bonny Dundee.'

'Eh?'

'That's her name. Well, actually her name's Flora, but everyone calls her Bonny.'

'For obvious reasons. Tell me, Roger, does everyone around here have a Scottish name?'

'There are a lot of them, aren't there? Also for obvious reasons. The whole area was originally settled by Scottish Presbyterians.'

'Good God. No wonder you can't find Suze in the liquor stores. What does Miss Dundee do?'

'She's my new executive assistant. Very capable. She started working for me at the beginning of this academic year.'

'So I'll be seeing more of her?'

'She has a very busy schedule,' said Roger firmly. 'And by the way – How is Henrietta? And Dorothy? And Nell?'

'Unsubtle, Roger,' Matthew sighed. 'Very unsubtle.'

The party grew noisier as the night progressed. Large lethal martinis, towering highballs, and cases of Miller Light and Molson Golden flowed down scholarly throats. Matthew switched recklessly from sherry to screwdrivers, and devoured half a tableful of canapés to balance out his alcoholic intake. Alison appeared at his shoulder with more loaded platters to replace the ones he had denuded.

'Really, Matthew,' she said, 'you still eat the way you did at Cambridge. But you're not a growing boy now. How you stay so thin beats me.'

'It's my metabolism, love. It's on overdrive all the time.'

'Lucky you. You'll need overdrive to get that play on. What did you think of your actors?'

'Well, there's a mousy little girl called Ursula who seems to have real talent.'

36

'Ursula Hooper.'

'Yes, that's right. Some of them seem a bit resistant, though. One in particular – a good-looking boy who wears an earring. Can't think of his name.'

Alison wrinkled her brow. 'A smallish young man?' she said. 'With light brown hair that flops over his forehead?'

'That sounds right.'

Alison popped a sardine canapé into her bright marmoset face. 'It's probably Cubby.'

'Cubby?'

'Cuthbert Kirkwood. Canada's future Al Pacino-cum-Jerzy Grotowski-cum-Harold Pinter-cum-cum-cum . . . The boy has a very inflated ego, but it's probably over-compensation for the fact that he lives in the shadow of a very famous father.'

'Poor little sod. Who's his father?'

'Hugh Kirkwood. He's a cabinet minister in the provincial government. Minister of Research and Technology – or something like that. Much touted as a future leader of his party.'

'Cabinet ministers' sons! We've suffered from them before, haven't we, Alison dear? Do you remember Whiffer Lucas-Croft at Magdalene?'

Alison giggled. 'Awful!' she said. 'Don't dare mention his name in front of Roger!'

And with a little conspiratorial wink, Alison disappeared into the crowd.

Matthew thoughtfully ate the rest of the canapés, wondering whether Cubby Kirkwood might not prove to be as much of a nuisance as Whiffer Lucas-Croft had been in that long-ago golden Michaelmas Term at Cambridge.

37

# Chapter Four

The Charles Heavysege Theatre at Wacousta University had been built in the sixties at a time when the enthusiasm for thrust stages and audience involvement was at its height. Veteran faculty members still remembered the days when naked students of both sexes had sought to break the barriers between the artificial world of the stage and the real world of the spectator by leaping off the platform and charging up the aisles with a great jiggling and bouncing of unfettered flesh. Though they looked back on those days with a kind of indulgent censure, the fact was that they were now stuck with a theatre space that did not lend itself easily to more conventional types of presentation. Fortunately for Matthew, it was ideally adapted to the free-wheeling, non-realistic structure of *The Armageddon Excuse-Me Fox-Trot*.

That afternoon, he was rehearsing the opening of the play. It began in the orchestra pit with a Dionysian chorus of the entire cast, out of which at the climax of noise and movement was to step Thespis, the first actor of the Greek theatre, played by Cubby Kirkwood. He was to be followed up onto the stage by the other members of the cast in their various characters: the old man, the matron, the hero's friend, the confidante, the villain and so on. As they mounted the platform, they were supposed to recite, each taking a fragment of the text, the first lines of Peter Brook's *The Empty Space*: 'I can take any empty space and call it a bare stage. A man walks across this empty space whilst someone else is watching him, and this is all that is needed for an act of theatre to be engaged.' At the end of this, Thespis was to climb onto his vine-bedecked cart and be dragged into the wings by the cheering revellers.

At first things went badly.

'Just do it,' Matthew said, 'and we'll worry about polishing it up later.'

He sat down in the front row of the auditorium with Calvin and Marie-Ange. In front of them was a wooden table which held a small desk-light, the director's prompt-book, the stage-manager's script, an ashtray and a collection of freshly sharpened pencils.

'From the top!' Calvin yelled.

Falteringly, the cast began the Dionysian chant, moving in an uncertain circle around the orchestra pit. They were hampered by their scripts and unsure of their choreography, but gradually the volume of the chant rose and the circle began to revolve faster and faster. Then with insolent agility, Cubby leapt up onto the stage, the working-lights overhead catching the glitter of his one dangling earring.

'I can take *any* empty space . . .' he announced, advancing to centre stage and spreading his arms wide.

There was a slight titter from several members of the cast and Calvin stirred uncomfortably at Matthew's side. The tittering died down as portly Wayne Goffman, the old man, lumbered up from the orchestra pit.

'. . . and call it a bare stage,' he recited as he crossed to Cubby's left.

'A man walks . . .' fluted Lulie Burns, the matron, moving with the exaggerated dignity of Margaret Dumont trying to ignore Groucho Marx.

'. . . across this empty space . . .' continued Joe Innocenti, the hero's friend, grinning at Cubby.

Gradually, the stage filled with actors, taking up positions in a half-circle around the leading man. When they were all assembled, Cubby moved downstage centre and began to repeat the whole speech to a hummed accompaniment from the rest of the cast. Going down on one knee, like Al Jolson singing 'Mammy', with one hand on his heart and the other which held the script extended towards the audience, he declaimed his lines. The cast's humming became ragged and several of the actors were clearly trying to stifle their laughter. It was only then that Matthew realised what was happening. He was being treated to a deadly accurate, though he thought uncharitably exaggerated, mimicry of his own vocal mannerisms. 'Dear Lord,' he thought, 'it's beginning. If I don't control this now, the whole thing will degenerate into a "get-the-director" session. How would Nell handle it, I wonder?'

The invocation of Nell Finnigan was a customary one for Matthew in moments of crisis in the theatre. Their relationship was intense, though sporadic, but his closeness to her didn't prevent him from having an objective sense of her mastery of the skills of acting and directing that had made her one of the leading new talents of the English stage. She was known to directors as a co-operative performer and to actors as a receptive and empathetic director, but she also dealt cleverly with fools and time-wasters. Gazing at the performers as they continued their scene, he called up a vision of Nell. She appeared, leaning over the table in a jade-green parachute suit and a matching jockey cap. 'What would you do, Nell?' he implored her, silently. 'Congratulate the little bugger,' she replied and briskly disappeared. Marvelling at her shrewdness, he interrupted the rehearsal.

'All right,' he yelled. 'Hold it, everybody!'

The scene stopped and the cast looked at him with wary

curiosity. Cubby Kirkwood broke his Jolson pose and, with an elaborate yawn, reclined on the floor.

'We have just witnessed a breakthrough,' Matthew said. 'Mr Kirkwood has found a way of enriching this scene which lifts it above a simple recital of the lines. He has put his finger, in fact, on exactly what the scene calls for.'

He paused, and noticed that not only had Cubby stopped yawning but that he and several other members of the cast were looking baffled.

'What does the scene call for?' Matthew went on, beginning to enjoy himself. 'Any suggestions?'

Ursula Hooper, the mousy girl with the beautiful brown eyes who had already impressed Matthew with her talent, promptly offered one. 'Funny voices?'

The tittering which threatened to break out again died away in the face of Matthew's obvious cheerfulness.

'That might be one thing,' he agreed. 'What the scene needs is everything. It needs to be a demonstration of all the resources of the performer. Cubby used one – mimicry – and I must say he's remarkably good at it. The best version of me I've heard since I was on a TV Quiz with Rich Little. It's probably a little esoteric for the average audience, however.'

Matthew turned his attention directly to Cubby. 'What you might try for Thespis, Mr Kirkwood, is a real ripe actor-ish voice – Sir Ralph Richardson, say, or – well – who, for instance, would be familiar to a Canadian audience?'

Reluctantly Cubby was allowing himself to become intrigued by the idea. 'Well, there's Douglas Campbell – or – or Tony van Bridge . . .' he said hesitantly, then snapping his fingers: 'No, I've got it! John Houseman. Everybody knows him from those Smith Barney commercials on TV. You know—'

41

And becoming John Houseman, Cubby proclaimed with a magisterial sneer: 'They make money the old-fashioned way – they *earn* it!'

'Hey, that's great, Cubby!' said Joe Innocenti.

The whole cast, by now, was lighting up as actors do when playable ideas start emerging, and Matthew began rapidly to pile more fuel on the small fire he had lit.

'Right – but as I said the scene needs everything. It has to be like a circus of performance. You can enter doing cartwheels; you can sing your line; you can do a soft-shoe; you can give us melodrama or the Method; you can be Pavarotti or Baryshnikov; you can do vaudeville shtick or commedia dell'arte *lazzi*. What we need is a carnival atmosphere that builds to a climax when you drag Thespis triumphantly off on his cart. Try anything you like now and we'll refine it as we go along.'

The atmosphere was crackling with energy as the cast began the show again from the top. Matthew breathed a small sigh of relief, Marie-Ange smiled at him and Calvin patted his arm.

'Way to go, *mon capitaine!*' he murmured.

'*Toujours l'audace,*' replied Matthew.

Matthew was the first to leave after the rehearsal. The performers went back to the dressing-rooms and the technicians took over the stage. Marie-Ange began an earnest discussion with the technical director about the absolute necessity of having certain props ready for the next rehearsal, and several members of the stage crew wandered around looking vaguely up at the fly gallery and the lighting grid. Calvin hung around for a few minutes and then, waving good-bye to Marie-Ange, headed backstage towards the men's dressing-room.

Inside, in the steamy mêlée, the actors clad in white

towels or nothing at all wandered in and out of the shower-room, sat before the mirrors combing their hair, or hopped about on one leg trying to put on their trousers. Calvin stood impassively in the doorway.

'What's this? Voyeurism?' said Joe Innocenti as he emerged dripping from the shower room.

'Where's Cubby?' Calvin asked.

'In the shower. Why?'

'Tell him I want to see him in the coffee shop.'

'What for? A slap on the wrist from the director – by proxy?'

'Just tell him I want to see him.'

Joe Innocenti dropped his towel, turned and thrust his bare buttocks towards Calvin.

'Why don't you just kiss my ass?' he demanded.

Calvin glowered, but made no response. The dressing-room was silent. Finally Calvin walked out. As the other actors hooted and applauded, Cubby came out of the shower room, his skin glowing pink as he briskly towelled himself.

'What's the big joke?' he said.

Rezi Yanouf snorted and pointed at Joe.

'Innocenti's ass.'

'Oh,' said Cubby, 'I would have said it was vulgar without being funny.'

'He showed it to Cal and told him to kiss it.'

Cubby threw his towel into a corner and began to climb into his underpants.

'Kiss it?' he said. 'I may lose my lunch. And what exactly brought all this on?'

The other actors became uneasy. Cubby wasn't laughing. His tone in fact was distinctly cool. Joe's face contorted in sudden Sicilian fury.

'He came in here throwing his fucking weight about; that's what fucking brought it on!'

43

Cubby walked calmly over to Joe, grabbed him by his dark curly hair and twisted it viciously.

'As the assistant director he has every right to come into the dressing-room. Now what the hell did he want!'

Tears of pain and rage were running down Joe's face. 'Fuck you! Fuck you!' he screamed.

Wayne Goffman, horrified out of his usual plump amiability, yelled: 'Cut it out, you guys! Cal wanted to see you in the coffee shop, Cubby – that's all!'

Cubby released Joe and smiled at Wayne. 'Thank you, Mr. G. All I wanted was a simple answer to a simple question.'

For a moment it looked as if Joe might hit Cubby, but two or three of the others interposed themselves and Wayne whispered something in Joe's ear. The tension in Joe slackened. 'Oh, what the shit . . .' he said dully, turning away from them. Cubby, with a marked air of indifference, continued to dress. He was still dressing when the others left.

Ursula Hooper was the last one in the women's dressing-room. She and Lulie Burns had been arguing about whether Glenda Jackson or Jane Fonda gave the better performance as Nora in *A Doll's House*. Lulie had continued dressing throughout the argument, but Ursula's phenomenal ability to concentrate single-mindedly on one activity at a time had the effect of leaving her standing in her underwear waving one shoe emphatically at Lulie's retreating back as she had the final and definitive word on the subject.

'Oh, hell,' she thought, looking at her watch in the empty dressing-room, 'I'll really have to hurry now if I'm going to meet Rezi before the movie starts.'

Rezi had invited her to an on-campus showing of Fassbinder's *Fox and his Friends*, and though Rezi wasn't an ideal date, being inclined towards aggressive groping, she really wanted to see the movie and she hated to go to a show on her own.

Hastily she pulled on her Arran sweater and her Gloria Vanderbilt jeans, ran a comb quickly through her mousy hair and bundled herself into the raccoon-skin jacket she had bought second-hand at the Bisbis Boutique on Queen St West. As she fastened the jacket, she heard a sound behind her. Thinking it was Lulie coming back to pick up something she had forgotten, she turned to speak, but her voice died in her throat. Confronting her, she saw a naked male figure, his face concealed by a ski-mask. She screamed and, snatching up her nail-file from the dressing-room counter, launched herself at him. This swift reaction was clearly not expected and the figure reeled back. Ursula, fleeing for the door, raked his chest and arm with the point of her nail-file, drawing a neat line of blood across the pale flesh. Then she was out in the corridor, shrieking for help, running blindly towards the stage-door. Suddenly arms closed around her and her heart quailed.

'What's this, Ursie? Rehearsing for *Friday the Thirteenth: Part Nine*?'

It was Cubby's voice. Ursula fell against him, feeling the comforting texture of his overcoat against her cheek. She trembled and gasped in his arms for a moment and then blurted out what she had seen in the dressing-room. Whatever might be said against Cubby, he was – for a relatively slightly built man – courageous. He went straight back to the women's dressing-room with Ursula and coolly flung the door open. There was no one there. He peered into the shower room. It too was empty, but as he stood there looking round at the damp tiles and the steam-dulled chrome, he heard an exclamation from the other room. Turning back, he saw Ursula examining something she had picked up off the floor. Silently she held it out to him. It

45

was a scrap of photographic print. He took it and held it to the light. It showed a girl's face against an indeterminate background.

'It's me, Cubby,' wailed Ursula. 'It's *me*!'

# Chapter Five

The second time Matthew saw Bonny Dundee – in her office next to Roger's – he became convinced that she was someone worth cultivating. She wasn't warmly domestic like his ex-wife, Henrietta; she wasn't briskly efficient like Dorothy; she wasn't vividly eccentric like Nell. She seemed rather to be a compound of contradictions: gently stern, quietly assertive, yieldingly firm. Her face fascinated him with its pointed chin, high cheek-bones and almost Oriental eyes, and her mouth – well, on anyone else it might have been ugly: the lips too full, the front teeth a little too prominent, but on Bonny it seemed the final masterly touch that confirmed her startling prettiness.

'You know, you don't look Scottish at all,' he said to her the day after his first successful rehearsal.

'What a silly thing to say,' she replied unemphatically. 'What am I supposed to look like? Red-haired and raw-boned, I suppose – with freckles all over my nose.'

'Something like that. Certainly not like a golden-haired Leslie Caron.'

'My, my! That dates you. I saw Leslie Caron in *Gigi* when I was six.'

'And that dates you – I saw *Gigi* when I was sixteen, so that puts you on the shady side of thirty.'

'An outrageous assumption,' she said, bridling exaggeratedly. 'I might have seen a revival.'

'Did you?'

47

'No – and yes, I am over thirty. And I'll answer your next question too. I *am* unmarried.'

'And proud of it,' said Matthew.

She gave him a straight, unsmiling look. 'Is this a professional visit? I mean, are you studying me because you think I'd make an interesting character in a play?'

'Absolutely not. I'm not saying you wouldn't, mind you,' he added quickly. 'But I had something more personal in mind. Such as, would you have dinner with me tonight?'

'Where?'

Matthew hadn't expected such rapid capitulation and, not knowing the local restaurants, was momentarily nonplussed.

'Where's good?' he said finally.

'Mirabeau's in Toronto. It's shockingly expensive and I only go there if someone else is paying.'

Matthew accepted that bravely.

'Mirabeau's it is. I'll pick you up at six-thirty. Where do you live?'

Moments later, Matthew was on his way to his playwriting class distinctly elated. The windowless classroom lowered his mood somewhat, but the students – to his relief – were not sitting dough-faced and sullen around the table as they had been at the beginning of his first class. Instead there was a sense of eagerness as they shuffled their manuscripts on the table. Meriel Kitt, the black girl, smiled at him; Ken Meldrum was all doggy enthusiasm, eyes bright and ears cocked; even the petulant Alithea Trudy Birnbaum seemed to have caught some of the fervour.

Matthew made some introductory remarks about not regarding the outline of a play as a strait-jacket but rather as a flexible body-brace that would allow freedom of movement while giving support. Some of them, like the jury in *Alice in Wonderland*, were scribbling down every word he said: others merely nodded agreeably.

'Well, let's get started,' he said when he had run out of apothegms and aphorisms. 'Who wants to go first?'

Trudy Birnbaum's hand clawed for the ceiling.

'Fine, Trudy – go ahead.'

Smirking with self-satisfaction, she began to read:

'A synopsis of the drama, *Triumphal March* by A. Trudy Birnbaum . . .'

Fidgeting more and more as she proceeded, the class attended while Trudy unfolded the tale of a talented, attractive girl from a well-to-do Jewish family who is constantly thwarted in her attempts to 'find herself' by her socially active mother, her business-obsessed father, and her revolting younger brother. Severing all ties with her family, she leaves for New York where she becomes a dazzling success as a performer in musicals and returns years later with her choreographer boyfriend to forgive her much-humbled relatives.

Matthew desperately tried to find some merit in it, but since none was obvious he turned to the class:

'Comments, anyone?' he said.

There was a strained silence, broken at last by the Italian boy, Tiberio.

'The leading character,' he said, 'she sounds like kind of a pain. All she cares about is what *she* wants. Maybe her father hates what *he's* doing, but he's doing it for the family. Maybe her mother had ambitions for a career too, and got stuck being a wife and bringing up children. Maybe her younger brother has problems – no friends, doing badly at school, whatever . . . All we get from you is how rotten they are.'

'I think Tiberio has a point,' said Matthew. 'You've made the mistake of weighing the scales too heavily in favour of your heroine. The audience is going to feel it's being manipulated. Now, if you showed her *trying* to understand the other characters' points of view, and gave them some more positive qualities, it would be a fairer contest.'

The comments then began to come thick and fast. Far from dismissing Trudy's plot as a piece of scandalously transparent wish-fulfilment, the other students made some shrewd and useful suggestions, based for the most part on their own real experience of family conflict. Trudy, who was inclined at first to be huffy, gradually became interested in what the others were saying, and even agreed in the end that her characters needed to be fleshed out.

Next Walt Dunn offered a grim fable of incest and suicide on an Ontario farm, Meriel outlined a children's play based on a Jamaican folk-tale, and Celia, the girl with the punk hairstyle (which had now changed from blonde to dark burgundy), entertained them with a farce about a small-town girl's misadventures in the world of big-city rock clubs. In many of the synopses, the sense of the dramatic seemed to derive from television sitcoms, action shows and soap operas. What Matthew found more surprising, however, was that for theatre students they had remarkably little grasp of the practicalities of theatre. On the whole, though, he was not utterly dismayed by their first exercises in plotting.

Ken Meldrum was the next one up. He seemed to be almost panting with excitement as he began to read. 'If he had a tail,' thought Matthew, 'it would be wagging.'

'I guess this is a sort of update of *Twelfth Night*,' said Ken, 'but it's set in the future. I have these twins – a brother and a sister – who're escaping from a totalitarian government. The girl dresses up in boy's clothes, borrowed from her brother, so that they can join a refugee convoy out of the country. The convoy gets attacked and they get separated. She's convinced that her brother is dead but she makes it across the border into neutral territory – a place called Illyria. She meets the rich heiress of a chocolate fortune, who takes pity on her and gives her a job as her private hairdresser. She thinks the girl is a guy, of course – kind of faggotty, but so what – she figures most hairdressers are. Anyway, the heiress has this boyfriend – a big-time banker – who meets the hairdresser and thinks he's going gay because he falls in love with him – er – her.'

'You're going to get all tangled up in your pronouns,' Matthew broke in. 'Why not call the girl "A" and her brother "B"?'

Ken grinned gratefully at him.

'Yeah – OK – thanks. Anyway, they're all on this big Hollywood-type estate in Illyria with, like, an Olympic-size swimming pool and everything. The heiress has a male secretary – a real creep – called Sowerby. Sowerby's really a secret agent for the totalitarian regime that A's escaped from and he gets suspicious of A. But there are these other guys in the house – the heiress's uncle, a big fat guy, and his friend, a goofy Englishman, and the heiress's protégé, a young stand-up comedian – and they're all counter-intelligence agents. They trick Sowerby into revealing himself and lock him up in the heiress's private aviary where he gets all covered in bird-shit. Meanwhile B turns up and they suspect him of being a totalitarian spy too, and they're about to lock him up in the aviary too when A turns up and tells them that B is her brother and that she is really a girl. This is a great relief to the banker who, of course, proposes to her – and the heiress hitches up with B – and they all live happily ever after. Except Sowerby. He gets deported back to the totalitarian country and they shoot him for incompetence.'

Ken subsided breathless in his chair and there was a moment's silence. Then Matthew said:

'Ingenious – but to what end?'

Then, seeing that Ken looked downcast, he hastened to qualify what he had said. 'You know, Shakespeare's play isn't just a farce about disguise and impersonation; it's also very much about the folly of choosing inappropriate love objects and of being in love with love or in love with self. Orsino is just as ludicrous as Malvolio in that respect. It's also a comedy with a dark side – the darkness of a joke that goes too far. By making Sowerby a total villain you lose the pathos and discomfort that Shakespeare creates through the character of Malvolio – a dignified man who becomes a fool and eventually a desperate and almost frightening figure: the only one who isn't included in the final harmonious resolution and the one who lingers in the mind to cast doubt on that apparent final harmony.'

'It's the same problem as Trudy's,' interjected Celia. 'You just haven't looked at Sowerby from enough different angles.'

'Anyway you can't get away with that girl-pretending-to-be-a-boy stuff nowadays,' Trudy said sniffily. 'Look how awful Julie Andrews was in *Victor Victoria*.'

The class broke into a wrangle at this point in which the performances of Dustin Hoffman in *Tootsie* and Linda Hunt in *The Year of Living Dangerously* were invoked. Matthew finally brought it to a halt by glancing at his watch and informing them that they had ten minutes to get to their next class.

At about three-thirty that afternoon, Bob Pfaff was in the voice studio exhorting his students to open up the resonators in their craniums when the alarm bell sounded. At first they ignored it, thinking that some prankster had set it off. The clamour went on so long, however, that Bob's never very even temper reached critical mass and exploded. He dashed to the studio door, wrenched it open, and bellowed at the top of his excellently developed lungs: 'What the fuck is going on?' In the process, he inhaled a noseful of noxious fumes and began to splutter and weep stinging tears. Ted Campbell came reeling down the corridor at that point, wagging his great beard and gasping:'Clear the building!' With streaming eyes, Bob dashed back into the studio and, deprived of speech, was forced to communicate with his students in mime, never one of his strengths. Eventually, as the tear-gas began to seep in through the door, they grasped his meaning and stampeded for the exit. By this time, the corridor was full of choking, weeping, screaming students, as well as frantic faculty members and panicky secretaries.

They fled down staircases and battled their way through emergency exits, and in a few minutes the Fine Arts Building was cleared. Passers-by on campus were alarmed to see a great eruption of hysterical and breathless people from the main entrance. True, the fine arts crowd were weird and unstable, but surely this was going too far. Many of the onlookers simply walked on, assuming that it was the 1980s equivalent of 'street theatre'. Fortunately, there were a few who realised that this was no experiment in avantgarde performance and, sensing that something had gone seriously wrong, hurried to the assistance of the victims. One, a humble Sri Lankan graduate student in applied mathematics, had the presence of mind to find a telephone and call both campus security and an ambulance.

Matthew was lucky. He had spent the last hour in the library looking up some details of the life of Oliver Cromwell for the second act of his play. As he crossed the snowladen expanse between the Learning Resources Centre and the Fine Arts Building, he heard the commotion and saw the disorder. Among the struggling crowd, he noticed Roger Mold, his hair ruffled and his eyes red, Ted Campbell, arms lifted trying to impose order, Julia Dean, comforting a weeping girl, Bob Pfaff, cursing and waving his fists, and several students from his play-writing class and from the cast of his play, milling about in confusion and alarm. He didn't, however, see Bonny. Breaking into a run, he made for the spot where Roger was standing.

'What happened?' he demanded, as he slithered and skidded to a halt.

'Tear-gas bomb,' Roger croaked. 'The whole building's full of fumes.'

'Did everybody get out?'

'Yes. I – er – think so.'

'Where's Bonny?'

Roger looked around, and then called to Ted. 'Ted, have you seen Bonny?'

Ted shook his head.

'Oh, my God – where is she?' exclaimed Roger.

All three of them made a rapid check of the crowd. But Bonny was nowhere in view.

'Wasn't she in her office when you left the building?'

'No, Matthew,' Roger wailed. 'I think she'd gone to the mail room.'

The next minute Matthew astonished Roger, Ted and himself by stripping off his duffel coat, jacket and shirt and trampling his shirt in the snow to soak it. He wrapped the wet shirt around his head and, vaguely aware of protesting voices behind him, charged into the building. Speed, he knew, was the important thing. He had been through this in OTC practice in public school: 'How to survive a gas attack'. The problem was that he didn't know the where-abouts of the mail-room. He raced down the ground-floor corridor, trying grimly to hold his breath. His eyes were prickling and his skin tingled.

'Mail-room?' he thought. 'There would have been other people in there. They wouldn't have left her.'

Where then? Where could she have been trapped, caught unprepared? He had a vision of a school fire drill when he had been surprised by the bell in the basement lavatory. That was possible. She might have been caught in the ladies' room – and there it was at the end of the corridor.

Well, it wouldn't be the first time he had stormed a ladies' room. There was that time in the Mirabelle on Curzon St, when Nell had disappeared in there after a row and refused to come out. Of course, he wasn't allowed in the Mirabelle any more, but—

He thrust open the door at the end of the corridor and found Bonny, prone on the white tiles, pale as a snowdrift. Coughing and gasping, he managed to hoist her in a fireman's lift. And then began the long, staggering run back to the main entrance.

Outside, the crowd, now calmer and less concerned about their own injuries, broke into a short-winded cheer as the shirtless figure of Matthew came weaving out into the sharp, frosty air bearing the limp figure of the chairman's executive assistant draped over one shoulder.

'Very Beau Geste, old boy,' said Roger, but Matthew heard nothing else, for he collapsed on his back in the snow with Bonny on top of him.

Matthew found it hard to understand what had happened to him that day. He was not, he felt, so much a man of action as an imaginer of action. Furthermore, he had come of age in the Cambridge of the early sixties, a time when the strains of the Modern Jazz Quartet, the anti-heroic stance of such film actors as Michael Caine, and the passionless detachment of the French *nouveau roman* had helped create a special blend of 'cool' to which he and his friends subscribed. To this day, he always felt he was over-acting if he raised his voice or waved his arms about, whereas the truth probably was that at all other times he was underacting, projecting an adolescent image of the restrained, ironic, unflappable man-of-the-world. What on earth would Henrietta have said about his exploit? 'Very capable, darling. I didn't realise you had such presence of mind.' And Dorothy? 'Interesting how people react in crises, but what made you sure the girl was still in the building?' And Nell? Ah, Nell! 'Pure Errol Flynn. I love the bit about you whipping your shirt off.'

And Bonny herself? 'Sorry about dinner,' had been her only comment before lapsing into unconsciousness. Later that evening he had called the hospital only to be told in a singsong Filipino voice that her condition was satisfactory, the nursing profession's jargon for 'No comment'. Roger, however, being her employer and the nearest thing to next of kin available, was allowed to visit her and reported to Matthew that she was recovering and had sent her thanks. Gratifying as that was, it made him feel that their relationship would be on an awkward footing from then on: he, the rescuer; she, the rescued. Nothing, as he knew from past experience, was more fatal to romance than a sense of obligation.

Eventually, the efforts of the day began to tell on him and he almost fell asleep in the armchair in his guest quarters. He thought for a moment of having a late-night stroll before turning in, but the prospect of tramping through snow dissuaded him. Aching with tiredness, he undressed, leaving a trail of clothes across the room to the bed. Just as he was turning out the light, he wondered 'Now, who the hell would want to gas-bomb a fine-arts building? Are we breeding a new and more violent generation of critics?'

# Chapter Six

Someone had watched the commotion outside the Fine Arts Building not with embarrassment or annoyance or even amusement, but with a sense of accomplishment. It had all depended on a series of lucky chances: a temporary clerical job at the local armoury; having access to the right keys; seizing the opportunity to make a wax impression of the one that opened the door to the tear-gas canister storage; being ready to act when the armoury guards were distracted by a sergeant who ordered them to help him move a filing cabinet from his office. The large gym bag that had carried the canister out of the armoury had been a familiar sight and aroused no more comment than the usual teasing about a hard day's work doing more good than any number of work-outs at a health club. Releasing the gas in the Fine Arts Building would normally have been harder, but fortunately the Dean had called a Faculty Council meeting that day and almost all the offices and classrooms were empty for more than an hour: time enough to make a careful survey, choose the ideal spot and get away before anyone noticed a gas-masked figure running towards the exit. The gas-mask, of course, came off and disappeared into the gym bag before anyone who happened to be passing the exit door outside could have glimpsed anything odd.

The effect of the gas attack had been predictably disruptive but somehow disappointing. It was too indiscriminate.

The really guilty ones had not been in serious danger. At first it had seemed right to punish the whole faculty, but now that notion had given way to an earlier one: the wrong could not be righted simply by spreading fear and alarm; the punishment must be individual and final. The photograph and the list were still there on the desk and what could be more sane and methodical than to start with the name at the top of the list. Yes, that one particularly – that big, lumbering, ugly cow – still here, still carrying on with her life, when the quick, light, pretty one had gone . . .

She would be first.

The campus security guard was understaffed; its members were poorly paid, badly trained and out of condition. The recent events on campus had brought their inadequacies into focus and had resulted in the students forming their own vigilante group to protect each other from the increasing muggings, acts of vandalism and sexual assaults that had been taking place in remote, unlit corners of the University's dreary vastness. One of the most dangerous areas was the network of underground tunnels that linked the student residences with the classroom buildings. This catacomb had been constructed as a means of avoiding the bitter cold and heavy snowfalls with which Wacousta was afflicted between the middle of November and the end of March. Women students in particular had been warned to avoid the tunnels at night, or, if that wasn't possible, to call the vigilante group and ask for an escort. It was foolhardy of Dodie Goldberg to ignore the warnings, but after a long night in the costume shop, struggling to finish a basque-bodice, she wanted to get to her room and go to bed as quickly as possible.

Not since she was fourteen, when she had punched Hirsch Zitner in the eye for trying to grope her at her cousin Murray's bar mitzvah, had any boy approached Dodie amorously. Her expression was forbidding and her physique awesome. So, if she had any misgivings about entering those tunnels late at night, she quickly shrugged them off, reasoning that no rapist would consider her sufficiently appealing, and that if one did, she could deal with him speedily without the assistance of a bunch of self-elected Captain Marvels from the student patrol.

Yawning, Dodie started down the staircase at the northeast corner of the Fine Arts Building towards the entrance to the first underground passage. Inside the first branch of the maze the lights burned steadily, but as she turned into the tunnel that led towards Lampman College Residence, the illumination became dimmer. Several of the bulbs seemed to be broken or burned-out, and her vast shadow, advancing before her, appeared and disappeared, assuming different shapes in each manifestation, like some terrible black djinn from the *Arabian Nights*.

She was halfway down the tunnel when she became aware of a noise behind her. Looking back, she saw a figure moving out of a patch of light and into darkness about fifty yards away. Dodie was unperturbed. Some other student taking the short way back to the dorm, she supposed. Whoever it was moved much more quickly and lightly than Dodie and in a few moments had drawn parallel with her. Dodie glanced sideways and saw a face framed in long, straight hair – a face which seemed somehow familiar. She was about to speak but the figure hurried on and in a very short time had passed out of sight around the next bend. Dodie was puzzled. There was something wrong about that face – something that made her feel it didn't belong in that place at that time. The face was associated with a submerged memory that, try as she might, she could not drag up to the surface.

Worrying away at the problem, she trundled on deeper and deeper into the shadowy labyrinth. At the next intersection, she grumbled to herself about the maintenance staff not replacing the lights, as well she might because a deeper darkness now stretched before her. She felt a momentary frisson, quite untypical of her usual impervious self, but it was only a step or two now to the staircase which led up to her own college residence. In her room there, safe and warm, she would heat up a can of chunky beef soup and consume it with three or four bagels and a mug of hot chocolate before toppling gratefully into bed.

She was grinning in anticipation of this, when it suddenly occurred to her where she had seen that face before. She stopped short in the middle of the tunnel, aghast. 'But it can't be,' she thought.

It was, in fact, Dodie's last thought, for the next moment something hard came crashing down on her skull and she fell monumentally, like a mountain sliding into the sea, down into the deepest darkness she had ever known.

The next morning students were annoyed to find that the entrances to all the tunnels were closed. They muttered and cursed as they floundered along snow-buried pathways on their journey to classrooms or the library. Campus security guards were stationed at the top of all staircases leading down to the underground corridor system, turning back anyone who tried to pass them and refusing to answer any questions. Only a few people saw the blanket-shrouded stretcher on which Dodie's body was carried out to the waiting mortuary van.

The body had been found at 4 a.m. by a third-year engineering student returning from a drunken evening in a house shared by three of his friends in the grubbiest section of Mapleville. He was feeling unusually mellow and at peace with the world, when he tripped over a bulky mass in the subterranean dimness, fell flat on his face, and broke his nose. The pain, and the terror that accompanied it when he discovered he was sprawling over a corpse, caused an abrupt reversal of mood. From a strapping, self-confident, cheerful twenty-two-year-old he regressed to a frightened infant, running bellowing through the halls of his residence, his face dabbled with blood and tears.

An hour later, the police were there, and by dawn Inspector Bain and Sergeant Kozetsky had arrived to take charge of the investigation. It was clearly a case of murder; the weapon which had clubbed Dodie Goldberg to death had been found hidden behind a soft-drink vending machine in the basement of Lampman College. It was a very curious weapon indeed.

The hysterical engineering student was taken in for questioning. On the face of it, he seemed the likeliest suspect. The engineers at Wacousta were notorious for the directness of their advances and drunken engineers were often prepared to forgo all other considerations than that the object of their passion be a member of the opposite sex, and even that consideration had sometimes *in extremis*, been abandoned. Dodie, on the other hand, had certainly possessed the necessary strength and aggressiveness to break the nose of a potential rapist. It all looked very bad for the boy.

Fortunately for him, the medical evidence proved that Dodie had been dead for at least an hour before he left the party, and his departure time was attested to, not by his equally drunken friends, but by a furious next-door neighbour who had been stark sober when he hammered on their door at a quarter to four in the morning to demand if they knew what son-of-a-bitching time it was. The grim neighbour had then watched the young suspect stagger out of the house and down the street. So Bain and Kozetsky regretfully let him go, cautioning him to avoid disturbing the peace in future. That left them with no suspects and one very odd instrument of murder.

That afternoon they were in Roger Mold's office, questioning him about the dead student and looking through her academic file, when Matthew walked in.

'Sorry. Didn't know you were busy,' he said, preparing to leave.

'Don't go, Matthew. I want you to meet Inspector Bain and Sergeant Kozetsky.'

They shook hands.

'Trouble?' Matthew asked.

He had slept late that morning and had breakfasted at the McDonald's on the highway (two Egg McMuffins and a coffee), so he had seen no one yet who might have broken the news to him. Roger explained briefly why the police were there and Matthew felt a pang of pity for the big ungainly girl, whom he had met a few times in the costume shop.

'It looks like a sex crime,' said Bain. 'Do you happen to know who she associated with?'

'A sex crime?' Matthew was incredulous. 'What makes you say that?'

Kozetsky threw a swift glance at his superior, who having just opened his mouth to answer closed it again. Roger intervened smoothly.

'I understand your discretion, Inspector. Let me just say that Mr Prior has had some experience of these matters . . .'

Bain raised his eyebrows. 'Of sex crimes?' he wondered.

'Of murder investigations,' replied Roger. 'You might recall the murder of the *Sunday Inquisitor* critic in England two years ago.'

Bain shook his head.

'Or the investigation into the death of Peter Parley, the television talk-show host?'

'Can't say I do.'

Matthew broke in hastily. 'And no discredit to you, Inspector. No reason in the world why you should have heard of them. Besides I'm here to teach play-writing and direct my play. I dislike murder investigations, and I hope very earnestly that I am never involved in another one as long as I live. Now, if you'll excuse me . . .'

He reckoned without Roger who was beginning to get the pale determined look that Matthew had first seen the morning Roger decided to propose to Alison. They had been standing on Garret Hostel Bridge and Matthew, for a moment, had thought that Roger was either going to be sick or throw himself into the Cam.

'Wait a moment, Matthew,' said Roger sharply.

Matthew obeyed.

Roger turned to Bain, the steeliness that lay hidden behind his mild academic mask making one of its rare and surprising appearances.

'Inspector, you may or may not be required – as we scholars are – to keep up with recent developments in your field of expertise, but I am surprised that two important murder cases which were given considerable coverage in the world press seem to have escaped your attention.'

Bain mumbled something about the *Mapleville Courier*, which Roger pounced on.

'I have no doubt the *Mapleville Courier* was too busy reporting some local hootenanny or regional pork festival to take much notice of events in the world at large – but the *Globe and Mail* carried regular reports of both investigations, and there was a feature article on Mr Prior in *Saturday Night*: "The Plot Thickens – The Playwright as Private Eye".'

Matthew signalled weakly at Roger to shut up. From past experience, he knew that Roger was liable to become a monster of verbose outrage, piling one elaborate denunciation on another until the only thing to do – as his fellow undergraduates had discovered years ago – was literally to sit on him. But Roger had developed such a fine head of steam that there seemed no stopping him.

'No, Matthew,' he continued, 'I will say my say . . . You may not realise it, Inspector Bain, but as a playwright Mr Prior has not only considerable insight into character and motivation but is also generally regarded as one of the most skilful plotters among the younger British dramatists. Anyone who can create the kind of complexity of action he can is surely able to unravel the complexities created by others.'

Matthew looked around desperately for something he could throw at Roger that would stop the terrible flow of pomposity. Fortunately, Inspector Bain seemed to be amazingly tolerant and unresentful.

'You may be right, Mr Mold,' he said, leaving Roger perched awkwardly at the very summit of his tirade. 'Mr Prior – as an outsider – could be an ideal observer and listener. He might hear and see things that me and Sergeant Kozetsky wouldn't be likely to. And since, as you say, he's had some experience in these matters . . .'

Sergeant Kozetsky smiled. The chief had taken the wind right out of Professor Mold's rhetoric. But the other one – the playwright – seemed no happier with the inspector's speech than he had with the professor's. In fact, he was again clutching at the doorknob and making ready to leave.

'Very flattering,' he said, 'but if it's a simple case of sexual assault, I doubt if you need me. Besides I'm going to be very busy.'

Roger looked stern. 'Matthew, it is everyone's duty to help the police.'

Matthew opened the door and walked out into the corridor.

'Matthew!'

Matthew turned and looked back into the room. Roger stood facing him, and Bain and Kozetsky sat watching them both with interest.

'Is this extra activity to be covered by my stipend for teaching and directing, Roger? Or are you going to pay me an additional fee?' Then – in his best Bogart voice – he continued: 'I get fifty bucks a day, plus expenses. See you around, sweetheart.'

Roger was nonplussed. 'You have to . . .' he pleaded.

'No,' said Matthew, and closed the door.

# Chapter Seven

Matthew was not being coy when he discouraged attempts to involve him in the investigation. His previous experiences had been far from pleasant. He had become entangled in one murder case because suspicion had fallen on his younger brother, Mark, and in another because of Nell Finnigan's friendship with the murder victim. In neither case did he feel that the cases had been solved through any natural skill on his own part, but the press, having found an 'angle' that would sell more papers, had inflated his role in those unlovely episodes and stamped an image of him on the public mind that far overshadowed his fame as a playwright.

So it was rather firmly that he shut himself into his office to work on revisions to the play. He wrote busily and uninterruptedly for about two hours and was just about to pack up and return to his guest room to freshen up before dinner when he heard a tap at the door. Matthew immediately became motionless. Perhaps if he waited very quietly, whoever it was would go away. This time there was a double rap, louder and more insistent. It might, he thought, be someone who needed his advice as playwright-in-residence about a point of dramaturgy. The knocking resumed. He hadn't the heart, he decided, to leave an aspiring dramatist standing disconsolately in the corridor. Giving in, he went to the door and opened it. It was Bain.

'Mr Prior,' he said, 'I wonder if I could have a few words?'

Ungraciously, Matthew waved him into the office. It was not a large room and most of it was occupied by his desk and some bookshelves. With two of them in there together, it was like being in an apartment-house elevator on moving day. Bain sat in the acid-yellow armchair upholstered in tufted acrylic, while Matthew slumped in the swivel-chair behind his desk.

'Where's your side-kick?' he asked rudely.

'Sergeant Kozetsky?' Bain's tone was mild. 'He's doing some routine questioning. So am I, as a matter of fact.'

'I must say I'm disappointed,' said Matthew.

Bain raised his eyebrows interrogatively.

'I expected a red-coat and jodhpurs and a boy-scout hat.'

'That's the Royal Canadian Mounted Police, sir. I'm OPP.'

'OPP?'

'Ontario Provincial Police. Mapleville's too small to have its own police force so we handle law enforcement here under contract.'

'Ah! A sort of franchise.'

'In a way, sir.'

They looked warily at one another across the desk. What was the score? Love all? Matthew spun round in his chair to face the narrow slit of window that looked out on a view of redbrick courtyard and a few snow-covered shrubs.

'Routine questions tend to get routine answers,' he said.

'Very true. But we're pretty good at listening between the words. I think in your business you call that the "subtext".'

'Fifteen-love,' thought Matthew, swivelling back and looking at the inspector with new respect.

'There might, though,' Bain continued, 'be a place for someone who could ask questions that weren't routine. Unorthodox questions. That's your line, isn't it? Asking unorthodox questions about human character and human action?'

Matthew shrugged helplessly. 'Yes, I suppose so. But I don't supply the answers. Even Shakespeare couldn't manage that.'

'I once read a short story in *Ellery Queen's Mystery Magazine* where Dr Samuel Johnson solved a murder case,' Bain offered, somewhat irrelevantly.

'By Lilian de la Torre. Clever writer ... Oh, really, Inspector, I honestly don't think I can help you much.'

Bain stared at him, good-natured but implacable. 'But you'll help as much as you can.'

Matthew nodded reluctantly. 'In my pitiful few moments of spare time, I'll try asking a few unorthodox questions.'

Bain smiled. 'Good. Now let me show you something.'

He pulled from inside his overcoat a transparent glassine bag, sealed tightly at the top. Inside it was a large club-like grey object, darkly discoloured at one end and with a few brunette hairs adhering to it. It looked organic rather than man-made and was peculiarly shaped, thick at one end and tapering slightly to a rounded apex with knots and gnarls along its length.

'The curious murder weapon,' said Matthew. 'But what is it?'

'Ah,' said Bain, 'that's what's so curious about it. You see, it's an ossified elephant penis.'

At the same time, Sergeant Kozetsky was having a stroke of luck. He had learned from the head of the maintenance staff that the cleaners often worked late into the night since certain classrooms couldn't be cleaned until evening extension classes were over at ten o'clock. Once it had been established which tunnel entrance would have offered Dodie Goldberg access to the shortest route between the costume shop and her college residence, it didn't take long

68

to find out which of the cleaners might have been in the area at the time she was passing through. There were two, in fact: Mrs Rozilda Botelho, a recent immigrant from the Azores, and Mrs Tussy Napoleon, a Jamaican who was already the happy possessor of a plastic Canadian citizenship card. Like most of the cleaning staff, they lived not in Mapleville but in a sprawling exurb of Toronto called West Darlington.

Sergeant Kozetsky, whose father had left Poland in 1945 and had worked himself to death trying to establish a dry-cleaning business, knew that for recent immigrants the arrival of a policeman on the doorstep was not a welcome event, recalling as it did oppressions fled from or heightening fears that the immigration authorities had found some excuse to ship them back. As he had expected, Mrs Botelho who was at home on the fifteenth floor of an ugly high-rise apartment building, looking after her eighty-year-old father-in-law and her oldest daughter's three children, was terrified into near speechlessness. What little English she knew seemed to desert her and Kozetsky's grasp of idiomatic Portuguese was minimal. After about half an hour and with the help of ten-year-old Rosario as interpreter, he managed to establish that Mrs Botelho had been working at the far end of the building from the tunnel entrance and that Mrs Napoleon had been much closer to the vital area. He then spent an extra ten minutes assuring Mrs Botelho that she would be allowed to continue her life in peace, before he left.

Mrs Napoleon, confident in her newly won citizenship, was a different matter. He tracked her down in a neighbourhood launderette where she helped out in the afternoons. A tall, striking woman, caramel-coloured and wearing a pink nylon overall, she boomed a welcome as she stuffed wet sheets into a dryer.

'Murder!' she exclaimed when Kozetsky had told her of the reason for his visit. 'Oh, God, that be ba-a-ad! Me leave that job, officer. Don't want no crazy man goin' after *this* child.' She tossed her handsome head, making her green glass earrings dance and shimmer in the fluorescent light.

'The point is – did you see anything?' said the sergeant. 'It would have been sometime between one o'clock in the morning and two-thirty.'

'Miz Botelho and me always finished that buildin' by half-past one.'

'Did you see anyone go down the stairs to the tunnel between one and one-thirty?'

Mrs Napoleon thought. She crinkled up her eyes, lifting a basket of washing from the floor and placing it on the wooden table to sort and fold it. Finally, she said:

'A big gal?'

'Large-ish,' agreed Kozetsky.

'Oh, God, mon, this was a *big* gal – like a hippo-pota-*mus*.'

'What time did you see her?'

'Jus' when I finish the main classroom on that corridor – the one with a clock over the platform.'

'The lecture hall?'

'Yes . . . and I look at the clock. I was gettin' tired and wantin' to get back to me home and I said: "Oh, God, fifteen more minutes".'

'It was one-fifteen?'

'Yes . . . and I come out into the corridor and I see this hippo-pota-*mus* in blue jeans and a big thick jacket. She go down the stairs toward the tunnel.'

'Good. That establishes the time. If the clock was right.'

'Oh, that's a good clock, mon. I go by that all the time.'

'Then you finished in that building and went home?'

'I go home and I say to me husband – "Oh, God, Edward, the gals at that school be gettin' bigger and bigger. One fat like your grandmother and the other one tall like a tele-phone pole." '

'The other one?' the sergeant said. 'There was another one?'

'About five minutes later. A tall one with long hair – and a tartan skirt.'

'Did you see her face?'

'No, jus' from back. They better fed than we was when we was young. That's why they grow so big.'

'You're not short yourself. She must have been very tall – the second girl – for you to take notice.'

'Very tall, mon.'

'But you didn't recognise her?'

Mrs Napoleon sighed. 'A lot of big girls around that place. A lot of them got long hair too.'

'Well, keep your eyes open. If you see anyone on cam-pus who looks like her, let me know.'

Mrs Napoleon folded a towel and placed it on the pile. Then she turned to him determinedly. 'Mon, I tell you – I not go back to that place for *gold*.'

'Thanks for your help, anyway,' said Kozetsky.

'Any time, officer,' boomed Mrs Napoleon, waving a pillow-slip and beaming with all her teeth as he left.

The more painful interviews were with Dodie's parents and her brother and sister, but none of them could add anything useful to the meagre store of information. She had no boy-friends as far as they knew, and no close girlfriends. Dodie, they said, was a work-horse. Whatever she was doing at any particular time, it occupied all her attention and con-sumed all her energy. They felt that in her first year she had been more involved with other students, had even gone on some trips with them, but in the last couple of years she had become more of a solitary. It began to seem evident that Dodie had been an arbitrarily selected victim.

71

As for the other girl, no amount of questioning by Bain and Kozetsky could unearth a single lead. It was true, as Mrs Napoleon had suggested, that height and long hair were not such rare qualities among the female students at Wacousta, and plaid skirts, though somewhat unfashionably "preppy", were not unknown. An appeal went out for the girl to come forward, but it went unanswered.

'Not necessarily a sign of guilt,' Bain said to the sergeant. 'She might not have seen anything and can't be bothered to come forward. She might have seen something and be afraid to come forward.'

'Because of possible reprisal from the killer?' said Kozetsky.

'If she saw *him*, he might have seen *her*. In which case he may have threatened her.'

'Or she may be dead too.'

'If so, he's done a marvellous job of concealing the body. And if one, why not the other. Why leave the Goldberg girl where she'd easily be found?'

'Too heavy to move?' suggested the sergeant.

'Maybe – and maybe he forced the other girl to go with him – to his car, perhaps – and drove her off campus and killed her somewhere miles away.'

'Except that no other girl has been reported missing. In which case we go back to the possibility that the other girl killed Dodie Goldberg.'

Inspector Bain frowned. 'Unlikely,' he said. 'Her skull wasn't eggshell thin. In fact, it was thicker than most. Not many women would have the muscle-power to do that kind of damage. Besides it's hard to believe that a woman would choose that kind of weapon.'

Sergeant Kozetsky looked sceptical. 'Isn't that a bit old-fashioned, sir? The traditional women's murder method is poison? Something subtle? What about Lizzie Borden?'

'She wasn't convicted.'

'What about female terrorists? The Weathermen? The Manson gang? Those women were brutal!'

Bain waved his hand dismissively. 'All right, all right: a woman could have done it. I just don't happen to think a woman did do it, and we can't waste all our time arguing. We have to talk to everyone who worked with the Goldberg girl in the costume shop that night, and everybody in the Lampman residence who might have been awake between one and two-thirty.'

'Can't we narrow the time a little further, sir? If Mrs Napoleon was right, she was alive at one-fifteen, and the other girl followed at one-twenty. If the girl with the long hair wasn't the one who murdered her, she must have passed her in the tunnel, because if she'd been dead at that point, the other girl would surely have raised the alarm.'

Bain shrugged. 'All right, between one-twenty and two-thirty — but somehow I don't believe the case is going to hinge on that. Are you a Freeman Wills Crofts fan, Stan?'

'Never heard of him.'

'Good. Don't bother to dig up any of his books. You're too hooked on timetables as it is.'

The curious weapon continued to intrigue Matthew. Its venue was not a mystery for long: it was established that it had been stolen from the office of a professor of anthropology some weeks before the murder. The professor himself had an impeccable alibi. On the evening of Dodie Goldberg's death, he had been in Berkeley, California, delivering a paper on Yuba burial rites. The weapon, or, as the professor preferred to call it, the fetish, had been found in a sacred cave in Africa which, like Mother Shipton's cave, transmuted anything organic into stone by the constant dripping of water through limestone. Thus, said the professor when Matthew questioned him, it was a petrified

73

– rather than ossified – male elephant's member.

What fascinated Matthew was why the murderer had chosen such an object. Clearly this was no random blunt instrument seized upon in the heat of the moment. It must have been chosen not for its heft and solidity, impressive though they were, but for its symbolic value. An elephantine girl, who according to some of her fellow students had an overt hostility towards men, had been despatched with an elephantine phallus. No reasonably sane person would have stolen a rare anthropological relic, carried it around with him for weeks, and then, on pure impulse, used it to bash someone's brains in. On the other hand, was it any saner to choose a weapon deliberately for its allusiveness? It was all very puzzling, but Matthew kept coming back to the point that there must be a sexual motive for the killing.

Lying on his bed in the guest room, Matthew went over it all again in his mind. What sort of sexual motive? It seemed improbable that Dodie had been wooed by a homicidal maniac, had rejected him, and had paid for it with her life. Sighing, Matthew turned over and punched his pillow. As he did so, he noticed that something had been pushed under his door. He was sure it had not been lying on the floor when he came in and he had heard no sound in the corridor. He swung himself off the bed, crossed the room and stooped to pick it up. It was a plain white envelope. Tearing it open, he found inside what looked like the stub of a theatre ticket. He took it over to the light and looked at it more closely. It was not just any theatre ticket. It was dated 6 April, 1983 and was for a seat in the upper circle of the Aldridge Theatre, New York, for a performance of his own ill-fated Broadway venture, *The Harmonious Blacksmith*.

# Chapter Eight

Bonny was back at her desk the following morning, not very much the worse, it seemed, for her experience during the tear-gas attack, but deeply shocked and dismayed by Dodie's murder.

'You must try to help, Matthew,' she said as he lounged in her doorway wolfing down a chocolate doughnut.

'That's what everybody says,' grumbled Matthew. 'Really, the reports of my investigative skills are greatly exaggerated. How I got cast in the role of Charlie Chan, I don't know.'

'Charlie Chan . . . Lesley Caron . . . you must have spent your entire childhood in the local Odeon.'

'And a lot of my adolescence – but not always watching the screen.'

'Ah, yes – "I Was a Teenage Wolf" – starring Matthew Prior.'

'Now a rather mangy and toothless middle-aged one.'

Bonny's glance was as cool as it was shrewd. 'You're married, aren't you?' she said.

'Divorced six years ago.'

'Children?'

'Two. Bryn and Sofia. They're twins.'

'Living with their mother?'

'Mostly. In a few years they'll be at university.' And doesn't *that* make me feel my years, he thought. The cycle he and Henrietta had begun when they met at Cambridge would be completed when Bryn and Sofia became under-graduates. They would encounter their own Henriettas and Matthews, and probably their share of Whiffer Lucas-Crofts, and eventually they would be the initiators of another cycle, while he and Henrietta tottered feebly towards their respective graves. In the meantime, God willing, there were Nell and Dorothy – and maybe even Bonny. Or, as he was beginning to feel, maybe especially Bonny.

'I still owe you a dinner,' he said, wiping his chocolate-smeared fingers on a paper napkin.

She nodded agreeably. 'So you do,' she said, 'but I'm a bit superstitious right now about your dinner invitations. I tell you what, though, I've been asked to a launch tonight. Want to come along?'

'What would they be launching at this time of the year – an ice-breaker?'

'It's a book launch. You've met Fraser McCullough, haven't you?'

Matthew admitted that he had.

'Fraser's on the board of Donaldson and Durie – the publishers – and they're giving a bash tonight for one of their authors. You'll meet all kinds of literary types.'

'I've *met* all kinds of literary types – and they're not exactly my idea of a fun crowd – but with you, I think I could face it.'

'I'll be sure to hold your hand any time you feel the least bit timid.'

'Won't you be too busy holding Fraser's?'

Bonny lifted both hands from the typewriter keyboard. 'See. I have two. One for each of you. Pick me up at six-thirty. Fraser's flying in from Winnipeg so he'll meet us there.'

Matthew sighed. 'Well, half a date is better than none, I suppose.'

'Now, get back to your students. I've got a report to type.'

★ ★ ★

76

The book launch was held at Casa Loma, an Edwardian folly built by a local tycoon to entertain a visiting monarch who failed to show up. It was a combination of Scottish Baronial and Transylvanian Gothic and had been rented for the occasion from the Lions' Club of Toronto who had bought it when the tycoon went bankrupt. The first thing that Matthew noticed as he drove his rented Dodge Aries up the driveway and parked it among the Porsches, Saabs and BMWs was a kilted Highlander marching up and down in front of the main entrance, playing a scalp-tightening version of *The Bluebells of Scotland* on the bagpipes. Matthew remembered a line of Shakespeare's about the effect of bagpipes on the bladder, and was glad that he had emptied his before leaving the campus.

'Fraser's method of welcoming us is a little excessive, don't you think?' he said to Bonny.

'Don't be silly,' she replied. 'That's not Fraser; that's the Pipe-Major from the Territorials.' Then, raising her voice as they mounted the steps to the entrance, she said: 'Hello, Andy. You must be freezing. When're you coming in for a nip of whisky?'

The piper withdrew his lips briefly from the mouth-piece, smiled and answered: 'Soon, lassie, soon', and then with scarcely a pause for breath, launched into *The Bonnets of Bonny Dundee*. Bonny bowed to him gravely before she and Matthew went inside.

'Could have sworn it was Fraser, but then all Scotsmen look alike in their kilts. Your eyes are drawn to their uniformly hairy legs and you don't notice their faces.'

'That's what passes for English wit, I suppose,' she said loftily. 'As a matter of fact, Fraser's legs aren't hairy – and I happen to think he's a fine-looking man in his tartan.'

By this time they had left their outer coats in the cloakroom and had passed on into the main hall which was crowded wall to wall with members of the Toronto arts establishment. Bonny pointed out various notabilities to Matthew. There was Hallan Clough whose painting of a half-gutted Winnipeg Goldeye had triggered the Magic Brutalist movement; his daughter, Faith Clough, who ran an art-movie house dedicated to black-and-white classics; St David Denbigh, an elderly man-of-letters of vaguely Chestertonian aspect, who had achieved a late-blooming celebrity with his *roman-à-fleuve, Angels and Archetypes*; Zoltan Zubescu, an exiled Romanian poet and blue-grass banjo player; Piers Plowden, a pop historian and television celebrity, noted especially for his award-winning television series, *The First Nail*, the story of the building of a pioneer hardware-store chain in the Prairie provinces. And of course there was Donald Donaldson himself, Canada's most adventurous publisher, with the author whose book was being launched, J. T. McLaughlin, a hearty red-bearded fellow with a piratical look. The book which was on display at a table near the bar was called *The Further Adventures of Zipper*.

Bonny and J. T. were obviously on a familiar footing. He greeted her with a hug and shook Matthew's hand energetically, giving off such emanations of friendliness that it seemed his beard might ignite from the fierce warmth of it. He pressed Rob Roys on to Bonny and Matthew and introduced them to Donald Donaldson. Donaldson had heard of Matthew and immediately began talking up an idea he had for a book about Canadians who had become famous figures on the English scene: Beaverbrook, Beatrice Lillie, Lord Thomson, Robert Ross. Matthew was able to supply several other names and proposed the name of a young Canadian writer in London who might be interested in such an assignment. By this time, Fraser McCullough had arrived. The sandy eyebrows and the kilt caught Matthew's eye several minutes before he reached their little group at the bar.

'Ah, there you are Bonny m'love,' he said hugging her more awkwardly than J. T. had. 'And Prior.'

'Call me Matthew,' Matthew said.

It was apparent that McCullough had not expected to see him there and, judging by the charged looks he and Bonny exchanged, he was far from delighted. However, he quickly assumed an air of cordiality which was a testimony either to his good manners or to his awareness that being cool to Matthew would not earn him any points with Bonny.

'How was Winnipeg?' Bonny asked.

'Windy and cold.'

'And Meg?'

'Calm but chilly.'

'Still no word of Heather, of course?'

Fraser's face stiffened. 'No. There'll be no news now. I've made my mind up to the fact.'

Bonny hastily changed the subject and began talking about the University, and the reaction to the tear-gas bombing.

'You showed great presence of mind,' Fraser said to Matthew. 'I'm glad you were on the spot – for Bonny's sake.'

Fraser was clearly grateful but seemed to feel awkward about expressing it. To change the subject, Matthew said:

'Terrible thing about the Goldberg girl, wasn't it?'

Fraser arched his eyebrows.

'Hadn't you heard?' Matthew continued. 'There was a murder on campus. One of the girls in the theatre department was killed.'

'Awful business,' said Donaldson. 'Surely it made the Winnipeg papers?'

Bonny attempted to create a diversion by asking J. T. loudly whether he had begun his next novel, but Fraser's attention was caught. 'I didn't get a chance to read any papers or watch any television. What happened?'

'A girl was clubbed to death in one of the underground tunnels,' said Donaldson. 'What was her name? Debbie Goldberg?'

'Dodie,' said Matthew.

A kind of shadow seemed to pass over Fraser's face. 'Dodie Goldberg? I know that name from somewhere.'

'You've probably heard me mention her, Fraser,' said Bonny quickly. 'She talked to me sometimes, poor girl. I don't think she talked to many people.'

'Dodie Goldberg . . .' Fraser repeated. 'No, I can't remember. But I don't think it was just hearing her name from you. There's something else.'

J. T. began to talk about his next book and eventually he and Fraser drifted away from the bar, while Donald Donaldson was seized by a tall grey-haired woman from one of the Toronto newspapers. Matthew and Bonny were left together.

'I wish you hadn't brought that up,' she said.

'Why not?'

'Because Fraser's just been visiting his wife in Winnipeg and she blames him for what happened to their daughter. All this about Dodie Goldberg being murdered doesn't help.'

'Why? Was his daughter murdered?'

'Nobody knows. She disappeared. They searched for her for more than a year – ads in the paper, posters with her picture, private investigators. Nothing worked.'

'A runaway?'

'That's what it looked like. But it didn't make sense. She didn't seem to have any problems at home or at school.'

'But what has all this to do with Dodie Goldberg?'

Bonny sighed. 'Meg thinks her daughter's dead – and so does Hamish, Fraser's son. Fraser prefers not to believe it. But every time he visits Winnipeg she keeps going on about it and it depresses him. I just didn't want him thinking about dead girls, that's all.'

'I'm sorry,' said Matthew. 'Poor Fraser.'

An hour or so later, the party began to break up. Fraser helped Bonny on with her coat.

'Can we give you a ride, Matthew?' he said. 'The campus isn't far out of my way.'

Matthew looked at Bonny and she shrugged guiltily.

'No, Fraser, thank you,' he said. 'I have my own car.'

Outside, he watched them get into Fraser's regal Lincoln and as it moved sedately down the drive-way through the whirling snowflakes, he saw Bonny's small hand waving to him in what he hoped was a regretful farewell.

'The hero's reward,' he thought resentfully. 'Half a date – and goodbye, Charlie.' Then he trudged through the drifting whiteness to his own car and drove sadly back to Mapleville.

Back in his guest room on campus, he decided to phone Henrietta. He dialled the international code, the local code and Henrietta's number. All he could hear on the line was the breath of the abyss, an echoing emptiness broken occasionally by what sounded like someone trying to play scales on a Moog synthesiser. This was followed by a long high-pitched whine. He hung up, counted slowly to fifty, picked up the phone and dialled again. The eerie sequence began as before and he was just about to give up in disgust, when he heard the familiar buzz-buzz of the ringing tone. There were five double buzzes, a click, and then Henrietta's sleepy voice on the line.

'Hello, who is it?'

'Darling, it's me.'

'Matthew! Wha . . . what time is it?'

'Eleven-thirty.'

81

Some scuffling noises came from the other end. Then Henrietta's voice again, tight with annoyance. 'It's four-thirty in the morning!'

'Eh?'

'Four-thirty a.m. You know – *ante-meridiem*?'

Matthew slumped. 'Oh, darling, I'm sorry. I forgot you're five hours ahead.'

'Honestly Matthew! And I have to be up at the shriek of dawn to take Sofia to the doctor.'

'Nothing serious, I hope.'

The chances were that it wasn't. Sofia had been hypochondriacal since she was three years old, and every other week, it seemed, she reported symptoms that sounded near-fatal but which turned out always to be quite innocuous.

'I think it's just pre-exam panic. This is the big one for the year coming up – and you know how she gets.'

Matthew laughed. 'But, Good Lord, it's months away yet,' he said.

Sofia was a brilliant student, but every test, every examination, produced the same symptoms of headache, pains in the stomach, and nausea, though not usually this early. Bryn, on the other hand, though less dazzlingly bright, maintained an easy nonchalance. Both of them invariably did well.

'Tell her if she fails she can always take a typing course and I'll hire her as my secretary.'

'Hm . . . I don't think that would work. She's very women's lib now, you know.'

'How's Bryn?'

'Fine. He's playing keyboard with a group from school. They call themselves the White Zombies. Matthew – why am I having this trivial conversation with you in the middle of the night?'

'Eh – Oh, I just needed to talk. I've been stood up by a girl I rescued from death.'

'Maybe she thought death was preferable.'

'Really, Henrietta, you might be just a little more sympathetic. I feel something quite different about this one. She's so – so real. But she's got a thing about older men.'

'Then you should be just her cup of tea.'

' 'I was hoping,' said Matthew stiffly, 'that I would get some sensible advice – not just a lot of cheap gibes.'

He heard a patient sigh from way across the Atlantic.

'The other man is even older, is that it?'

'Yes.'

'A father figure?'

'Yes, I suppose.'

'And she's a dear little girl who needs protecting?'

'No, she's not like that at all. She's very adult, very much in charge of her life.'

There was a pause, followed by something that might have been a yawn.

'Well, then, Matthew,' Henrietta said, finally, 'your only hope is to convince her that you're an adult, too. Good luck with that, darling – and good night.' The uninterrupted buzz that followed told him that the connection had been broken.

Matthew replaced the receiver with dignified restraint. Really, what were ex-wives for if not to be a fount of wisdom about navigating through the trickier shoals of human relationships? Who could possibly know him better and advise him how to capitalise on his strengths? And all he got was smart banter about his weaknesses. Oh, well, sleep might help. Some of his best ideas came to him after a good rest.

Matthew undressed, and as he was hanging up his suit he checked the pockets of his jacket. In the inside one on the left, he felt something rustle and pulled it out. It was the envelope that had been pushed under his door the previous night – the envelope containing the ticket-stub for *The Harmonious Blacksmith*. He must have slipped it in there with all the other junk from the top of his dresser and forgotten about it. Now he wondered what its message was and what connection it might possibly have with Dodie Goldberg's murder.

Whistling a few bars from 'The Anvil Chorus', he put on his pyjamas and went to bed.

# Chapter Nine

There was a caste system in operation in the theatre department at Wacousta U. It was unofficial but rigid and had grown up in spite of efforts by the faculty – sixties liberals to a man – to emphasise the equality of all students. Briefly, a three-level hierarchy had evolved: at the top were the performance students, the princes and princesses of the discipline; in the middle were the production students without whom no show would be lit, decorated or costumed; at the bottom were the peons – the historians, theorists, critics and dramaturges, scholars by default because they had neither the talents of the performers nor the skills of the technicians. The scholars were mildly resentful but carried on writing their papers on the influence of Jarry on Ionesco or David Belasco's theatrical realism. The major conflict, however, was between the performance students and the production students. Each group felt that the plays staged by the theatre department were principally for its benefit: the acting ensemble believing that they were vehicles for their vocal and physical displays and the technical crew that they were opportunities to dazzle the audience with the polish and precision of the *mise-en-scène*. That they ought to be mutually supportive seemed rarely to occur to them. Their interaction was mainly in terms of complaints – from the actors that their faces weren't lit or their costumes were awful and from the technicians that the actors didn't show up for costume fittings or misbehaved during cue-to-cue run-throughs.

Calvin Knox, though he had done his undergraduate work elsewhere, was aware of this, so he might well have been surprised when he saw Cubby Kirkwood in the lighting booth entangled in an embrace with the lighting designer, Shana Pilton. Calvin, hovering in the doorway, was uncertain whether to break in on them or to retreat quietly. The problem was resolved for him when Shana opened her eyes and saw him over Cubby's shoulder. Cubby turned his head, following her gaze.

'Oh, hi, Calvin,' he said.

Calvin was silent.

'Whew!' Shana exclaimed. 'Talk about being caught in the act. Old cat-foot Cal crept right up on us.'

'I came to check that the dimmers were patched in properly. We're going to try a few of the lighting cues at tomorrow's rehearsal.'

'I know that, Cal,' said Shana. 'Sure they've been patched in properly. What's the matter? You don't trust me?'

Calvin moved silently to the board and operated a few switches. The lights over the stage faded up and down on several different areas.

'Fine,' he said, getting ready to leave the booth, 'I'll catch you tomorrow.'

Shana grinned. 'Not like tonight, you won't.'

Calvin left without replying.

'What's eating him?' Shana asked.

But Cubby just shrugged and put his arms around her again. Soon the two figures sank down onto the floor. Outside the booth, the theatre was empty and silent.

The rehearsal next day was supposed to begin promptly at two, but as usual some of the actors straggled in late. Matthew tried to conceal his impatience, but when Rezi Yanouf, the villain, sauntered in at two-fifteen, he blew up. The speech he made to the cast damned them for their lack of professionalism, their unwarranted arrogance, their failure to co-operate with each other and with him, and their general negativism. Throughout the rehearsal period, each advance had become by the next day a retreat; each surge of energy and confidence had collapsed into inertia and indifference. He ended by saying that he had worked with some of the best professional actors in the world, many of them renowned for their bloody-mindedness, but never had he worked with a more infuriating group of irresponsible egotists in his life.

The outburst relieved Matthew's feelings but did little for his relationship with the cast. He had laid, as they would have said, a heavy guilt trip on them and the only result was to make them subdued and resentful. He turned despairingly to Calvin.

'Let's get this damned rehearsal going,' he muttered.

Calvin stood up and was about to speak when he stopped and turned back to whisper to Matthew. 'Cubby isn't here yet.'

'Oh, for the Lord's sake!' Matthew groaned. 'What the hell is the use of starting without the bastard leading man?'

Calvin turned back to the cast. 'Has anyone seen Cubby?' he asked.

But no one had. Cubby's room-mate in residence, Joe Innocenti, claimed that Cubby had not slept in his bed the night before, and Wayne Goffman added that he hadn't been in class that morning. Marie-Ange, the stage-manager, went off to call the residence to see if Cubby had returned there, and Lulie Burns offered to telephone the University Health Service to see if he'd reported sick. Neither of them brought back news of the missing actor. Since Cubby's work was central to the play, Matthew's rehearsal plan had to be abandoned and he left Calvin to take the cast through a line rehearsal. Matthew himself set off for Roger's office to indulge in a session of complaint and reproach.

So it wasn't until late in the afternoon – when one of the props makers went to the storage room to put away an elaborate papier-mâché Holy Grail he had been making – that Cubby was found.

'Pink and blue tights!' said Inspector Bain disbelievingly.

'I'm told it was part of a costume for an Italian comedy the kids did last year: one leg pink and one leg blue.'

Sergeant Kozetsky and Inspector Bain were sitting in the small office they had been allotted in the theatre department as their incident room. It was strewn with photographs and reports to do with the Dodie Goldberg murder. Now on top of that case, they were faced with an apparent suicide.

'Funny thing to hang yourself with,' mused Bain. 'Plenty of rope backstage. Why would someone go over to the costume shop, pick up a pair of tights, and then go all the way back to the props storage room to hang himself?'

'Come to that, if you were going to the costume shop, why not get a strong leather belt?'

But the fact was that Cubby had been found hanging with one leg of the tights knotted round his neck and the other leg fastened round an overhead pipe. It had been an overwhelmingly horrifying sight for the third-year student who had found him, with his head lolling to one side, his face dark with blood, his tongue protruding . . . and one earring swinging gently to and fro. Later, when the medical examiner arrived, a further discovery was made. Tucked inside the pink noose was a small square of photographic print. The face in the print was Cubby's.

'Pink and blue tights – and a bit of a photo! Does any of this make sense, Stan?'

Inspector Bain rubbed his face exasperatedly and turned back to Cubby's student file. There were grade reports, confidential assessments by his performance teachers, records of his high-school career, and a snapshot of a much younger Cubby – eighteen years old and looking like a startled choirboy. Bain turned a page and read on, humming.

'What *is* that, sir?' Kozetsky asked after a few minutes.

Bain looked up impatiently. 'What's what?'

'That tune you were humming.'

'I wasn't humming anything.'

'You were, sir. It went like this.' Kozetsky tried to reproduce the sounds that Bain had been making.

'What on earth is that supposed to be? It sounds like a Hoover that's gone on the blink.'

'It's what you were humming,' said Kozetsky through gritted teeth.

Bain's face cleared. 'Wait a minute,' he said. 'Are you sure it wasn't this?' He hummed the melody again.

'Yes,' said Kozetsky, rolling his eyes to the ceiling. 'That's it exactly.'

'That's funny,' Bain said, chuckling self-indulgently. 'I shouldn't laugh really but it tickles me the way your mind throws up strange things. I haven't heard that song in years.' He seemed inclined to go on chuckling and shaking his head in wonderment, but Sergeant Kozetsky's impatience was becoming apparent.

'What song?' he almost snapped.

Bain looked pained. 'I don't remember the name of it, Stan. All I remember is a few lines:

My grandmother used to say
In her quaint old-fashioned way:
'Pink for a little girl;
Blue for a boy'.

Sergeant Kozetsky slapped his forehead. 'That's it!' he yelled.

'What's it?'

'Colour symbolism. The tights. Half-pink, half-blue. Sexual ambiguity!'

Bain stared at him for a moment in alarm, then his eyes narrowed and he began to ponder aloud.

'Colour symbolism? A message from him to us? The elephant whatnot. Another message from him to us. Are you saying, Stan, that this lad – all mixed up about which way he's going sexually – first bumps off this very butch-looking girl and then strings himself up because he's sorry for what he's done?'

'Whoa, you're way ahead of me, sir. I was just offering a possible motive for suicide – sexual confusion – not uncommon at that age. You're saying the boy's suicide and the Goldberg murder could be connected.'

Bain patted his sergeant on the shoulder. 'It's a theory. And a very lovely theory. A bobby-dazzler of a theory, in fact. There's just one problem.'

'What?'

'No suicide note.'

Sergeant Kozetsky gave a fretful shrug. 'Not all suicides leave notes,' he argued.

'The ones that get drunk and drive their cars at ninety miles an hour into concrete walls don't, that's true. But ninety-nine per cent of your overdosers, your gas-oven merchants, your window-jumpers, and your hangers do.'

'What about the ones that half-hang themselves to get some kind of sexual kick and then can't control it?'

Bain shook his head. 'Well, then, Stan, it's not suicide, is it? It's accidental death.'

'Was this? What about the bit of photo inside the tights?'

'God knows, Stan. Narcissism? But if it wasn't an accident, and it wasn't suicide, then we've got another murder on our hands.'

'And Hugh Kirkwood and the rest of the Ontario Provincial Cabinet on our backs.'

Bain groaned. 'Spare us, Stan. I don't know about your back, but mine's too frail for all that weight.'

The two men stared gloomily out of the window as a fresh fall of snow began to blanket the campus.

At the far end of the theatre department corridor, Roger Mold was staring out at the same snow. Matthew, who had equipped himself with a large carrot-oatmeal muffin, two butter tarts, a bagel with cream cheese and a cup of hot chocolate, was munching and gulping his way through this not untypical mid-afternoon snack.

Roger turned away from the window and eyed him with distaste. 'Is this the man who insisted on nothing but quails' eggs and sparkling Vouvray for breakfast after the May Ball in 'sixty-five?' he asked.

Matthew devoured a butter tart and lavishly licked the treacly residue off his fingers. 'I believe in eating the cuisine of the country – the out-of-the-way local specialities. In Japan, I eat sushi; here I eat butter tarts.'

'Ugh,' said Roger.

Matthew noted that Roger really did look queasy. His normally sallow complexion was mottled with greenish tints like a late Van Gogh self-portrait, and though the office was not overheated a dew of perspiration gleamed on his forehead and upper lip.

'Are you all right, old man?' he asked. 'You look like death.'

'You're a marvel of tact, Matthew. No, I do *not* feel all right. Two of my students are dead. One of them had close ties to the Provincial Government. The University's funding comes from the Provincial Government. I am being pressured by the Dean, the Chairman of Senate, the President and the entire Board of Governors. They feel that there may be a certain weakness in the running of this department that allows its students to be exposed

91

to maniac killers or drives them to suicide. And all *you* do is lie around wolfing down nasty sticky pastries. Does it surprise you that I feel unwell?'

Matthew took a deep draught of hot chocolate. 'I take it that the sub-text of this harangue is: get up off your backside, Matthew, and do something. You seem not to understand that I do *not* consider myself a sort of trans-sexual Miss Marple. True, I got involved in a couple of unpleasant incidents and made a couple of lucky guesses – but I don't wish to make a habit of it, as the dress designer said to the nun. The police will handle it, Roger. Leave it to them. All I've promised to do is to keep my ears open and maybe ask a few unorthodox questions.'

Someone knocked at the door.

'Excuse me, sir.'

Ken Meldrum stood in the doorway, looking like a worried Borzoi.

'Yes, Ken – what can we do for you?'

Ken hesitated and then came into the office and closed the door behind him. His bright-eyed doggy face was uncharacteristically clouded.

'I – I heard about Cubby.'

'Yes?'

'I saw him late last night.'

Matthew stopped in mid-gulp and set down his hot chocolate. 'You did?' he said. 'Where?' It was not very unorthodox, as questions go.

'In the theatre lobby. I'd been up in Miss Dundee's office using her typewriter...' He looked momentarily guilty. 'She said I could, Prof, and I had to get an assignment typed for Mr Prior's class.'

Roger waved his hand impatiently.

'I finished typing I guess about ten o'clock and went downstairs. There's a water-fountain down there just around the corner from the auditorium entrance, and I

92

was feeling thirsty so I stopped to drink. I must have been partly hidden by the announcement board – and besides the lights on that side of the lobby were out. So they didn't see me.'

'They?' Matthew asked.

'Cubby and Shana. They came across the lobby and went up the stairs to the lighting booth.'

Roger bristled. 'Why was the theatre open at that hour?'

'I don't know, Prof. Maybe Calvin opened it.'

'Calvin?' It was Matthew's turn to be startled.

'Yes. He came out of the men's room at the other side of the lobby and went up the stairs after them.'

Matthew's chocolate was left to grow cold. A half-eaten bagel lay abandoned on a paper plate.

'But Calvin didn't say a word about seeing Cubby last night.'

Ken looked from Matthew to Roger and back to Matthew like a friendly puppy half-afraid he may have chewed the wrong bedroom slipper. 'He might have been ashamed, Mr Prior.'

'Ashamed?'

'That he was on the downside of the triangle.'

Matthew's eyes narrowed. 'The eternal one?'

Ken nodded reluctantly.

'Cubby, Shana and Calvin?'

Roger intervened. 'You mean Cubby and Calvin were both in – er – love with Shana?'

Ken lowered his eyes and blushed. 'No, sir,' he said. 'I mean Calvin and Shana were both in love with Cubby.'

Roger gulped and Matthew raised his eyebrows. 'A very modern triangle,' he said. 'How did you know about it?'

Ken looked even more embarrassed. 'Department gossip. I guess everyone knew – except maybe Shana and Cal.'

'And Cubby?'

'Cubby thought it was a big joke – keeping them both on the string without them knowing it. Neither of them had a really close friend who would tell them.'

'Oh, my God,' said Roger. 'This is beginning to sound like one of the nastier Jacobean tragedies.'

There was an awkward silence in which Matthew moodily crumbled his bagel, Roger stared frozenly at the wall, and Ken shifted uneasily from foot to foot.

'I thought I should tell someone, Prof,' he said finally. 'I figured it might be important.'

'Yes, yes, Ken. You did the right thing. Mr Prior and I will handle it from here. You'd better go now – but for Heaven's sake, don't say a word about this to anyone else.'

Ken was about to leave when Matthew stopped him. 'You say you saw all three of them go into the theatre. Did you see anyone come out?'

'Oh, no, Mr Prior. I didn't hang around. I went straight back to the residence.'

Matthew had no more questions, so Roger ushered the boy out, patting him reassuringly on the shoulder.

'Well,' he said to Matthew when they were alone again, 'I suppose someone should tell Bain.'

'I will,' said Matthew. 'At least he'll know I'm keeping my ears open.'

# Chapter Ten

Matthew did not go directly to the incident room to speak to Bain. Instead he decided to look for Calvin. At that time of the afternoon, he was usually to be found in the meditation room in the student centre. Looking in there, however, Matthew saw no one but an elderly political science professor stretched out on a couch and a girl who looked like the young Virginia Woolf, practising yoga breathing exercises. Matthew ducked hastily out again and was about to try the next likeliest place – the graduate students' lounge – when he ran into Marie-Ange. Her pretty oval face lit up when she saw him.

'Mr Prior! What luck bumping into you! I was just on my way to see you about the rehearsal schedule. I need to know who's taking over from Cubby.'

'Oh, right,' said Matthew. 'I think it'll have to be Joe. He's dark, which isn't really right for the hero – but I think he can handle it. We can always get him a blond wig. Alan Bernstein can move up to hero's best friend – and get one of the third-years to do the utility man. Professor Mold has already suggested a boy called Duncan Hogg.'

'Oh, yes – Duncan will be great. He did a terrific Ralph in *The Knight of the Burning Pestle* last year.'

'That's that, then. Oh, by the way, do you know where I can find Calvin?'

Marie-Ange shook her head. 'Sorry. You might try asking the graduate secretary. She keeps tabs on where the grad students are.'

Waving good-bye, Marie-Ange went off to sort out the rehearsal schedule for the following week, while Matthew headed for the pay-phone near the cafeteria to call the graduate office.

This time he found out what he wanted to know. Calvin had gone into Toronto to research some eighteenth-century music scores at the Metro Reference Library. Matthew considered waiting till he got back to campus but then decided that a trip to Toronto would give him a much-needed change of scene.

The sky had cleared, and for the first time in several days the campus looked brighter under the pale winter sunshine. The snowy land dazzled the eye with reflected light and the air was clean and sharp. Matthew had snatched up his heavy tweed overcoat and his brief-case before he left the office and now, as he trudged along the slushy pathways to the parking lot, he looked around him at the throngs of students in their vividly coloured anoraks and parkas, cheerful in the unexpected sunlight, and could hardly believe that anything sinister had grown in such wholesome ground. But two, not so unlike themselves, were dead, and one, very unlike themselves it was to be hoped, was that ultimate solipsist, a taker of lives.

The trip to Toronto was not unpleasant in spite of slippery roads and several traffic jams on the freeway caused by messy but non-fatal car accidents. Matthew drove along the shore of Lake Ontario, past the deserted pleasure gardens of Ontario Place, the Canadian National Exhibition grounds, the slender, sky-piercing CN Tower and eventually turned down the exit ramp at York Street and up the broad boulevard of University Avenue, its impressive prospect closed at the top by the dirty pink of the Provincial Parliament

96

building at Queen's Park, as elaborately ugly as a raspberry shape made for a Victorian banquet. He found a parking space eventually in a quiet tree-lined street near the University of Toronto campus and walked up to Yorkville Avenue with its smart boutiques and expensive restaurants. Where this street met Yonge Street, the city's main thoroughfare, stood the red brick and glass building that housed Toronto's central reference library.

The wind blowing up Yonge Street was piercing, so he crossed hurriedly and pushed his way through the glass doors into the warm interior. Inside, the atmosphere was part greenhouse, part cathedral. Green plants flourished around reflecting pools in the foyer and in the main body of the building a central atrium rose five storeys to a glass roof through which the wintry light filtered down. The glass elevator which Matthew took up to the music department was an acrophobic's nightmare, offering a dizzying view of the lower galleries as it sped up the side of the atrium. Slightly shaken, Matthew stepped out at the appropriate floor and almost immediately spotted Calvin sitting at one of the long tables, his head bent over a large music folio.

Matthew slipped quietly into a seat next to him and whispered: 'Hello, Calvin.'

Calvin looked up startled, and Matthew saw the traces of sleeplessness and grief on his face.

'Hello, Mr Prior – er – Matthew. I didn't know you were coming into town.'

'I wasn't. I came to look for you.'

Calvin's eyes grew guarded and he tugged nervously at his moustache. 'Was it about the music? I think I've found something – a terrific bit of Arne – from *Artaxerxes*. We could re-orchestrate it. Give it a kind of heavy metal feel. It would be really wild!'

'Fine, fine,' said Matthew, 'but that wasn't what I wanted to see you about.'

Calvin's face paled. 'Is it about Cubby?'

'Yes, and I think we'd better find somewhere else to talk. People over there are making shushing noises.'

Matthew led Calvin to the elevator and soon they had found a small peaceful restaurant a few blocks away. They sat in a booth and ordered coffee. Matthew, giving way once again to his craving for carbohydrates, called the waitress back and ordered a slice of pecan pie and a piece of carrot cake as well. Then he turned to the purpose of the interview.

'Calvin, at the rehearsal yesterday – why didn't you tell me you'd seen Cubby the night before?'

Calvin blinked and looked frantically around the restaurant as if searching for a way of escape.

'The night before? Who – who says so?'

Matthew didn't reply.

'It was Shana, I suppose,' Calvin said bitterly. 'Well, she was still with him when I left, so she's the one you should be asking the questions.'

'No, it wasn't Shana as a matter of fact – and I *will* talk to her – but you must see, Calvin, that in the circumstances you should have said something.'

'Oh, shit,' exclaimed Calvin, and buried his head in his hands.

It was Matthew's turn to look nervously around the restaurant. Two young men sitting at a table near by had clearly drawn their own conclusions about what was going on. They smiled knowingly at Matthew and then began to whisper to each other with obvious relish.

'Come on, Calvin,' said Matthew uneasily. 'Calm down.'

Calvin gulped and turned his swollen, red-rimmed eyes on Matthew. 'That's easy to say,' he croaked. 'You don't know what it was like!'

'Maybe not. What was it like?'

'You wouldn't understand.'

'Try me.'

Calvin blew his nose on the paper napkin and stuffed it into the pocket of his jeans. The expression of soggy despair on his face was replaced by one of brave defiance.

'I'm gay,' he said.

'And the Pope's Catholic,' said Matthew. 'What's the big deal? Let me tell you something, Calvin. For two romantic years at Cambridge, I was as gay as a goose. A lot of sweet agonies in an idyllic hothouse. Then I met Henrietta – and that seemed to work all right. Not that I don't feel the occasional fleeting lust for a well-put-together male, but I dare say I'm not as unusual in that respect as most people would like to believe.'

Calvin began to look interested. 'You know, Matthew, you're the first straight man I've met who's ever admitted anything like that.'

'Damn "straight" and "gay"! People don't divide that neatly into groups. Don't let your pink triangle ideology blind you. I imagine that's what got you into trouble with Cubby. You thought he belonged in a neatly labelled box with you.'

Calvin sighed. 'And he kept hopping into other boxes. Yes, you're right. I loved him and I guess I was fooling myself into thinking he was as gay as I was – Sorry, that he was *like* I was. I should have known from the beginning that Cubby took his kicks where he could find them.'

'Polymorphously perverse.'

'I suppose. Anyway, it was the night before last that I realised how true that was. I went to the lighting booth to check some pre-sets and found Shana and Cubby together.'

'Did you have a row?'

Calvin shook his head. 'No. I checked the lighting board and left.'

'Shana and Cubby were still there?'

99

'Yes. That was the last time I saw him . . .'

Calvin showed signs of being about to break down again so Matthew swiftly went on to the next question.

'Do you think Shana knew about you and Cubby?'

'I don't think so. She didn't react that way. She just behaved like I was intruding.'

Matthew was silent. The restaurant noises around them suddenly seemed magnified: the rattle of spoons in cups, the hiss of the espresso machine, the scrape of chairlegs on the floor, the ping of the cash register. Matthew leaned forward and looked Calvin squarely in the eyes.

'Calvin, do you think Cubby killed himself?'

'No,' said Calvin. 'He loved himself too much to do that.'

'Hmm,' Matthew said. 'Do you remember what Oscar Wilde wrote in *The Ballad of Reading Gaol*?'

Calvin looked at him inquiringly and Matthew recited:

> Yet each man kills the thing he loves
> By each let this be heard
> Some do it with a bitter look
> Some with a flattering word.
> The coward does it with a kiss
> The brave man with a sword.

'The love that dare not speak its fucking name!' said Calvin savagely. 'Fuck Oscar Wilde. Cubby was a Lord Alfred Douglas if anything – a bloody troublemaker and a survivor.'

'Except that it looks as if someone decided he had survived long enough. I hope, Calvin, that it wasn't you.'

Sergeant Kozetsky was waiting for Matthew in his office. The sergeant and Inspector Bain had discussed the significance of the pink-and-blue tights till they had given each other headaches. Kozetsky felt that a fresh view of the subject might be valuable and had come looking for

Matthew with that in mind. Bonny had assured him that Matthew had an appointment with a play-writing student in about fifteen minutes, so he was sure to be back soon. Kozetsky, therefore, made himself comfortable in the acid-yellow armchair and began to browse through a copy of William Archer's *Playmaking*. He had just begun the chapter on 'Exposition: Its Ends and Its Means' when Matthew walked in. Matthew masked his surprise with a polite smile, squeezed behind his desk and sat down.

'Interesting stuff, this,' said the sergeant. 'Exposition. Something you don't think about when you're watching *Dynasty* on television.'

'Ah, yes,' said Matthew, 'but, of course, a lot of modern playwrights don't bother with it much. All that careful planting of information, casual revelation through dialogue so the audience knows where it is, what time of the year, who the characters are, and what they've done in the past. A sort of orientation device really. Not very useful if you want your audience disoriented, though.'

'Like Pinter,' the sergeant suggested tentatively.

'Some Pinter. Some me, for that matter.'

'It's a bit like investigation in reverse. Planting the clues, setting up the signposts.'

'Yes. There's another device called foreshadowing. It gives the audience a kind of pre-echo of a forthcoming event.'

Kozetsky shifted in his chair and closed the book. 'I suppose,' he said, 'that sometimes the signposts are set up by the playwright to fool the audience – to lead them to expect something that doesn't in fact happen.'

Matthew smiled. 'Well, that's more my brother's line. Paul Prior. He wrote *Cadaver* and *Habeas Corpus*. Big successes. Made him lots of money.'

'I saw the movie of *Cadaver*. Now that was very ingenious. I was sure Tom Courtenay was the murderer until the last five minutes when it turned out to be Albert Finney. Of course it's not the kind of thing we run into much in the OPP. Most murders turn out to be very simple – or so random that they're impossible to solve.'

A sudden gust of wind outside shook the window. Kozetsky waited expectantly. Matthew stared back at him.

'Is all this leading somewhere, sergeant?' he asked.

'This way to the egress,' Kozetsky said.

Matthew looked baffled.

'Sorry, Mr Prior. I thought you might recognise the reference. P. T. Barnum – a great American showman. He wanted to keep the crowds moving through some exhibit of his – so he could get more people in and make more money. So he put up a sign: "This way to the egress". People thought it pointed the way to another exhibit – an exotic bird or something – but when they followed it, they found themselves outside on the street. They didn't know "egress" was just a fancy word for "exit".'

Matthew's interest quickened. 'And *you* think, sergeant, that somebody may be doing that to us. Elephant penises and pink-and-blue tights. Deliberately chosen to send us barking up the wrong tree.'

'It's worth thinking about.'

Matthew applied his mental brakes hurriedly. 'Wait a minute,' he said, 'wait a minute. You're trying to pique my interest – get me more and more involved in this damned investigation. I've promised to keep my ears open and ask a few questions – *when* I have time. That's all – and I'm sticking to it.'

The sergeant rose to leave, shaking his head regretfully. 'It's a pity, sir. I think you could be a real help. In fact, I think you're kidding yourself, if you don't mind me saying so. You've got a whiff of the chase. I don't think you'll be able to stop now.'

102

After the sergeant left, Matthew sat cursing silently. The significance of the pink-and-blue tights hadn't escaped him, and now his mind, the brakes released, began to career furiously ahead. What connected those things: the elephant penis, the pink-and-blue tights, the theatre ticket, the scrap of photograph, Cubby's bisexual affairs? Or were they connected? Was Dodie's murder the random act of a maniac? Was Cubby the murderer and was his suicide the result of remorse? Or was his suicide due to some other cause? Was it a suicide after all, in fact? Damn the sergeant; he was right. Matthew's curiosity was aroused. But that didn't mean he was going to involve himself any further. One thing he might do, though, which wouldn't cost him much time or commit him any more completely was to have a little chat with Shana Pilton. A quiet director-to-lighting-designer chat over a coffee and a muffin.

There was a shy tap at the door. It was time for his session with Walt Dunn, who was trying to write a play about incest on an Ontario farm between a grandfather and a granddaughter.

'Come in,' he said, preparing himself for an hour of brain-drenching gloom.

It was while they were deep in a discussion of whether the central situation was really plausible, given the mores of rural Ontario, that Matthew remembered that he hadn't told Kozetsky about Cubby's involvement with Calvin and Shana. 'Oh, Lord!' he thought, 'the less I want to get involved the more difficult it gets. Now I'll have to find Kozetsky and tell him, which will look like I've decided to play "amateur-sleuth-helping-police", or, if I don't, face the possibility of being charged with concealing evidence.' Impatiently he turned his attention back to Walt Dunn.

'Sort of like Electra,' Walt was saying.

'Eh? Electra,' Matthew seemed to have lost the thread.

'Or Oedipus in reverse.'

he had wound up at La Freluche International Academy in Lausanne. His career there hadn't been distinguished either, but since it was little more than a holding facility for rich juvenile delinquents from all over the world, his behaviour had not seemed quite so out of place.

Cubby had returned to Canada when he was eighteen and ready for university. But Hugh's alma mater, the University of Toronto, had flatly refused to admit him and so had McGill, Queen's, Carleton, Guelph, York, Western, Brock, Trent and various other institutions across Canada and the USA. In the end it was a toss-up between the University of Miami and Wacousta. Hugh was on the Board of Governors at Wacousta, and Miami – in Hugh's opinion – offered Cubby too many opportunities for becoming either a beach bum or a cocaine trafficker. So Wacousta it was.

Cubby was clearly never going to make it as a lawyer like his grandfather, a doctor like his uncle, or a businessman and a politician like his father. What he did have were the qualities of a first-class con-man and, primary among those qualities, the ability to assume convincingly a different persona for any given set of circumstances. Consequently, though actors ranked, in the Kirkwood world, somewhere slightly above used-car salesmen, Cubby had entered the performance programme in the Wacousta theatre department. Even there he had barely skirted disaster several times. In his first year, on a class trip to New York City, something had happened that could have blown up into a major scandal, but Hugh Kirkwood's influence had been exerted strenuously to hush it up. The incident still troubled Hugh, but he argued to himself that the girl had probably decided, like so many of her generation, to drop out of society and take to the road. She was probably somewhere in California selling handmade crafts to tourists. What had upset Hugh even more was Cubby's gradual involvement in a sub-culture of young people who exalted androgyny, eccentric clothing, and a kind of kamikaze attitude to the arts. He had long had doubts about Cubby's sexual orientation and this affronted his old Toronto, Presbyterian-tinted masculinity.

Now all his worries about the boy, the tensions, the irritations, and the occasional moments of pleasure when, for instance, they had sailed together from the family dock on Lake Laurent, were ended. Cubby was dead. For a moment an uncharacteristic weakness overcame the minister and his vision blurred as the tears welled up and spilled down his cheeks. The elevator stopped and the doors opened. Kirkwood hastily pulled a handkerchief from his breast pocket and dabbed at his eyes as he stumbled out, almost colliding with a tall, thin, vague-looking man who was biting into a large cinnamon Danish.

'Excuse me, old boy,' the man said in an unmistakably English accent, and squeezed past Hugh into the elevator.

'Goddam Brits!' Kirkwood muttered to himself, and stalked off towards the Dean's office.

Dean Ripper was a man of considerable ambition. He had been born in Streaky Bay, South Australia, right on the Great Australian Bight, and had left there at eighteen for Adelaide where he became apprenticed to a photographer. One of the photographer's clients, the rich widow of a sheep farmer, took a fancy to young Vernon, or 'Vern' as she preferred to call him, and had sent him to university. There, he became involved with some young film-makers, and in 1963 their first effort – *Koala Summer* – won a national student film award. After graduation, and a very difficult parting from the widow, Vern Ripper left for the States and enrolled at UCLA, where he earned a master's degree in cinematography. From there it was a short step to Hollywood, so in those heady days when California was awash in flower children and psychedelically decorated Volkswagen vans, young Vern with his dark hair down to his shoulders, his jeans jacket decorated with peace symbols and his hashish pipe in his haversack, arrived on Sunset Strip.

The Australian film industry had not yet astonished the world, and his arrival in the kingdom of shadows was greeted with condescending amusement rather than awed admiration. But young Vern was brash, energetic and loud. It was hard to ignore him. After a few months of scuffling around, sleeping with a few influential people, and supplying good-quality Panama Red to a front-office man at Astral Studios, he was given a job as second-unit director on an exploitation movie called *Hellcat in Leather*. Years later it earned the distinction of winning a Golden Turkey Award from the Medved brothers. At the time, however, it did very little for Vern's career.

A stroke of luck brought him to Canada. It was 1967 and the World's Fair was being held in Montreal. The Australian Pavilion on the Expo '67 site had, among its several attractions, a mini-movie theatre showing classic Australian movies. There, in repertory with *The Overlanders*, *Eureka Stockade* and *The Siege of Pinchgut*, *Koala Summer* was being screened. Vern, as the only one of its co-creators able to attend, was invited to be a representative of the Australian arts for the run of the fair. It was through meeting young contemporary film-makers from Toronto, Vancouver and Quebec in his official capacity that he became one of the midwives at the rebirth of Canadian film – or rather of what appeared to be a rebirth. In retrospect, it could more easily be seen as a hysterical pregnancy.

Nevertheless, it was his direction of *Beverage Room Blues*, a study of four unemployed sewer-workers who masquerade as members of the Greek Olympic Darts Team and are given a civic reception by the mayor of Ottawa, that brought him to the attention of the Canadian media. Had he been Canadian by birth he would have been quickly forgotten, but as an exotic outsider, trailing clouds of international film glamour, he was able to parlay his brief celebrity into an ongoing career as a popular savant, appearing on television panels and radio talk-shows, and contributing voluminously to every arts periodical and newspaper entertainment section in the country. In next to no time he had become one of those who were famous for being famous, and was invited to sit on arts commissions, advisory boards and film award juries. In 1974, he was asked to join the film department at Wacousta as its chairman and three years later he became dean of the faculty.

To say he made a formidable dean would be an understatement. His loud Australian breeziness made his more introverted Canadian colleagues cringe and sent his prim English colleagues into a huff. The Americans on the faculty dealt with him as if he were a Texan, which seemed to work well enough, but generally they were all flattened by the steam-roller of his personality. So Dean Ripper, confident in his ability to handle all comers, felt no qualms when the Hon. Hugh Kirkwood was ushered into his office.

The office itself would have intimidated a lesser man than Kirkwood. It was the size of a small aircraft hangar – with a cathedral ceiling and windows twenty feet high. It contained a massive desk of brushed steel and plexiglass which could easily have been exhibited at a gallery of modern art as 'Arrangement of Planes No. 2'. The walls were decorated with huge blown-up posters for some of the films the Dean had been associated with as well as a shot of a younger Vern in swimtrunks on the Great Barrier Reef. There was a conversation pit with rolled-up futons and a short-legged Japanese table lacquered in black and gold. One wall held a projection screen and near it there were shelves full of film and videotapes. Other shelves held every volume of *Screen World Annual*, as well as hundreds of technical and historical volumes about the film industry. The wall-to-wall carpet was deep plum and the several comfortable armchairs placed about the room were upholstered in a grey and lilac figured material. The office had been designed as a sculpture studio, but the Dean had commandeered it on his appointment and furnished it with money that he had diverted from various departmental budgets.

Hugh Kirkwood entered and, apart from making a mental note that his own office in the Parliament Buildings looked positively dingy in comparison, took no further notice of his surroundings. He marched straight across to Dean Ripper, who was pretending to complete a transatlantic call ('Bon soir, François, et mes remercies à Mademoiselle Moreau'), and confronted him.

'Vern, what the hell kind of operation are you running here?' he demanded. 'You and all the goddam members of your faculty are supposed to be *in loco parentis* to the kids here. They're supposed to go about getting an education without being raped, or gassed, or attacked by homicidal maniacs!'

The Dean stood up and made various deprecating gestures with his large, well-manicured hands. 'Hughie, I've got to tell you how sorry I am about Cubby. It's been a blow to us all. He was a wonderful . . .'

Kirkwood stopped him in mid-sentence. 'He was a pain in the ass, a troublemaker; he was a disappointment to me all his life – but goddam it, he was my son!' He ended on what was almost a howl of anguish and the tears started to his eyes again.

'Easy, Hughie,' said the Dean firmly and then bared his large teeth in the semblance of a reassuring and sympathetic smile.

110

'Easy!' snarled Kirkwood. 'How can I be easy? I won't be easy till I know exactly what's been going on here.'

The Dean walked round his desk and threw open his arms in an extravagant gesture of entreaty – an effect known to his colleagues as his 'Zorba the Greek pose'.

'Hughie, I know it's a sad and terrible thing, but it's not so mysterious. Young men at that age are very unstable; the pressures of university life, fear of failure, anxiety about identity, uncertainty about peer acceptance – these things cause many of them to crack up and commit suicide.'

Kirkwood thrust his face into the Dean's and yelled: 'It was *not* suicide. Cubby would never have committed suicide. Do you think he gave a damn about peer acceptance or any of that claptrap? He was far too goddam pleased with himself ever to commit suicide.'

The Dean sighed. 'You knew the boy best, I suppose – but surely you don't seriously believe that we have a homicidal maniac on the loose here?'

'You have every kind of goddam screwball on the loose here. This whole goddam faculty is full of maniacs. I should have sent him somewhere to study computer programming.'

The Dean inwardly had to admit that the faculty did encompass a number of borderline psychotics, a few cases of *folie de grandeur*, several manic-depressives, and at least one example of multiple personality. Nevertheless, he was reasonably sure that none of them were homicidal. 'What is it you want, Hughie?' he asked after a moment's pause.

Kirkwood knew exactly what he wanted and he told him.

'I want to be the next premier of this province – and I mean to be. No goddam scandal is going to take that away from me. I want this thing cleared up and I want

111

it done quietly. I've spoken to the commissioner of the OPP and I've had a word with senior management of all the news media. I want *you* to make sure that none of your screwballs gives any interviews to reporters and I want full co-operation from everybody in this nut-house with the men who are conducting the investigation. If I don't get what I want, I think you know what'll happen, Vern.'

The Dean's smile froze, a reaction that Kirkwood noted with pleasure.

'One of my great buddies in the cabinet, Vern, as you know, is the Minister of Colleges and Universities. You might have to say "bye-bye" to that fat grant for expanding the fine arts complex.'

Since Dean Ripper had spent the better part of five years getting approval for the construction of new studio and theatre spaces on campus, and since his reputation, his *amour propre*, and perhaps even his future rested on the successful completion of this project, Kirkwood's threat was a very potent one. The Dean had, however, not reached his present comfortable position of prestige and privilege without developing, along the way, sharply honed techniques of survival.

'Hughie,' he said, slapping Kirkwood on the back, 'I don't think you have a thing to worry about. As a matter of fact, right here on this faculty we have a distinguished visitor who's made a bit of a name for himself as a private investigator. Do you remember the Peter Parley murder case in England?'

Kirkwood grunted. 'Peter Parley? Yes. I felt like flying over to London to shake the murderer's hand. I never liked that smarmy Brit – always greasing up to dead-beat ex-Presidents on his TV show.'

The Dean beamed. 'Well, it was Matthew Prior who identified the killer.'

112

'Matthew Prior? Is he a tall, skinny Brit with a rah-rah accent?'

The Dean agreed that this was a fairly accurate description.

'Then that's the jerk who nearly knocked me over getting off the elevator. Called me "old boy" – bloody arrogant s.o.b.!'

'Clever, though,' said the Dean. 'Keen eye for detail. He could help to wind this mess up very quickly and very quietly.'

'Prior?'

'Prior.'

Kirkwood nodded grudgingly. 'All right. If there's any special help he needs, I'll see he gets it. Just keep him away from me.'

'Done, Hughie. Now, how about a drop of good Kentucky bourbon? I know it's your favourite.'

Looking in on them later, the Dean's secretary saw the minister snoring on a futon in the conversation pit with a half-empty bottle of Jack Daniels beside him on the Japanese table, while Dean Ripper sat behind his desk playing happily with a handsome scale model of the proposed fine arts extension.

# Chapter Twelve

The pathologist's report established once and for all that Cubby had not committed suicide. There was a fracture-dislocation of the second and third cervical vertebrae and a rupture of the spinal cord – all of which were consistent with a hanging death – but the hyoid bone in the throat was also broken and the thyroid and cricoid cartilages were damaged, all indications of manual throttling before the hanging occurred. Once Matthew had passed on his information about the rendezvous in the lighting booth, suspicion focused on Cubby's two lovers, Calvin and Shana, and since Shana was slightly built, Calvin seemed the more likely suspect. Matthew remembered the murder of a fellow playwright, Joe Orton, by his lover, Ken Halliwell, and concluded gloomily that such violent conclusions to homosexual love affairs were not to be discounted – but somehow he could not quite believe in Calvin as a murderer.

Inspector Bain and Sergeant Kozetsky were less doubtful than Matthew. In fact they considered Calvin to be an all-too-likely candidate, particularly as he had no absolute alibi for the night of the murder. So it was with some expectation of success that they entered Calvin's room in the graduate student residence to conduct a search. The room was, in many ways, a remarkable one. The walls were covered from floor to ceiling with posters, postcard reproductions of famous paintings, photographs, sketches of sets and costumes, handbills of plays, and beef-cake pin-ups of such youthful film and television stars as Lorenzo Lamas, Tony Danza, Tom Cruise and Matt Dillon. Almost the whole of the wall-space above the bed was taken up by a bullfighter's suit of lights and cape, spread out and pinned to a panel of white velvet. The bed itself was draped in a black spread, sewn all over with the signs of the zodiac in silver thread, and piled with magenta cushions. In a chair by the window sat an artist's lay figure, dressed in motor-cycle leathers and with a Harlequin mask over its face.

'If this is a picture of what the inside of his head's like,' said Bain churlishly, 'he'll probably get off on an insanity plea.'

'Hardly get off, sir. An insanity plea could land him in the bug-house for a lot longer than most convicted murderers do in the slammer.'

'Slammer!' snorted Bain. 'Where do you pick up your slang? Mickey Spillane?'

Kozetsky decided to let that one pass and began a rapid but systematic search of the room, emptying drawers, turning up the rugs, and looking under the mattress. Bain meanwhile was studying the pictures and other memorabilia on the walls.

'Funny, I don't see any pictures of his boyfriend,' he said when he had finished his survey.

'Plenty of signs of a rich fantasy life, though,' said Kozetsky, pointing to a cache under the mattress of various magazines with titles like *Stallion* and *Torso*, all of them featuring naked males in provocative poses.

Bain's face registered disgust. 'Why they want to look at pictures of hairy thugs with their drawers off beats me,' he said.

Kozetsky knew better than to offer any explanation that would smack of night-school psychology classes. No amount of explanation would leave the Inspector other than resolutely and glumly baffled. Bain, like many police-men of his generation, had never accepted the liberalisation in 1969 of the laws against homosexuality. Kozetsky, who had grown up during the summer of love and peace and who had even been to Woodstock, was committed to at least a theoretical tolerance.

'Nothing much here that's any help,' he said when he'd finished turning things over. 'Nothing that tells us anything we didn't know already. Here's his diary, for instance . . .' He held up a small leather-bound book. 'It's really just a list of appointments. Nothing for the night of the mur-der except "Check pre-sets", and we know he went to the theatre to do that.'

'All right,' said Bain. 'Let's go. No point in wasting any more time here.'

As they began to leave, Bain's sleeve caught something on top of Calvin's work table and sent it clattering to the floor. It was a small brass pot with a perforated lid. Stan Kozetsky recognised it from his long-ago nights in crash-pads on Yorkville Avenue as an incense burner. Stooping to pick it up, he saw a small square of shiny white material lying on the carpet beside it.

'Here's something,' he said. Straightening up, he held it to the light. It was a segment of photographic print. 'Take a look, sir. Is that who I think it is?'

Bain peered at the piece of photograph and then whis-tled in surprise. 'Well, darn my socks! It's a picture of the Goldberg girl!'

Shana Pilton was not someone who had impressed her-self much on Matthew's consciousness, despite her bizarre appearance. He had seen her at the first production meet-ing and thereafter only dimly as a figure up in the lighting booth. Calvin's greater competence in lighting design and other technical details had persuaded Matthew to leave

116

most of the liaison work in those areas to him. Now that he was face to face with Shana for virtually the first time, he realised that she was, leaving aside the stark white makeup, the black rimmed eyes and the multicoloured spiked coiffeur, a very attractive girl. She was not, however, very polite.

Matthew had persuaded her, with some difficulty, to meet him in the quiet and little-used faculty lounge belonging to the School of Anthropological Studies, a venue he had been introduced to by the professor whose African relic had been used to murder Dodie Goldberg. It was at the very top of the Life Sciences Building, hidden away at the end of a long corridor so that few knew of its existence. Even the few who did were not always prepared to make the long trek to reach it when there was a perfectly adequate cafeteria on the ground floor. For Matthew, it had some of the atmosphere of a London club – cosily panelled in pine stained to look like dark oak, with bookshelves full of leather-bound collections of anthropological magazines and paperback copies of novels by Jean Auel, Pierre Boulle and William Golding. To say that Shana looked exotic in such a setting would be less than adequate, and the lady behind the counter who dispensed sandwiches and glasses of Canadian wine said as much with her eyebrows. The effect on Shana was negligible. Clearly disapproval was something she had learned to ignore, if indeed she didn't actively seek it out as further confirmation of how hide-bound society in general was.

Matthew settled down in a corner of the room, far removed from the two or three other lunchtime customers. Shana sat opposite him and looked disdainfully from her small plate of salad and bean sprouts to his trayful of corned beef sandwiches, potato chips, pickles, and Boston cream pie.

117

'You'll be dead by the time you're forty,' she pronounced.

'Impossible,' said Matthew. 'I'm past forty already.'

'I suppose you expect me to say "Really! You don't look it!"?'

'Certainly not,' said Matthew. 'I dislike insincerity.'

'Well, you don't look it,' said Shana aggressively. 'It's probably because you're one of those Peter Pan types who've been protected all their lives by a lot of motherly women.'

Matthew summoned up the images of Henrietta, Nell and Dorothy. Henrietta, of course, *was* a mother, but surely neither Nell nor Dorothy could be called motherly. On the other hand, in all justice, he could see that each of them had protected him in one way or another. Hastily, he sought solace in a mouthful of corned beef on rye.

'We're not here to psychoanalyse me,' he mumbled with his mouth full.

'Just as well,' said Shana. 'I can't think of anything more boring.'

'You can't? I can. Gratuitous rudeness, for example. An occasional dollop of it might add a little zest to conversation, but unremitting, repetitive impoliteness is paralysingly dull.'

'Pardon me for living,' Shana said vulgarly.

'You're pardoned,' said Matthew. 'Now, how about if I asked you a few questions, and you endeavoured to answer them without any impertinent addenda.'

Shana suddenly grinned at him. 'You sure know how to sling the old vocabulary around. OK – you're on. Ask.'

'When did you last see Cubby?'

'On the night he – died.'

'What time did you see him?'

Shana shrugged. 'I don't know. Around eleven-thirty I guess. I wasn't keeping my eyes on the clock.'

118

'Where was he when you left him?'

'Still in the theatre. He said something about trying something out on the stage.'

'And Calvin? Did you see him that evening?'

Shana frowned. 'Yes, earlier. He burst into the lighting booth when we were in the middle of what I guess you'd call "making out". He must have snuck up on his little tippy-toes. We didn't hear him till he was on top of us.'

'Did you know Cubby was sleeping with Calvin?'

'Sleeping?' she snorted. 'That's not exactly what they were doing. No, I didn't know till – later.'

'Later?'

'Cubby told me just after we'd finished making out on the floor.'

Matthew looked at his plate and realised he didn't want to eat any more. Thinking about Cubby took away his appetite. 'Did you see Calvin again that evening?' he asked wearily.

'No.'

'Did you see anyone else near the theatre?'

'No.'

Shana finished her salad and began to gather her things together. 'I've got a humanities class at two,' she said.

'Thanks for coming,' Matthew said, 'and if you think of anything else . . .'

'Wait a minute,' said Shana. 'I've just remembered. I did see somebody. I was on my way through the lobby to the main door when I saw the door of the women's john open. Whoever it was closed the door again quickly but it looked like a tall girl with long straight hair – nobody I knew, though.'

'In jeans or a skirt?'

'A skirt I think. Some kind of plaid number. Not what your typical fine arts student would wear.'

'But you didn't recognise her?'

Shana shook her head impatiently. 'I already said it wasn't anyone I knew.' Then she paused, a faint look of bewilderment passing across her face. 'There was *something* about her. Something familiar. Like someone I had imagined – or dreamt about maybe.'

Matthew stood up. 'If you see her again, let me know right away. Come on, I'll walk you as far as the Humanities Building.'

Matthew was deeply depressed by his interview with Shana. The more he heard about Cubby, the more heartsick he became. It was evident that he was among those at whose centre is a spreading darkness, a darkness that shrivelled what it touched. A fair face, a charming manner when he wished to use it, a background of wealth and privilege all of which had been directed towards ends that were self-defeating. Matthew remembered his old tutor at Cambridge, Mr Peascod, a gentle Victorian with side-whiskers, saying about a similar young man, Wilfred Lucas-Croft, 'I don't care who he sleeps with, dear boy, or where, or how often, if only he would remember that it involves more than two bodies: two histories intersect at every coital thrust.' Somewhere along the line in Cubby's life two histories had not merely intersected, they had collided and now Cubby was part of the wreckage.

As he wandered back to his office, his eye lit on two familiar figures. He almost didn't recognise Fraser McCullough who instead of his ceremonial kilt was wearing a leather car-coat over a well-cut tweed suit. The other figure was more immediately recognisable in his regular attire of blue jeans and bomber jacket. What puzzled Matthew was how Ken Meldrum came to be on such friendly terms with a member of the Board of Governors. As he drew nearer, they both recognised him and he thought he saw a look of alarm on Ken's face.

'Hello, Fraser . . . Ken . . .' he said, pausing beside them. 'Not a very comfortable place to have a conversation. It must be below zero.'

'Hello, Matthew. Ken was just telling me about the Kirkwood boy. Rotten business. Here, why don't you walk back to the theatre department with me. I have to see Roger about something.'

They said good-bye to Ken and walked on.

'I'd no idea you knew Ken. He's one of my more promising play-writing students.'

Fraser looked pleased. 'Is he? Good for him.'

'How *do* you know him?'

A sharp gust of wind blew Fraser's hair over his eyes, and he swore as he brushed it back. 'Damned wind tunnels on this campus!'

'Family friend, is he?' Matthew persisted.

Fraser shot him a look out of the corner of his eye. 'I used to know his mother,' he said shortly.

Treacherous ground, thought Matthew. Perhaps she was one of Fraser's lost loves, and promptly changed the subject.

'You must know Cubby's family, too?' he said.

'Very well at one time. It's not surprising the boy turned out so badly. His mother was a delightful woman but she died young. Hugh Kirkwood has always been a pompous self-centred jackass. Still, it's a thing I wouldn't have wished on him. His only son, you know, dead at twenty-two. I know what it's like to lose a son – and a daughter.'

They walked on for a moment in silence and then as they reached the entrance to the Fine Arts Building, Fraser made a startling announcement.

'By the way, Matthew, I'm not really going to see Roger. I'm taking Bonny to lunch. I'm going to ask her to marry me. Thought I ought to give you the straight of it. I fancy you're after her yourself, so I'm warning you off. See you later, Matthew. Better luck next time.'

He left Matthew standing in the freezing wind and marched on through the door.

# Chapter Thirteen

Thanks to the efforts of Hugh Kirkwood and Dean Ripper, a heavy blanket of security surrounded the investigation. The newspapers had reported Dodie's death, but without sensational details. Cubby's was given a small paragraph in which it was described as accidental and his relationship to a leading figure in the Provincial Government was played down. There was, of course, a great deal of gossip on campus, but a memo had gone out from the President to all faculty members asking them to emphasise to their classes that any indiscreet chattering to reporters which could be interpreted as either slanderous or as impeding the work of the police would be dealt with severely. This, coupled with the directives that came down from managing directors to editors of the local news media, succeeded – at least for a time – in suppressing any widespread public speculation about the events at Wacousta.

'Senseless to start a panic,' the President told his vice-presidents.

'We don't want to damage the image of the university,' the vice-presidents told the chief administrators.

'Let's avoid hysteria among the students,' the chief administrators told the deans.

Nevertheless, there was an atmosphere of unease on campus. The student patrol was overwhelmed with requests from single female students for escort services, and, after nightfall, if it were at all possible, students – male and female – arranged to move from place to place in groups of three or more.

Bain and Kozetsky, after the discovery of the scrap of photograph in Calvin's room, had decided that there was a clear link between Dodie's death and Cubby's. They would have been equally convinced that Calvin was responsible except for the fact that though he had no alibi for the night when Cubby was killed, he had a seemingly unbreakable one for the time of the attack on Dodie. He had been baby-sitting for a fellow graduate student and his wife, who had picked him up in their car from campus, driven him to their small farmhouse fifteen miles away and left him there while they attended a party in Toronto. The children had been annoyingly wakeful and were quite insistent under questioning that Uncle Cal had been with them until their parents returned at about one in the morning. The parents testified that they had insisted Calvin spend the night with them and had driven him back to campus the next morning. There was no way, they said, that Calvin could have left in the middle of the night and returned again. He couldn't drive – so he couldn't have used their car – and besides they were both light sleepers and would have heard him moving about.

This left Inspector Bain and Sergeant Kozetsky with a choice of several theories: that Calvin had murdered Cubby while Dodie's death was the work of someone else; that Calvin and Shana had conspired to murder both Dodie and Cubby; that Shana alone had committed the two murders; that Cubby had murdered Dodie and been murdered in revenge by Calvin or Shana or someone else; or that both killings were the work of a person or persons unknown. As far as Bain was concerned both Calvin and Shana were kinky enough to have thought up the bizarre murder methods. Furthermore, Shana's story, passed on by Matthew, of having seen a mystery girl hiding in the ladies' washroom could have been invented by her to tie in with the report Mrs Napoleon had made about the girl who had followed Dodie into the tunnel. A description of the girl had, after all, been circulated when the appeal went out for her to come forward.

'Bloody murder cases, Stan,' complained the Inspector. 'They give you nothing but grief. Ten years away from retirement, maybe my last chance for promotion, and I get stuck with this – this – can of worms!'

Kozetsky sighed sympathetically. 'It's a mess all right, sir – but there's got to be a logical connection. The negatives link them; the murder methods link them. Someone has to have some idea about what ties them all together.'

'Someone? Who? Let's face it, Stan: the Goldberg girl's death seems completely motiveless; the Kirkwood boy's death looks like the result of a love triangle. The negatives, the pink-and-blue tights, the girl in the skirt could all be part of an attempt to confuse us – to make us *think* that the deaths must be linked.'

Stan groaned inwardly. Round and round, he thought, like rats in a maze. This way and that, looking for an exit only to find ourselves back in the middle. This way to the egress – huh!

Bain got up and moved towards the door. 'Come on, Stan.'

'Where are we going, sir?'

'We're going to question Mr Knox and Miss Pilton again. And again and again, if necessary, till we get somewhere.'

Rehearsals were continuing inside the Charles Heavysege Theatre, not without a touch of hysteria. The cast changes that had been made meant that a lot of scenes which had been more or less 'set' were now being re-staged. Ursula, as usual, was dealing with the crisis intelligently and professionally, but Joe Innocenti was finding it difficult not only

125

to learn the lines for the leading rôle but also to forget the lines he had already learned for his previous rôle. He and Alan Bernstein were in the middle of a scene of mock-Victorian melodrama, Joe as good-hearted Ben Bowsprit, the innocent sailor lad, and Alan as Jack Mainbrace, his loyal shipmate. For the eleventh time that afternoon, Alan stopped the scene.

'Joe, you just said *my* line again. What the fuck am I supposed to do? You're driving me schizo!'

'I'm doing my best, you goddam asshole!' screeched Joe.

'Oh, Lord!' yelled Matthew, beating on the director's table with both fists. 'Bloody well *concentrate*! Don't shriek at each other like fishwives. I've seen more concentration at a tiny tots' talent show on Bognor beach.'

'Shit! Shit! Shit!' screamed Joe, flinging his sailor hat down on the stage and stamping off into the wings in a fury.

Matthew closed his eyes and leaned back in his chair. 'Nasty temper that boy's got,' he said to Marie-Ange and Calvin who were sitting on either side of him.

'He's a dirty little beast,' said Calvin.

Wayne Goffman, who had overheard this, began to snigger. 'You're just saying that 'cause he showed you his ass, Cal,' Wayne said.

Calvin blushed but didn't reply.

'Isn't that right, Cal?' Wayne persisted. 'Everybody in the dressing-room had a good laugh at that. Cubby didn't think it was funny, though.'

Matthew opened his eyes slowly and looked at Wayne who was sitting on the edge of the stage wearing his admiral's hat and an epauletted uniform jacket over a T-shirt and blue jeans.

'What was this all about, Wayne?'

Wayne shrugged. 'Oh, just some fooling about in the dressing-room.'

'Which Cubby wasn't amused by?'

'Amused by? He and Joe got into it so bad we thought they were going to kill each other. We had to hold Joe back.'

'Kill each other?' Matthew murmured.

Wayne gradually registered the implication of what he had said.

'Oh! – n–no – I didn't mean . . . It was just an expression. I mean, I don't think Joe would have . . . Joe and Cubby were room-mates – friends!'

'Dr and Mrs Crippen were room-mates,' offered Matthew.

Wayne shook his head thoughtfully. 'Joe sure was mad, though. But he brought it on himself. Cubby had chewed him out before about mooning and stuff.'

'Mooning?'

'Yeah! Hanging a moon – showing your bare ass to people. He'd do it out of car windows to a bunch of girls. He did it out of the dorm window once when the Lieutenant-Governor was on an official visit.'

'Vulgar little Italian punk,' Calvin muttered. 'He's got no business at university at all. He should be waiting tables in a pizza parlour.'

'Hey, sometimes he'd show more than his ass,' Wayne went on, now in full spate. 'Do you remember the time he streaked the end-of-term dance concert?'

'Streaked?' said Matthew faintly.

'Yeah, they were doing some real classical piece – all these dance department faggots up on their toes prancing about – and Joe comes bombing through, right across the stage, stark fucking naked. He had some ski-mask or something on, so the profs couldn't be sure who it was – but *we* all knew it was Joe.'

They were all startled to hear a loud intake of breath behind them. Matthew turned and saw Ursula Hooper two rows back, eyes wide with shock and her hand to her mouth. 'Ski-mask? Did you say ski-mask?'

'Sure,' said Wayne. 'Ski-mask.'

The conversation had by this time attracted several listeners. Lulie Burns, who was among them, said:

'You remember, Ursie. It was two years ago – just after the New York trip.'

'No, I don't remember. I was sick after the trip and I was out of school for a few weeks. I wasn't at the concert. All I heard when I got back was "Wow – you should have seen the stunt Joe pulled in the middle of *Les Sylphides* – streaked right through the *corps de ballet*".'

'So what's the big surprise?' said Wayne.

'I didn't know he streaked in a ski-mask.'

'OK, now you know – so what?'

'I'll tell you so what,' Ursula said angrily. 'He pulled the same stunt on me in the dressing-room a couple of weeks ago. Except I didn't know it was him. I thought it was some maniac-rapist and I was scared to death.'

Matthew broke in. 'For God's sake, Ursula, why didn't you say something at the time? If you thought it was an intruder, you ought to have reported it to me or Cal.'

'Cubby persuaded me not to,' she admitted.

Wayne laughed. 'That's because Cubby knew it was Joe. In fact Cubby probably put Joe up to it.'

'That,' said Lulie Burns, 'would have been just like him.'

By this time, Matthew realised that the rehearsal was in a shambles. Joe had disappeared, Ursula was upset and the rest of the cast were in a state of undisciplined excitement. He contemplated trying to get them to re-focus their energies by playing some concentration games, but at that moment Inspector Bain and Sergeant Kozetsky came tramping down the centre aisle.

'Sorry to interrupt your work, Mr Prior,' said Bain, 'but we'd like to have a few more words with Mr Knox and Miss Pilton.'

128

Matthew made a despairing gesture. 'All right, everybody,' he yelled. 'Take a half-hour break. Be back here no later than a quarter to four.' Then, turning back to Bain, he said: 'Calvin's here but Shana is in a design class right now. Before you talk to Calvin, though, I'd like to have a word with you myself. Let's go into the house manager's office. Calvin, wait here till we're through, would you? And Ursula, you come with us.'

Ursula's story left Bain yawning and Kozetsky examining his thumbnail intently.

'Well?' said Matthew. 'What about it? Doesn't it widen the field of suspects a bit? It was the night before Dodie was murdered. And here's a boy with a very volatile temper trying to scare – or perhaps sexually attack – a girl in her dressing-room, and being thwarted. Maybe he was so frustrated that he set out to prowl the tunnels and find another victim. That happened to be Dodie. And Cubby somehow guessed, and had to be kept quiet.'

Bain and Kozetsky were silent.

'Well?'

'And maybe,' said Bain, 'he just happened to have an ossified elephant penis handy?'

'Petrified – not ossified.'

'Whatever.'

Matthew sighed in exasperation. 'Why shouldn't he have been the one to steal it from the anthropology department? Maybe he was going to bludgeon Ursula with it.'

Kozetsky cleared his throat. 'Excuse me, Mr Prior,' he said mildly. 'I don't think that's very likely. I went through Professor Breithaupt's class lists for the past three years and Innocenti wasn't on them. The only theatre students were Kirkwood, Pilton, Goffman, Yanouf, Meldrum, Burns, Dunn, and Hogg. They are the only ones likely to have visited his office. Knox was the only graduate theatre

129

student he had ever met. In fact, Knox was in his office several times asking questions about African tribal life, apparently for a production of the *Agamemnon*, set in an African village.'

'But surely,' Matthew interjected, 'Joe could have found out about the damned penis from one of the others.'

'Maybe so, sir, but he'd hardly have the opportunity to get it. You see Professor Breithaupt is a very distrustful man. According to his secretary, he locks his office up – even if he's just going to the john. And because he has quite a few rare items in there, nobody else – not even a member of the cleaning staff – has a key.'

'So you've decided that Calvin's it,' said Matthew bitterly.

'Not necessarily, sir. He does appear to have an alibi for the Goldberg murder.'

Matthew turned in desperation to Ursula. 'Ursie, was Joe carrying anything when you saw him in the dressing room?'

Ursula shook her head.

'Could he have had something hidden?'

'He was naked! His face was hidden, but he couldn't have hidden any kind of weapon. It was lucky for me, maybe. I managed to slash him across the chest with my nail-file and get away.'

'Did you draw blood,' asked Bain intently.

'Yes. The scratch was bleeding.'

'There probably wouldn't be any sign of it by this time. But we can check. Are you absolutely sure it *was* Innocenti?'

Ursula's eyes clouded, and she bit her lip. 'How can I be?' she said. 'But the coincidence . . .'

Bain laughed good-naturedly. 'Circumstantial evidence,' he said, 'nowhere near convincing enough for a conviction – but it gives us something to go on. Now, what else did you notice? I mean, Innocenti strikes me as a typical Italian male – swarthy, hairy, dark. Did you notice the colour of the body-hair on this joker in the ski-mask?'

Ursula looked doubtful. 'You mean – like – chest hair?'

'Or in other locations,' said Bain comfortably.

'I don't think he had any.'

'What?'

'It was all very fast – and I was scared – but I think that all his body hair had been shaved off.'

'Good Lord!' said Matthew.

'Not an uncommon fetish, Mr Prior,' Sergeant Kozetsky said, clearing his throat again.

Bain snorted. 'This case gets kinkier and kinkier. So the attacker's body was smooth as a baby's bum, he wore a ski-mask, and he wasn't carrying anything. Is that right, Miss Hooper?'

Ursula hesitated. 'He may have been carrying something,' she said.

'Damn it! I thought we just went through all that. There was no place he could have hidden a weapon.'

'Oh, not a weapon,' said Ursula hastily. 'It's just that when Cubby came back with me to the dressing-room, we found something on the floor.'

Ursula fumbled in her bag, and after searching through her wallet, she pulled something out and handed it to Bain.

'It's part of a photograph,' she said, 'with my face on it.'

# Chapter Fourteen

So there were now three pieces of photographic print, two bizarre murder weapons, a mysterious girl in a plaid skirt, a bisexual love triangle, and a hairless flasher. A nice pot of unappetising scraps for Bain to take home with him and stew in. His wife, Olive, was surprised that he had arrived in time for dinner, their meal-times so rarely coincided, but if she hoped for an evening of togetherness and domestic chat, that hope was dashed at least temporarily. As soon as he had swallowed the sole véronique with crunchy nouvelle-cuisine vegetables and a helping of airy raspberry mousse, Bain took his coffee into the family room and sat staring unseeingly at a re-run of *The New Avengers*. John Steed, with his usual insouciance, was solving a mystery in which scientists all over England were stricken by a strange plague which caused them to throw up their jobs, leave their families, and hire on as ice-cream men for a new and powerful conglomerate called Yummycone International. The outré ramifications of the plot passed by Bain unregarded. Even if he had attended to them, they would have seemed humdrum compared to the case he was working on.

After an hour of silence, broken only by the nattering of the television set and the slurping on Bain's part of lukewarm coffee, Olive looked up from her copy of Liv Ullman's autobiography and remarked brightly:

'It must be fascinating working with all those theatre

people. You usually get stuck with such dull jobs.'

Olive was a handsome, brown-haired woman of forty-five. Apart from their house, which she had managed to turn into a quite passable imitation of a colour spread in *Better Homes and Gardens*, and her cooking, a craft which she practised with all the enthusiasm of a minor Borgia dabbling in new poisons, her great interest in life was amateur theatricals. She was a long-time member of the Mapleville Players' Guild, one of the oldest amateur groups in the province and a frequent prize-winner at the now-defunct Dominion Drama Festival. Her speciality, always a surprise to people who knew her less than intimately, was eccentric character roles: comic housemaids, tipsy tarts, and venomous spinsters. As well as being an enthusiastic actress, she was an indefatigable theatregoer. No road company of a Broadway show arrived at the Royal Alexandra or the O'Keefe Centre, no interesting new Canadian play opened at the Tarragon or the Toronto Free Theatre, no Mapleville High School production of *Oklahoma* or *Carousel* was staged without Olive somewhere in the audience, clutching her programme and beaming with anticipation. Her delight in these things, however, was not shared by Bain himself. On the few occasions he had been persuaded to accompany her – once to Stratford, Ontario, to see *Much Ado About Nothing*, once to the Shaw Festival for a production of *Mrs Warren's Profession*, and once to a straw-hat theatre in the Muskokas for a revue called *Fairer and Warmer* – he had fallen asleep before the intermission and snored so noisily that members of the cast had glowered at him from the stage. Few people could claim his record of being glowered at not only by Brian Bedford and Maggie Smith but also by Paxton Whitehead, Kate Reid and Carole Shelley.

Given his formidable uninterest in all things theatrical, it wasn't surprising that his response to Olive's remark was a look of blank disbelief.

'Interesting!' he grunted. 'That's not what I would call it.'

'Oh, what would you call it, dear?' asked Olive, keeping her tone determinedly light.

'If I called it what I *would* call it, you'd make me wash my mouth out with soap.'

'I'm sure I would find it interesting,' she said, ignoring his last remark. 'Didn't you say that Matthew Prior was giving you a hand? He's a very well-regarded playwright, you know. The Guild was thinking of doing *Swine Fever* last year but some of the old guard thought the language was a bit much so we did *Witness for the Prosecution* instead. You remember – I played the barrister's nurse.'

Bain grunted again.

'Funny,' said Olive, not put out by this rather meagre response. 'This case you're working on is a bit like an Agatha Christie. *Ten Little Indians.* Somebody is killing off people connected with Mr Prior's play, one by one.'

Bain responded to that all right. 'Poppycock!' he said. 'There have been two deaths, woman, and that doesn't exactly amount to a wholesale extermination. Besides we've no idea whether the deaths are connected or not.'

'Don't call me "woman", Murdoch. Of course they're connected. You're not going to tell me that it's pure coincidence that both of those poor children were theatre students and both of them were working on the same production.'

'I suppose you'll tell me next that Prior bumped them both off. That's the sort of solution your Agatha Christie would concoct. The least likely suspect! – Bah!'

'Please don't "bah" at me, Murdoch, just because you're stuck for an answer. Now, why don't you tell me the facts and maybe *I'll* come up with something.'

Bain knew that if he didn't just tell her the facts, he would be badgered and huffed at until life at home would seem much less like *Better Homes and Gardens* and more like *Judgement at Nuremberg*, so briefly and grudgingly he complied. When he had finished, Olive looked pale. The facts were a great deal uglier than she had imagined, but she was a modern woman and had at least dipped into Krafft-Ebing.

'So your chief suspect is this homosexual boy? Are you sure that's not just prejudice? Some of you old buffaloes on the police force are quite dreadful about things like that, sending hundreds of policemen to round up a few sad lonely men in a steam bath and wasting the tax-payers' money in the process.'

Bain's exasperation was about to get the better of him, so he slowly lit his pipe, an act of defiance which Olive frowned at. Pipes were to be smoked only in the den.

'Olive, you're talking through your hat,' he said. 'Anyway, the steam-bath raids were the Metro police, not us. And as for Mr Calvin Knox, he'd be under arrest now if I could break his alibi for the night of Dodie Goldberg's murder, whether he's straight, gay or a flipping celibate monk.'

'Well, I think you're wrong. If you ask me, that boy who goes around exposing himself is capable of anything.'

At that moment, the telephone rang. Bain put his pipe down on one of Olive's ceramic dishes and went to answer it. Olive, muttering testily, picked the pipe up again and put it on top of the *TV Guide* on the television set. *The New Avengers* had come to an end, so she switched over to the educational channel where a programme about the gardens of English stately homes was in progress. She was just settling down to watch it when Bain re-entered with a troubled look on his face.

'Who was it, dear?' Olive asked.

'I don't know,' he said.

'You don't know?'

'The voice was muffled. I'm afraid it's trouble though. I'll have to go out.'

'What's wrong?'

'I'm not sure. It might be a hoax. But whoever was on the line has just promised me another murder.'

The voice had in fact done more than promise. It had identified the time and the place, though not the victim. After all, there had to be some element of surprise for the police. But the voice had been confident: there would be a murder in fifteen minutes' time, and it would happen in Leslie Frost Park.

The park was something of a trouble spot in Mapleville. It had been created in the early sixties as part of a suburban development and had been named after a former premier of the province. In theory it provided playground space for the local children and leafy walks through a winding ravine for nature-loving adults. In practice, at night certainly, the playground was taken over by teenage gangs who dealt in drugs and pursued their complicated feuds, while the thickly wooded ravine was quietly alive with the watchful figures of males, young, old and middle-aged, prowling for sexual adventures with members of their own sex. The proximity of the two groups sometimes led to violence. The teenage boys in a random fit of malevolence would descend from the playground into the ravine for an evening of queer-bashing. Sometimes, though, they were surprised to find themselves confronted by a group who called themselves the Gay Guardians, who had been trained in the martial arts for just such a situation. The warfare that broke out would be overheard by suburbanites whose bedroom windows overlooked the park and the police would be called. At other times, the police would conduct their own private raids and surprise groups of three or more in various states of undress, enjoying an alfresco orgy. A surprising number of married men were rounded up in these putsches and the resulting embarrassment and exposure had effects which reverberated through the community.

Stan Kozetsky himself had found his life touched by the park problem. His brother-in-law had been arrested in the ravine two years before and had later been divorced by Stan's sister. Now, when he went anywhere near the park, he remembered the look of sick dismay on Charley's face when he had been brought into the detachment office. So, when Bain called and asked him to meet him at the park, he felt again the residue of shock and disbelief that Charley, good-natured, frisbee-throwing, beer-drinking Charley, Charley the family joker, Charley the surely completely loving husband and father, had been hiding his fundamental self from all of them for so long.

It was ten-forty when he got Bain's call, and ten minutes later he had parked his black Ford Tempo on the side street that led to the park. Bain was waiting in his ancient Buick Cutlass and got out as he saw Stan approaching.

'It's probably a crank trying to get a rise out of us, Stan,' he said, 'but we'd better check.'

It was too cold and snowy for teenagers to be in the playground and it was scarcely the weather for dalliance in the ravine. They took the icy path past the park-keeper's shed and began to climb down the wooden steps that hugged the ravine's edge. Bain kept a gloved hand firmly on the rail, for the footing was slippery. Apart from the whistle of the wind through bare branches and their own cautious movements, there was nothing to be heard. At the bottom of the steps, they entered the darker area of the park. Even the faint glimmer of the streetlights, which had illuminated their path at the playground level, was too distant now to penetrate the tangle of growth that sprang up around them. Bain took a torch from his pocket and switched it on. By its light they could see the trail in front of them packed hard with frozen snow.

'There won't be much chance of incriminating foot-prints on this stuff,' Bain murmured under his breath.

Kozetsky shook his head. 'This is crazy, anyway,' he said. 'There's miles of pathway here and lots of hiding-places among the bushes. How are we expected to find anything?'

'I hope we don't, Stan. I hope we're either here early enough to stop anything happening – or that someone has brought us here on a wild-goose chase.'

'How do you chase a wild goose? I've often wondered.'

'We'd better cut the chat. The less warning we give the better.'

Silently, they moved on, but they saw no figures moving among the trees, no matchflare or cigarette-glow, sig-nalling need, as there would have been on those firefly nights of summer when the love-seekers were abroad. Occasionally, there was the soft impact of snow sliding from a branch to the frost-stiffened undergrowth below. As the path wound on past clumps of bush and outcrops of rock, the moon sailed briefly from behind heavy cloud illuminating an empty clearing and an ice-bound creek. More and more, they became convinced that they were the only night travellers in that cheerless dusk.

'Damn,' said Kozetsky, stumbling against a tree stump.

'Shhh!' said Bain.

Somewhere ahead of them, they heard a faint scrabbling sound. It could have been a raccoon on a night-foraging expedition. It could have been stones sliding down a bank, released by the sudden collapse of some natural barrier. But just possibly it might be someone ahead of them in the darkness. At the end of the path, there was a large stretch of open ground, at the far side of which they could see the dim outline of a small building.

'Hell,' said Bain. 'I might have known. Where – on a miserable night like this – would a gay be cruising down here? The bloody park toilet, of course. Come on!'

'You mean you think it's Knox?'

'You're dam' right it's Knox. Come on! We may still be in time to stop him.'

Stan was confused. He wasn't at all convinced that Bain was right, but he followed as rapidly as he could across the treacherous ice-meadow. Suddenly, the building was in front of them: a brick oblong with a flat roof and two entrances. They entered the black opening of the Men's side, Bain swinging his torch around at the urinals and the graffiti-covered walls. Shadows danced in corners, but no human figure appeared in the roaming light. Kozetsky pushed open the doors of the toilet stalls. They were all empty. Then, chillingly, they heard what sounded like a stifled cough from behind the dividing wall.

'Quick, the Women's side!' said Bain, and led the way.

When Kozetsky entered, Bain was already bending over something huddled half in and half out of one of the cubicles.

'Jesus, Jesus!' Bain exclaimed. 'Stan – you know the Heimlich manoeuvre – Do it!'

Kozetsky pushed past Bain and saw who it was, lying there clutching at his throat, eyes bulging, face darkening rapidly. It was Calvin Knox.

Kozetsky moved quickly. He flipped Calvin over, formed two fists and drove them hard into the cavity beneath the ribcage and upward towards the breastbone. There was an extraordinary snorting gurgle and out of the young man's mouth something flew, mixed with a slimy rope of saliva and vomit.

'How is he?' asked Bain.

'I'm not sure,' said Kozetsky, turning Calvin's head to one side to make it easier for him to breathe.

139

'What happened, son?' Bain asked, looking into Calvin's terrified eyes.

Calvin's breath came ragged and slow. There was an ugly rasping in his chest. Kozetsky, whose ear was nearest to the gasping mouth, heard something, and then – like a machine abruptly switched off – the breathing stopped.

'Bugger it!' yelled Bain furiously. 'I'm sick of this. It's got to be stopped. Poor little sod. I wish I could—'

He broke off, shook his head at Stan, and walked quickly outside into the cold untainted air. Stan rolled Calvin over onto his back again and began deftly but urgently making use of his CPR training. When it was clear that Calvin's heart was never going to beat again, Stan bowed his head and, alone in the dank and fetid stillness, covered his eyes for a moment. Then, picking up the object that had come from Calvin's throat, he went outside to join his chief.

'He'd been lured there, obviously,' said Matthew to Sergeant Kozetsky the next morning.

'Probably, Mr Prior, and it wouldn't have been difficult. Knox was certainly familiar with the park and what went on there. We've already talked to some of the Gay Guardians and they've identified his photograph as someone they'd seen roaming the ravine at night.'

'Surprisingly co-operative of them,' said Matthew.

'That's one of the few times they'll help the police – when one of their own is murdered. Try to get them to talk about other cases in the gay community and they clam up.'

Matthew wondered privately whether clamming up wasn't a perfectly natural reaction when you had so little reason to love or trust the forces of law and order, but aloud he said:

'Really? So you've established he might have been per-suaded to meet someone there – a fine and private place

140

where they could – er – "get it on" is the phrase, I think.'

'That's our speculation at any rate.'

'And you've lost your chief suspect. I suppose you're not going to tell me that *he* committed suicide?'

Kozetsky frowned. 'No, and I'm not going to tell you it was an accidental death, though I suppose in a weird way it could have been.'

Matthew shot him a sharp glance. 'I thought you said he was strangled.'

'Well, asphyxiated would be more accurate perhaps. He choked to death on an object stuck in his throat. If we'd been there a minute or two sooner we could probably have saved him.'

'Damn!' said Matthew. 'What a bloody waste!'

Kozetsky pulled a transparent bag from his anorak pocket and laid it on the desk in front of Matthew.

'This is what killed him, Mr Prior.'

Inside the bag were three white plastic balls, about an inch and a half in diameter, connected to each other with a length of black cord.

'Good Lord! Ben-wa balls,' Matthew exclaimed.

'Is that what you call them, sir?' said Kozetsky.

'Benoit balls?' muttered Bain. 'What're they? One of Madame Benoit's recipes for ground beef?'

Sergeant Kozetsky smiled patiently. 'Ben-wa balls, sir,' he said. 'B, E, N, W, A.'

'I'm no wiser, Stan. What do you do with them?'

The shiny white spheres lay between them on Bain's desk-top.

'Er . . .' said Kozetsky. 'Well, sir . . .'

'Yes, yes! Get on with it, man.'

'According to Mr Prior, sir, they're sexual aids – from Japan.'

'Sexual aids!'

141

Bain glared at the balls in disgusted bafflement. His imagination failed him. How these things that looked as if they might have been designed for some as yet uninvented version of ping-pong could aid him or Olive was unfathomable.

'I don't understand,' he admitted sadly. 'The things that people get up to nowadays . . . Would you mind explaining, Stan, how exactly these doo-dads work?'

Sergeant Kozetsky did mind, but stifling a sigh, he made the effort. 'Apparently, sir, the – er – objects can be inserted in the vagina or the anus, and at the moment of climax can be pulled out by means of the cord to intensify the pleasure.'

'I'm sorry I asked. To intensify the *pleasure*, you say?'

'Some people find it has that effect; yes, sir.'

Bain rolled his eyes upwards. 'Mr Prior told you this, did he?'

Sergeant Kozetsky nodded. In fact, he was being disingenuous. His own experience, working for 52 Division in Toronto, had included keeping an eye on sex shops and massage parlours. Once Matthew had identified the balls, he recalled seeing similar things among the sexual paraphernalia offered along the Yonge Street strip. Still, for the moment, it seemed better to give the impression of borrowed worldliness.

'Mr Prior recognised these things immediately, did he?' asked Bain.

Kozetsky nodded again and Bain looked depressed.

'I suppose him being a writer – a man with a naturally enquiring mind – and, of course, working in the theatrical profession . . . Damn it, Stan! I thought I was pretty well clued in to the nastiness that goes on in the world – but ben-wa balls!'

'I don't think they're much in use in Mapleville, sir,' said Kozetsky reassuringly.

Bain picked up his Bic pen and poked at the things gingerly. 'So somebody stuffed them down Knox's throat? He couldn't have been trying to swallow them?'

'Unlikely, sir. If he'd been high on drugs, or if it was a suicide attempt, maybe. But the gag reflex would probably make it very difficult – if not impossible. Anyway, the evidence points to someone using force on him. His shirt collar was ripped and there was a sizeable bruise on his left wrist.'

'Murder, then,' said Bain. 'And some kind of pattern. First the elephant thing, then the tights – now this.'

'Yes, sir, it *does* look like a pattern. The question is whether the killer means us to see the pattern or not.'

Bain was silent for a moment. Then he said: 'This way to the egress.'

Kozetsky blinked. 'I beg your pardon, sir?'

'P. T. Barnum, Stan! A great showman. Wanted to keep the crowds moving through one of his exhibits, so more could get in. What does he do? Puts up a sign that says "This way to the egress". The idiots thought it was pointing to some exotic animal's cage – so they followed it and found themselves out on the street. Didn't realise "egress" was just a high-falutin' word for "exit".'

Kozetsky was speechless. It was a bit much having one of his favourite stories fed back to him almost word for word, particularly when he was sure Bain had heard it from him in the first place. Finally he swallowed and said: 'In other words, a misleading sign?'

'Right, Stan,' Bain said with satisfaction. 'Or a series of arrows pointing in the wrong direction.'

The third murder destroyed all the careful efforts of Hugh Kirkwood and Dean Ripper to keep the press at bay. For one thing, the Gay Guardians seized on it as one more evidence of society's violence against homosexual men

143

and linked it with a whole string of still unsolved gay murders in the Toronto area. The protests that they mounted outside OPP headquarters and Metro police headquarters were covered by television news teams and reporters from the major dailies. The next day, headlines in the *Globe and Mail* and the *Toronto Star* referred to Wacousta as 'Murder U.' and 'the Campus of Terror'. Frantic parents began to flood the Registrar's office with hysterical phone calls, and a considerable number of students took unauthorised leave.

There were more unavailing appeals for the mysterious girl to come forward. Instead Kozetsky and Bain were inundated with unreliable reports of a kilted girl leaving the scene of the crime on a motor-cycle, throwing a mysterious object into the Don river, buying an airline ticket for San Francisco, buying a train ticket for Edmonton, buying a bus ticket for Sudbury, checking in at the Sheraton Four Seasons, and throwing up in the ladies' room at the Diamond Disco. On top of that there were the usual crank confessions from all the people who regularly claimed responsibility for all murders in Southern Ontario. None of this got them any further ahead.

Matthew, meanwhile, though heartsick at Calvin's death, struggled on with rehearsals for *The Armageddon Excuse-Me Fox-Trot*. Marie-Ange took over as assistant director and proved to be not only wonderfully cool and competent but also tactful and sensitive in the face of a cast of actors who were on the verge of total demoralisation. To Matthew, who was beginning to wonder if there was any point in going on with the play, given the ugliness that now surrounded it, she gave quiet support. Towards the end of the first rehearsal after Calvin's death, Matthew wandered up to the lighting booth to check on a lighting cue that didn't seem to be working and caught Shana, looking like a female Pagliacci with her white makeup and multi-coloured hair, sobbing over the control board. It seemed to him, given his slight knowledge of her, so remarkable a display of vulnerability that he was momentarily speechless. Shana, sensing him standing there, swiftly suppressed her tears and turned towards him with a defiant sniff or two and a forbidding scowl.

'All right,' she snapped. 'I'm sorry about that last cue. It won't happen again.'

'Screw the cue,' said Matthew inelegantly. 'You seem to be having other problems.'

Shana's body went slack and her eyes lost their fire. 'Problems? Me? Are you kidding? Oh, no . . . After all, what problems can the third side of a triangle have when the other two sides have been rubbed out? I mean – I'm just a free line floating in space, now. So what problems?'

'Perhaps you're afraid of where the eraser will strike next.'

Shana brushed her eyes with the back of her hand, leaving an unattractive smear of eye-liner.

'Forget it. I've got protection. I'm not going anywhere alone from now on.'

'And who's your protector?'

'That's my business. It's someone I trust. That's all you need to know.'

Matthew sighed. 'OK, Shana. But please be careful. I don't know what's going on yet, but you were involved with both Cubby and Calvin, and whoever it was who hated them so much might just hate you too.'

'I wasn't involved with Dodie.'

Matthew sighed again. 'That's true, I suppose. Oh, Lord, what a mess it all is. Let's just try to forget it for a while and get on with the show.'

At the end of the rehearsal, as Matthew was going over some notes with Marie-Ange, he happened to glance over his shoulder and see Shana leaving through the auditorium door, accompanied by Joe Innocenti.

'Is that her protector?' he wondered. 'Or is that the eraser?'

One thing that baffled Bain and Kozetsky – or rather one of the many things that baffled them – was the way in which Calvin's murder broke the pattern in a couple of significant ways. First, it was the only murder of which there had been advance warning, and second, though they had subjected the toilets in Leslie Frost Park to a microscopic search, had combed the park itself with trained dogs, and had examined not only the clothes Calvin was wearing but every piece of clothing, every book, every conceivable hiding-place in his room, they had found no section of photograph with Calvin's face on it. They had already pieced together the sections that showed Cubby and Dodie as well as the piece Ursula had handed over, and it was clear that they all came from the same group photograph. Where it had been taken, or who else might be in the group, so far remained a puzzle. The fact that such a photograph existed, however, had created another possible direction for the investigation.

'I'm not throwing out sexual jealousy as a motive, sir,' Kozetsky said, 'but it does look as if there's some kind of systematic serial killing going on. Two people in the photograph were killed, one was attacked, and – assuming Calvin was on it too—'

'We can't assume anything, Stan,' Bain interrupted. 'The photograph may be another spanner thrown in the works to ball everything up.'

'But even if it is, sir, it suggests one mind behind all the killings.'

'One mind, maybe – but possibly many hands.'

'What!'

'You were the one who brought Manson up a few days ago. Good old Charlie and his band of loonies. I might also mention Dean Corll.'

'Dean who?'

'How quickly we forget, eh, Stan? Dean Corll of Houston. Had a little torture and murder ring going. Killed a lot of boys – with a little help from his friends.'

'Yes, chief, but crazy as those murders were they had a definite purpose and a clear pattern. Manson was promoting some lunatic radical notion of class warfare. Corll was a homosexual sadist. Neither of those patterns fits this. Two of the victims were homosexual – or bisexual – but one of them was a girl.'

'Stan, I must say I never thought to hear such a simple-minded statement coming out of such a smart mouth. You've heard of dykes, haven't you? Couldn't the Goldberg girl have been a lesbian? I've seen some tough old bull-dykes in my time and I tell you she had all the makings. Now, suppose we're dealing with a loony who's got it in for gays generally – male and female.'

'In that case, it would mean that Ursula Hooper was gay.'

'Well, we drew a blank on the Goldberg girl's private life, but now we've got a new tree to bark up I think we should backtrack on her and take a look at Miss Hooper's extra-curricular activities as well.'

'Meaning?'

'Meaning that *you*, Stan, will pay a visit to a few of the better known lesbian clubs in Toronto.'

In the Blue Turtle, one of the many snack-bar-cum-pubs on campus, a scattering of students sat at the scarred, beer-ringed tables, eating bean sprout and tofu salads or tuna sandwiches, and drinking Molson's Light straight from the bottle. The air was full of over-amplified rock music, yet miraculously conversations were being held. At one table in particular, a rather intense exchange was in progress.

'You mean I don't rate,' Joe Innocenti was saying to Shana Pilton, his good-looking face marred by a dark Sicilian scowl.

'What I mean is you don't inherit me just because you were Cubby's room-mate.'

Joe reached out and grabbed Shana's hand, squeezing it in his sinewy grip.

'Fuck that shit,' he sneered. 'You think you're some priceless heirloom or what? We're not talking about who was screwing who when; we're talking about now. And if you're worried about my dick – it's bigger than Cubby's was.'

Shana snatched her hand away, wincing with pain. 'Jesus, you're sick!' she gasped. 'You know that? You're out of control. You need help. And since you're so interested, let me tell you I'm busy tonight, and I'll be busy tomorrow night and the next night. And my date could make two of you, you creep. So just *leave . . . me . . . alone!*'

And with that, Shana pushed her chair back and fled, attracting several interested glances as she left. The eyes that had followed her turned next to Joe, who flushed a dull red under his normal sallow olive. The music of the Clash reached a shattering crescendo and the conversations around the room gradually resumed. But if they had watched a little longer, they would have seen a pair of lustrous tears slowly tracking their way down Joe's swarthy cheeks.

It was snowing again when Matthew crossed the campus to return to his office. Shuddering, he pulled up the collar of his quilted parka and cursed the bitter wind that swept down on him around the corner of the Central Administration Building. The light was fading and the outdoor standard lamps suddenly came on. Around the acid glare at the top of each pole, an aureole of brightness illuminated the drifting snowflakes, giving them a temporary significance like a group of dancers moving through a theatrical spotlight.

Inside the Fine Arts Building, the mustard-coloured walls of the corridors seemed uglier than ever. Matthew wondered, not for the first time, how a faculty supposedly dedicated to the improvement of aesthetic standards could bear to spend their working lives amid such hideousness. Perhaps that was why most of the offices were deserted except for those times when the faculty members absolutely had to be there. This early evening was no exception. Most of the doors on Matthew's corridor were shut. Only the door to the Chairman's office stood open, and from beyond it, Matthew could hear Roger's voice.

'Yes, Vern. Yes, I know, Vern,' he was saying. 'Yes, it's certainly going to play hell with enrolments for next year ... I understand; you're under pressure ... But I honestly don't know what more can be done ... Keep them all in after school until somebody confesses? ... Sorry, yes, it's not funny ... Hugh is what? ... Going berserk? ... I'm not surprised but I'm afraid at this point the lid has blown right off and not even a cabinet minister can put it back ... Goodbye to what? ... Oh, the fine arts complex extension ... I wouldn't be surprised ... All right: goodbye, Vern.'

Matthew heard Roger groan as he replaced the receiver.

'I was eavesdropping,' he said, entering the office. 'Ripper giving you a hard time, is he?'

Roger was sitting behind his desk, clutching his hair which had spiked up in all directions. He looked at Matthew over his spectacles and groaned again.

'Fat lot of good you are,' he complained. 'The great detective, huh! I'm beginning to think you couldn't detect a sausage in a sausage roll.'

149

'If it was a British Railways sausage roll, I probably couldn't. Come on, Roger – pull yourself together. You've handled worse things than the dementia of a dean.'

'You don't understand, Matthew. He sees his career in a shambles and, make no mistake, Ripper's like one of those ancient Asiatic tyrants. If he comes down, he's going to try to pull the whole bloody lot of us down with him.'

'He can't do that, can he?'

'I don't know,' Roger wailed. 'He's devious. He's cunning. God knows what he mightn't do. Matthew, you've got to get this mess sorted out.'

Matthew exploded. 'I'm a goddam playwright – not a magician. I can't wave a magic wand and make everything all right.'

Roger began to look calmer. He smoothed down his hair and straightened his tie. 'Sorry, old man,' he said. 'I suppose I was being a bit unreasonable. Still, you know, I don't see why a couple of first-class minds like ours shouldn't be able to get to the bottom of this. After all, we used to be able to do the *Guardian* crossword in ten minutes.'

Matthew took off his parka, threw it across a chair, and sat down. 'All right, Roger, I'll give you ten minutes. First clue?'

Roger looked annoyed. 'Well, if you're going to be flippant!'

'Thirty seconds gone, Roger. First clue?'

'Oh, I don't know – the photograph.'

'A group photograph. We know that at least three people were on it: Dodie, Cubby and Ursula. Judging by the general dimension of the pieces we've found, there can't have been many more in the group. Three at most.'

'A small group photograph. Taken where?'

'Somewhere on campus, I suppose.'

'Is there anything in the background that would help?'

Matthew scratched his head. 'I don't think so. It looked like an outdoor shot. They seemed to be standing against a wall.'

'Anything identifiable on the wall?'

'I'm not sure. I wish I had the bits in front of me . . . Wait a minute. I think there was some kind of lettering. Part of a sign. L . . . something. It might have been L . . . A.'

'Los Angeles? I doubt if they ever ventured that far as a group.'

'No, it didn't look like L dot A dot; it looked like part of a word.'

'L . . . A . . . something. Pity we don't know how many across. I wonder if it could be a campus sign. What is there on campus that begins L . . . A . . .? La-la-la-la . . .'

'And a hey nonny no. I don't think this is getting us anywhere.' Matthew pointed to his watch. 'Three minutes, Roger.'

'Lampman!' Roger shrieked.

'Eh?'

'Lampman College. Dodie Goldberg lived in Lampman College Residence!'

Matthew pulled at his lower lip thoughtfully. 'Could be,' he said, 'but where would that get us? Calvin certainly didn't belong to Lampman College.'

'No, but Ursula might remember. She might remember posing for a photograph outside Lampman with Dodie and Calvin – and she might remember who else was in the group.'

Matthew stood up. 'Roger, you were right. Two fine minds working together can solve more than crossword puzzles. I'm going to see if I can find Ursula – and while I'm at it, I'll see if I can get another look at those bits of photograph.'

# Chapter Fifteen

One of the reasons why Leslie Frost Park was such a popular place of assignation for gay males in the Mapleville area was that Mapleville offered no other venue: no gay bars, clubs, discos or steam baths. But while they had at least the park, uncertain and dangerous as it was, Mapleville's gay women had nowhere at all to go, except for the occasional discreet gathering in a private home. For more public encounters, the nearest promising places were in Toronto. There, a long-established gay community supported a variety of establishments, many of them cheerful and well-run. But even in Toronto, lesbians had fewer choices than gay men.

Stan Kozetsky's assignment was, therefore, not an onerous one, and though he had expected to feel uncomfortable – a lone male adrift in a sea of tough-looking women in suits – he discovered that in the enlightened eighties, the occasional male presence was tolerated good-humouredly. He also found that, for the most part, the women he met dressed and behaved much like his sister, his girlfriends and his mother. Nor were they deceived by his attempt to pass himself off as a worried relative looking for a missing girl. As one of them said: 'Feller, you've got cop written all over you.' But this didn't make them unco-operative. In fact, once they realised that he was investigating Dodie's murder, they were sympathetic and helpful. Nevertheless, he drew a blank everywhere until he reached the last and most popular of the places – Gertrude's.

Gertrude's was a large bar-cum-disco with a decor part art nouveau, part art deco, meant to suggest Paris in the twenties. Above the bar counter was a huge blow-up of a Man Ray portrait of Gertrude Stein. The bartender, a woman in her early thirties called Evelyn, dressed in the style of a Montmartre *cabaretier*, gave Stan the only lead he turned up that evening. He showed her pictures of both Dodie and Ursula and after studying them carefully she put them back on the counter.

'This one,' she said, pointing to Ursula's picture, 'little Miss Mouse. If she's one of us, she's probably a closet case. Definitely not on the scene around here.'

Then she indicated the other photograph. 'This one I know – Miss John Deere Tractor of 1933. Dodie – was that her name? Yeah, I remember now.'

'She's the one who was murdered.'

Evelyn looked stricken. 'Damn, I'm sorry. Shouldn't have made fun of her like that.'

'Where did you know her from? Was she a lesbian?'

'Lesbian.' Evelyn wrinkled her nose and gave him a cool stare. 'You sound real Victorian, you know that?'

'OK. Was she gay?'

'No. I'm pretty sure she wasn't.'

'Where did you meet her?'

Evelyn wiped the bar and emptied an ashtray into a bin under the counter. 'We worked together,' she said finally. 'Two summers. When I first met her she was on her first summer vacation from university – two years ago? No, two and a half. We were both waitressing at Mr Greenjeans in the Eaton Centre.'

'Did you get to know her well?'

Evelyn looked thoughtful. 'Not real well,' she said. 'But that first summer she was a lot of fun. She had a way of coming out with things. You know? – deadpan. She was always breaking me up. It got her fired in the end. That and the fact that she was getting beefier by the day and didn't fit the svelte image of Mr Greenjeans waitresses.'

'Seems a bit unfair.'

Evelyn waved her hand dismissively. 'She got another job real fast – at Laura Secord's.' Then she laughed. 'You can imagine what that did to her figure. Cramming candies into her mouth all day long.'

'You said you worked with her two summers?'

'Yeah. The next summer I got a job at a health food restaurant – the Sprouts n' Such – in the Yorkville area. And there she was . . . I was real glad to see her again, but – I don't know – she wasn't the same.'

'How do you mean?' said Stan, but he had to wait for the answer until Evelyn had served banana daiquiris to a couple of middle-aged women.

'How was she different?' she said, moving back down the counter towards him. 'Well, she seemed to have lost her sense of humour. She was kinda grim, you know? And kinda depressed too.'

'Love trouble?'

'No. She wasn't that type. She had no time for men – or women either. Not in that way anyhow. It was something that had happened to her before the summer vacation. And I know *where* it happened but I don't know *what* happened.'

Stan nodded and waited for her to go on.

'It was funny how it came up. A girlfriend of mine had asked me down to New York for the weekend. I was feeling sorry for Dodie, and though I was pretty sure she wasn't one of us I thought it wouldn't hurt to ask her along too. But she turned me down flat. Said she'd never set foot in New York again as long as she lived. Said it was a rotten place and something terrible had happened the last time she was there.'

'And that's all?'

'That's all, sergeant. Now, if you don't mind, I've got a job to do here.'

At about the same time that Sergeant Kozetsky was interviewing the bartender at Gertrude's, Shana Pilton drove a rented Honda into the forecourt of a motel on the lakeshore between Mapleville and Toronto. Like its nearby competitors, Slumber Lodge and the Rest-U-Well Motel, the Morpheus Arms – while catering generally to happy family groups touring the province in comfortable sedans – was also known to accommodate local couples bent on a few hours of sexual pleasure. They were discreet about this because of Ontario's infamous 'bawdy house' laws, which were not only ill-defined and confusing but also likely to be applied whimsically by the police. Shana, for instance, might be arrested and charged as a 'found-in' if other people were entertaining each other sexually in her presence, even though she was behaving chastely herself.

On this occasion, however, Shana was expecting to find only one other person in Room 16 which was at the opposite end of the building from the motel office. She approached the door and knocked. There was no reply. She waited for a moment, shivering slightly in her leather jacket as the gusts of cold air from the lake swooped around her, then pulled a note from her pocket to check the number. Finally, with an exclamation of impatience, she tried the door-handle. The door opened. Nobody, however, was inside the room. Shana checked the bathroom. There was no one there either, but she noticed a portable VCR and a small TV set, placed – it seemed clear – so that they could be viewed easily from inside the tub.

Shana shrugged and smiled, then walked back into the bedroom. It was at this point that she saw, in a small recess that held the automatic coffee-maker, an ice-bucket containing a foil-capped bottle with an envelope propped up against it. She opened the envelope and found another note.

'Hi!' it said. 'I forgot the snacks. Have gone to All-Night 711 on Sherbourne. Back soon. Meanwhile do me a favour. There's bubble-bath stuff in the bathroom and a sexy tape in the VCR. Make my fantasy come true. Let me come in and find you naked among the bubbles watching hot action on the TV. And I'll join you in the tub!!! How can you resist? Please!

Love,
Me.'

Shana put the note down with a sigh that was half-exasperated, half-amused. She began to reach for the champagne bottle, but changed her mind and went back into the bathroom instead. For a moment she stood and looked from the bathtub to the VCR and back again. 'Talk about your adolescent fantasies,' she thought. 'Oh, well – What have I got to lose?' Grabbing the package from above the sink, she turned on the bath-taps with a flourish and began to sprinkle bubble-bath crystals into the swirling water.

'Sorry to bother you at this hour,' Matthew said.

Ursula, who had opened the door of her room in Lampman College with some caution, relaxed and grinned when she saw him.

'That's OK. I was just trying to read *Man and Superman* for my Lit. class. You can give me a quick synopsis instead.'

Matthew followed her into the room which was in such disorder that it immediately reminded him of Bryn's bedroom in Belsize Park. There were clothes, shoes, books, the sleeves of record albums, empty Coke bottles, and binders full of lecture notes scattered over every available surface. Ursula had to sweep a pile of theatre magazines off a chair so that he could sit down.

'Would you like some tea?' Ursula said.

'What is it: Red Rose?'

'Celestial Seasonings. Raspberry Leaf Tea. It's just right for you. You're a thyroid type.'

'Are you being rude?'

Ursula laughed. 'No, no. It's your dominant gland. I can tell from your physique. You've got a basketball player's body. Tall and – er – lean.'

Matthew preened and patted his stomach. 'But why the interest in glands? Don't tell me you're planning to transfer to medical school.'

'Oh, no. It's just that I've been reading this terrific fitness book by some California doctor. I'm really into it. It says I'm a pituitary type. Unfortunately.'

'Why unfortunately?'

'Well, we tend to be a bit underdeveloped physically. I'll never be a Playboy centrefold.'

'But you may very well one day make a good Rosalind or a good Viola. Playboy centrefolds aren't likely to be offered rôles like that. For one thing, they'd look ridiculous dressed as boys.'

Ursula gave him a quick glance and then lowered her eyes. 'You think that I might be good enough, one day?'

Matthew nodded firmly. 'Yes, I think you'd be good enough. You're a director's dream. You're talented but not temperamental. You have an intelligent insight into characters but you don't over-intellectualise. You're open to other people's ideas. In fact, if I may say it without embarrassing you, you're a pleasure to work with.'

Ursula *was* embarrassed. 'Don't tell me you came all the way over here just to tell me how great I am. Did you want that tea, by the way?'

'No, thanks ... and no, I didn't come by just to tell you you're great. You're *not* great. Yet. I came because I thought you might be able to help me.'

Ursula's look of embarrassment changed to one of wariness. 'Sure. Any way I can.'

Matthew paused for a moment and then leaned forward towards her.

'It's about the photographs,' he said. 'Or maybe I should say "photograph". That bit that you found on the floor of the dressing-room matches bits that showed Dodie and Cubby. They were obviously part of the same photograph. The problem is: who else was on it and where was it taken?'

Matthew watched her face but there was only doubt and puzzlement there.

'It's no good. Those two policemen already asked me. I just don't remember. You see, we hung around together a lot the first year or two here. And we were all supposed to keep illustrated journals for our performance course. So we were all clicking away with Instamatics or doing pencil sketches or whatever, all the time.'

'Did the police ask you about the lettering on the wall?' Matthew persisted.

'Oh, yes. I couldn't help with that either.'

'There were two letters on the pieces that were found. An "L" and an "A". Could the building have been Lampman College?'

Ursula laughed nervously. 'Heavens, no. At least I don't think so. This university is terrible about putting signs up. The freshmen always complain. You practically have to have a licensed guide to find your way around in first year. As far as I know there's never been a sign on the outside of this college. But you could check with the people in the Physical Plant Office. They would know.'

'Physical Plant,' said Matthew absently. 'It sounds like

a carnivorous tropical flower. What's wrong with a good old-fashioned word like "buildings"?'

The interview seemed to have come to an end, so Matthew stood up.

'Well,' he said, 'I must be getting along.'

'Not before you've given me a synopsis of *Man and Superman*,' Ursula said determinedly.

Matthew groaned and sat down again. 'Oh, very well. Let's see . . . There's this girl called Ann Whitefield who's decided to marry this pompous ass called John Tanner . . .'

# Chapter Sixteen

Inspector Bain knocked politely on the open door of Bonny Dundee's office and walked in. It was nine-thirty in the morning and the pale winter sunlight was filtering through the window. Bonny, who had been clattering away on her IBM Selectric, stopped and looked up.

'Sorry to disturb you, miss,' Bain said awkwardly, 'but I thought you might be able to help us.'

Bonny switched off the machine, silencing its quiet hum. 'Certainly, Inspector. If I can, I'd be glad to. And please call me Bonny – and for heaven's sake have a seat.'

Bain sat down and pulled out a pack of MacDonald's Export. 'Smoke?' he said offering them to her.

'I don't,' she said, 'but go ahead. I have an ashtray some-where.' She rummaged in her desk drawers and found a metal ashtray with the Wacousta arms stamped on the rim.

'It's about Mr Knox,' Bain said.

'Calvin? Yes?'

'Well, we've searched his rooms and his clothes, and a storage locker belonging to him in the graduate residence. And so far we haven't found much to help us. I was won-dering – is there anywhere around the offices here where he might have kept things – a desk drawer, a filing cabinet, a lock-box?'

Bonny pondered. 'The grad students have an office they share,' she said. 'But they don't usually keep anything per-sonal there. The desk drawers are full of typing paper and carbons and things. And, of course, their mail boxes are in there, but they usually clear them out every day.'

'Might as well check anyway,' said Bain. 'Where is it?'

Bonny grabbed a bunch of keys from her desk-top. 'Come on, I'll show you.'

The graduate students' office was in an obscure corner next to a broom closet. After knocking, to make sure no-one was inside, Bonny unlocked the door and switched on the light.

'No windows in here,' she explained. 'That's why none of the faculty wanted it. Grad students are second-class citizens.'

'What about the undergrads?'

'Oh, definitely third-class. All they get is a student lounge. Well, poke about as much as you want. The mail boxes are over here and – oh, that's odd!'

Bain turned quickly. 'What is?'

'Calvin's box. It hasn't been cleared.'

Bain crossed the room swiftly and grabbed the sheaf of mail that Bonny held out to him. Quickly sorting through it, he saw that there were circulars from the Graduate Students' Association, a bill from the campus bookstore, a couple of flyers advertising new plays and one innocuous-looking white envelope. The postmark was a week old – five days before Calvin's death. Inside the envelope was a fragment of a photographic print showing Calvin's face and behind him on the wall the letters 'C' and 'O'. There was also a sheet of plain white paper and on it the words: 'You're next.'

'Damn the Canadian post office,' said Bain. 'He should have got this before he went to that park – even if it *was* posted in Winnipeg. Maybe he'd have shown it to us – and we could have done something.'

Bonny's pleasant face was suddenly pale and drawn. 'Did you say "Winnipeg"?'

161

Bain showed her the postmark then took a transparent glassine bag from his pocket and put the envelope and its contents inside.

'And the photograph?' said Bonny. 'It proves Calvin was one of the group. It's systematic murder. He's picking them off one by one.'

Bain gave her a sharp look. 'How do you know about the group photograph?'

'Matthew told me. He thought I might be able to suggest where it was taken. Of course he made me swear not to tell anyone else about it.'

'Very thoughtful of him. And why did you say "*He's* picking them off one by one"? How do you know it's a "he"?'

Bonny's eyes widened as he stared back at her, but she made no reply. The silence seemed likely to endure indefinitely, but at that moment Matthew poked his head into the room and said: 'Definitely not Lampman College.'

Bain was too startled to respond with anything but 'Eh?'

'The photograph,' said Matthew impatiently. 'I was talking to Ursula . . .'

Bain waved him to silence. 'Mr Prior, if you have anything to tell me, I think it should be in my office. It pays to be careful.'

Matthew looked inquiringly at Bonny and shrugged. Bonny turned away silently.

'All right, Inspector,' he said, 'your office it is.'

When they were settled down in the incident room, Matthew studied the piece of photographic print Bain had found.

'So Calvin was in the photograph after all . . . And the letters behind him could be the first two letters of "College".'

Bain waited impassively.

'But which college?' Matthew went on. 'It can't be Lampman. I checked that with Physical Plant and there's never been a sign like that outside Lampman. But on the other hand, it's the only college on campus that starts with an "L".'

'What makes you think "L" was the first letter of a word?'

'The spacing,' Matthew said promptly. 'There's a larger space before the "L" than there is between it and the "A".'

The inspector grunted and pulled out his pack of MacDonald's Export again. He offered it to Matthew, who shook his head. Then he began to fumble in his pockets for a match.

'And what makes you think that the second letter was an "A"? Damn it! I've left my matches in Miss Dundee's office.'

Matthew produced a matchbook with an advertisement for the BiggaBurger on the outside and tossed it across to Bain. 'Well, wasn't it an "A"? Of course, I only got one good look at the bits of print, but I could have sworn it was an "A".'

Bain reached into his inside pocket and pulled out a folded piece of paper. It was a Xerox blow-up of the pieces of photographic print. They had been arranged like a jigsaw puzzle with some of the pieces missing. The second letter, which was high on the wall and to the right of Dodie's head, was only partly visible. All that could be seen, in fact, was a vertical downstroke, which, judging by the style of the other letters, seemed unlikely to be the first arm of the letter "A".

'Oh, Lord,' said Matthew. 'I *have* been barking up the wrong tree. It's got to be a vowel, unless it's a Welsh word, and the only vowel it could be part of is "E".'

Bain exhaled a cloud of grey smoke with huge satisfaction.

'Ah, now,' he said, 'there's your amateur detective all over – leaping to conclusions. Couldn't it also be a complete vowel? Like an "I" for instance? And furthermore

163

couldn't the "L" – whatever – be the beginning of the second word before "College"? Let's say, for the sake of argument, the Annabel Lee College or the Harry Lime College.'

'Got me, Inspector,' admitted Matthew. 'I suppose that means we spread our net at least as far as Baltimore and Vienna.'

The Inspector frowned. 'That's not irony, Mr Prior. That's just cheap sarcasm.'

'I'm sorry, Inspector – but it's so frustrating. Just when we seem to have a lead, it evaporates.'

They both lapsed into silence, Bain puffing thoughtfully, Matthew gazing absently out of the window. The sound of footsteps in the corridor outside aroused them both. The next moment Sergeant Kozetsky entered. He looked pale and heavy-eyed.

'What a night!' he said. 'I was up till three in the morning.'

Matthew got up from his chair. 'Here, Sergeant; your need is greater than mine. Besides I have a play-writing class in five minutes.'

Just as he was leaving, he paused in the doorway and turned back to the Inspector. 'One last thought,' he said. 'We don't know that the "C" and the "O" are the first letters of "College". The word could be "Court". And not all signs retain all their letters permanently – so maybe the first word is "Police".'

Bain and Kozetsky looked at one another. 'Police Court!' they chorused.

It was an effective exit line, and Matthew waved cheerfully to them as he left.

The play-writing class went exceptionally well. Trudy Birnbaum had completely rewritten her script so that now, instead of being about an insufferably self-righteous Jewish princess who triumphs over an unfeeling family, it was about a long-suffering Jewish family who gradually teach an egotistical daughter the value of considering other people's wishes and feelings. Not surprisingly, in the course of writing it, Trudy had discovered much about herself and her own preconceptions.

Walt Dunn's exercise in Canadian Gothic had also been transformed. His play was now a lively comedy about the confrontation between a multinational corporation which plans to build a theme park in rural Ontario and a group of farmers whose land is threatened. Meriel's Jamaican folk-play had sprouted a framing device about a story-telling contest which allowed her to incorporate several legends within one dramatic structure, and Celia's picaresque adventure set in the world of punk had shed most of its sit-com devices and become a surprisingly moving piece about social dislocation.

The most disappointing work came from Ken Meldrum. His puppy-like enthusiasm was linked, unfortunately, with a restless dissatisfaction. The *Twelfth Night* modernisation had long ago been abandoned and since then he had toyed with an idea about the revolt of the machines against humanity, another one which dealt with a kind of land-locked Bermuda Triangle through which people disappeared only to emerge in an alternative universe, and a third – on which he seemed to have settled at least temporarily – which was an updated version of *The Spanish Tragedy* set in the world of Canadian high finance.

The other members of the class were unenthusiastic about it.

'You should write about what you know, Ken,' Trudy told him in her most sententious manner.

'I *do* know about it,' he protested. 'My dad's into all that stuff – takeovers and mergers and all that.'

'Fine,' said Matthew, 'but what you're giving us here is a revenge tragedy. Do you really think that – outside

165

the Mafia families, maybe – people behave like that any more?'

But Ken was stubborn. 'It's always been part of human life,' he argued. 'Look at President Reagan.'

The class discussion was transformed for the next fifteen minutes, in spite of Matthew's efforts to get it back on track, into a wrangle about American retaliation in the Middle East, the situation in South Africa, and the threat of world terrorism. By the end of the hour, Ken was still unmoved, so when the class broke up, Matthew decided to walk with him across campus and continue their discussion. It was such a cold day that they chose to make their way back to the Central Administration Building by way of the tunnels, which were now open again.

'You say your father's involved in high finance?' Matthew said when they had penetrated well into the underground maze.

Ken nodded non-committally.

'Would you say he was a very vengeful man?'

Ken gave Matthew a quick sideways glance. 'Not very,' he admitted.

'Then perhaps you should try to see the world as he sees it.'

Ken stopped and looked at Matthew quizzically, then smiled. 'It wouldn't be very interesting, Mr Prior. I'm sorry, I'll have to run now or I'll be late for my psychology class,' he said.

Leaving Matthew standing there, he sped away, and his slim agile body was soon lost to sight around the next bend.

'Hell!' said Matthew helplessly. 'Abandoned in the labyrinth. Now, how do I get out?'

He had to wait till another student came by, who, with the sort of kindly consideration he might have given to a bewildered octogenarian, led Matthew gently to his destination.

\* \* \*

Bonny was just getting ready to go to lunch when Matthew arrived at the door of her office.

'Let me treat you,' said Matthew. 'Where were you planning to go?'

Bonny shrugged. 'I was just going to grab a sandwich in the cafeteria downstairs.'

'Boring!' said Matthew. 'Let's get off the damned campus. We'll drive into town and find a place.'

Bonny was unusually acquiescent. She followed him silently to the carpark while he rattled on about his playwriting class.

When they reached the main street of Mapleville, they were faced with an unexciting choice: the Dodge City Steak House, the Golden Pagoda, the BiggaBurger, or Pozzo's Pizza Parlour. Bonny clearly had no preference, so Matthew parked in the Dodge City lot. Inside the restaurant, there was a curious mixture of effects: weathered barn-siding and steer-horns on the walls, but pink napkins and pink-shaded lamps on the tables. The waitresses, all of whom were homely middle-aged women, wore Annie Oakley outfits, while the maître d' and the wine steward sported powder-blue tuxedos and string ties. It was as though the decorator for the chain of restaurants had contrived a shotgun marriage between the OK Corral and Miami Beach.

While they were sipping their mimosas, Bonny relaxed a little and directed a sceptical smile at Matthew and his drink.

'Not exactly a man's cocktail, is it?' she said.

'You mean in this two-fisted Western ambiance I should be drinking Jack Daniels with a beer chaser?'

'Something like that.'

'I'm sorry. I like my drinks sweet – and preferably sticky too. It doesn't exactly match the private-eye image, I know – but there it is. It probably all goes back to my nanny who used to keep me quiet by dipping my pacifier in sweetened condensed milk and sugar.'

Bonny managed a faint laugh. 'She should have been reported to the RSPCC,' she said.

'She was eventually. But that was after they caught her deliberately forcing my head between the park railings. She was in love with a fireman and it gave her an excuse to call the local Fire Brigade.'

Bonny's laugh was more genuine this time. 'You're a terrible liar, Matthew Prior.'

'You should set that to music,' he said. 'Besides, I'm not a terrible liar. I'm a very good liar. And you're a very troubled young woman. Now, what's the matter?'

Her eyes clouded and she turned her head away. 'What would be the matter? It's just this awful business on campus. It's getting me down.'

Matthew reached across the table and patted her hand sympathetically, almost upsetting a trayful of steak and french fries that the waitress was about to unload in front of them.

Having wiped a few drops of gravy from his tie, he tried once more to probe the cause of Bonny's unease.

'I think it's depressing everyone. Roger's been very sombre lately. But I think we're beginning to get somewhere. I'd like very much to know if there was any connection between that group and Joe Innocenti or Shana Pilton.'

'Joe and Shana? No more than between them and other fourth-year students, as far as I know.'

'Are Joe and Shana an item – as the gossip-columnists used to say?'

'You mean are they going together? I don't know. Believe it or not, I don't spend all my time snooping into the students' private lives.'

She was beginning to sound indignant so Matthew made conciliating noises.

'Of course not! It's just that I happened to see them together and I wondered if any of the other students had said anything – you know, some casual remark which you might just accidentally have overheard.'

Bonny tightened her lips in mock exasperation. 'You don't give up, do you? Well, if you want my opinion – and it's just an opinion – Joe *is* interested in Shana and she has no time for him.'

Matthew chewed a piece of steak thoughtfully. 'No time for him, eh? But Shana *did* have time for Cubby – and Cubby's dead. Cubby had time for Calvin – and Calvin's dead. Would you say Shana had violent impulses?'

'How would I know? When they come to see me they're usually on their best behaviour because they want something – permission to use the typewriter or an appointment with Roger to complain about grades. My impression of Shana is that she's a fierce little woman – and then she's – as they say – "into punk" – all that slam-dancing and safety-pins through their earlobes.'

Matthew went on chewing the steak which was distressingly tough. 'I think slam-dancing and safety-pins are a bit passé. What about Joe's temper? I can see him setting out on a vendetta in the old Italian style. Perhaps this whole thing *is* a revenge tragedy after all.'

Bonny pushed away her plate and dabbed at her lips with the pink napkin.

'You haven't finished,' said Matthew. 'Would you like something else? Coffee? Black Forest cake?'

'No, I really don't feel very hungry. I'm sorry, Matthew – but thank you for lunch anyway.'

Matthew looked at her troubled face and his heart gave one of those disorienting lurches which signalled that it had passed the point of no return and that from then on it would be dancing to the melody of a new voice. Henrietta, Nell and Dorothy appeared momentarily before his mind's eye, wagging their fingers reproachfully (or in Nell's case satirically), but he mentally waved them away and tried to swallow the sudden painful constriction in his throat.

'Bonny,' he pleaded, 'for heaven's sake, tell me what's wrong.'

She crumpled her napkin and dropped it on the table. 'You're the wrong person to tell, Matthew, but you're also the best person to tell. I'm frightened and I'm worried – about Fraser.'

'Fraser!' Matthew exclaimed.

'He asked me to marry him.'

'I know,' Matthew said dully. 'He told me he was going to.'

'You remember the night we went to the book launch?'

'Yes.'

'And Fraser joined us?'

'Yes.'

'What was the date?'

Matthew pulled out his pocket diary and flipped through the pages. 'January the fifteenth,' he said when he had located the entry.

'Fraser was just back from visiting Meg and Hamish in Winnipeg.'

'So you told me.'

Bonny paused, and then with some difficulty went on. 'The letter Inspector Bain found in Calvin's mail-box was postmarked "Winnipeg" and dated January fourteenth. Matthew, I can't think of anyone else remotely connected with the case who would have been in Winnipeg on that particular day.'

The drive back to campus was almost entirely silent. Matthew had tried in the restaurant to reassure Bonny that there were many ways in which the letter could have been posted in Winnipeg without Fraser being implicated.

But even as he offered his reassurances, he couldn't think of anyone in the cast or crew of *The Armageddon Excuse-Me Fox-Trot* who would have had time between rehearsals to fly to Winnipeg and back. Nor could he conceive of any one of them going to the length of dangerously involving some relative or friend in that city in a deception solely for the purpose of planting such a stupidly misleading clue.

The puzzle was no nearer a solution when they drew into the University parking lot and pulled neatly into a space between a battered Jeep and a glossy BMW. They didn't get out of the car immediately but sat wordless, staring through the windscreen as the snowflakes settled thickly on the glass.

Bonny was the first to break the silence.

'You know, Matthew,' she said, 'Fraser is one of the unhappiest men I've ever met. He once told me that the last time he was happy – the last time all of them were happy – was at their summer cottage on the lake, the summer before Heather disappeared.'

'Unhappy, and perhaps vengeful,' Matthew thought, but all he said was: 'Don't worry, Bonny. I think you should forget the Winnipeg business and I wouldn't bother Fraser with it either.'

They left the car and Matthew helped Bonny across the snowy ruts and hillocks that covered the surface of the parking lot. So concerned were they with watching their feet that they weren't aware of anyone approaching until they heard a hoarse shout. Skidding and stumbling through the snow towards them came Bain and Kozetsky, grim-faced and breathing hard.

'Oh, Lord!' said Matthew. 'What is it now?'

Bain raced on to the unmarked police car but Kozetsky paused beside them. 'Another one,' he gasped. 'Shana Pilton. Dead in a bathtub at the Morpheus Arms.'

# Chapter Seventeen

The manager of the Morpheus Arms was an unhappy man. His life up to that moment had not, as he was fond of telling everyone, been a cakewalk. He used obscure and dated idioms like that because he had learned most of his English from old *Liberty* magazines which had been donated to his orphanage in Lebanon by a retired New England schoolmistress. After growing up in Beirut, he had moved to Australia in the late thirties where he had tried to start a Lebanese restaurant. The Aussies, however, were at that stage in their culture when beer and beef were staples and spicy concoctions of lamb and sticky confections of filo pastry were greeted not just with indifference but with outright scorn. After the war, he tried the USA and became a night clerk at a fleabag hotel in Chicago, but the immigration authorities caught up with him and deported him as an illegal alien. Canada's immigration quotas happened at that time to be liberal, thanks to Prime Minister Louis St Laurent, so Mr Ampagoumian entered as a landed immigrant in the early fifties. Nevertheless, he never felt secure. He lived in terror that he would unwittingly do something that would enrage Canadian officialdom and cause him to be cast out again to wander the airlanes and seaways of the world like a twentieth-century Flying Dutchman. The death in Room 16 seemed to him another unfair hurdle placed in his path by some distant committee of immortals who had determined that his life was to be one long and exhausting decathlon.

Terrified though he was of the police, he summoned up all his stubbornness and obduracy when he was confronted with them. 'An accident,' he kept saying. 'It's gotta be an accident.'

Sergeant Kozetsky took a deep breath. 'Not likely, Mr Ampagoumian. The young lady was very familiar with electrical equipment. She would have understood the risk – and she'd have been careful.'

'Everybody makes mistakes,' insisted the manager.

Bain tried a different tack. 'Did the young lady make the room reservation?'

'Nobody made the room reservation,' Mr Ampagoumian yelped. 'The room was *not* supposed to be occupied.'

'Could someone have stayed in the room earlier, and just walked off with the key?'

'If they do that, we change the lock immediately.'

'But you wouldn't have known,' said Sergeant Kozetsky, 'if someone had checked into the room and had a wax impression of the key made to use later?'

Mr Ampagoumian shook his head. 'You should know better than most, Sergeant – if someone's determined to commit a crime, they'll find a way.'

A particularly ugly crime, this one, Bain thought. That poor girl with her body arched and twisted, her face purple, her teeth clenched, her eyes staring as if still watching the television set submerged in the water.

'I want a list of everyone who has registered in that room in the last year,' he said. 'And I'm afraid the room will have to be sealed till we've finished with it.'

Mr Ampagoumian spread his hands in a gesture of resignation. 'At this time of the year, Inspector, I'm lucky to rent half a dozen rooms a night. So seal the room. But,

173

do me a favour – try to keep the name of the motel out of the papers, will you?'

'We'll do our best, Mr Ampagoumian. Now, if you don't mind – let's get started on that list.'

Valu-Video proved to be less of a dead-end. The videotape Shana had been watching when she was electrocuted was a pornographic feature called *Debbie Does Dallas*. The cassette case had a label inside which gave the name and address of the video store from which it had been rented. Bain gave Kozetsky the job of interviewing the store clerk, prompting him to mutter that he might just as well be on the Vice Squad.

The store itself was situated in West Darlington in a suburban shopping mall. It was a typical one-room, one-man operation. The walls were lined with Beta and VHS tapes arranged by category: Horror, Western, Comedy and so on. The pornographic tapes were in a discreet corner by themselves.

It didn't take long for the clerk, who was a young man with shoulder-length hair and a tattoo on his left bicep, to locate the rental slip. He handed it over to Kozetsky who looked at it and sighed. It read: 'H. Ibsen, 12 Wild Duck Drive, West Darlington'.

'How do you rent these tapes?' he asked. 'Do you have to have a membership?'

'Sure,' said the young man. 'We issue a membership card. Then if some goof-ball doesn't return the tape we can track him down.'

'I suppose you're careful to get proper identification.'

'Right on. We ask for a driver's licence or a major credit card.'

'You're very careful about that, are you? What if someone came in who didn't have either? You'd refuse to rent?'

The young man began to look a little shifty.

174

'We-e-e-ell . . .' he said. 'I mean, business isn't that great, you know. We can't afford to turn customers away.'

Kozetsky decided to put on a little pressure.

'So on what kind of flimsy piece of fake ID would you let minors rent X-rated movies?'

The young man reacted with some small signs of panic – swallowing, lip-licking and a nervous tremor at the corner of his eye. 'Hey, man! Hey, man!' he said. 'No way! And this was no minor, believe me.'

'So what was the ID? You'd better think hard.'

The young man gulped. 'I'm trying to remember, man. I'm tryin'! Wait a minute . . . It was a library card. A Metro Library card . . . that's it!'

'With that name and address on it?'

'Yeah. I copied it down.'

'Have you ever heard of a playwright called Ibsen?'

'No, man . . . I don't think so. Does he write for CBC?'

Kozetsky made no comment. 'Well, what about Wild Duck Drive?' he went on. 'Did you check to see if there was any such address in West Darlington?'

'Hey, man, there's all kinda streets named after birds – a whole section: Loon Lane, Hummingbird Drive, Killdeer Crescent.'

Kozetsky silently pulled out his pocket *A to Z* of the area and looked in the index. He put his thumb on the line where Wild Duck Drive would have appeared if it had existed and held the book in front of the young man's face.

'Wild Cherry Lane, Wilder Drive . . . No Wild Duck Drive.'

'How about that!' said the young man with exaggerated amazement.

'A library card must be one of the most easily forged pieces of ID in existence. Don't you think you've been just a shade careless here?'

175

Visions of prosecution for renting pornographic video-tapes to minors dancing in his head, the young man began to bluster and swear.

'Ease off, tiger,' said Kozetsky. 'You haven't been too smart, but if you help us with our inquiries I'll see you don't get hassled. Now, what did this character look like?'

The young man thought for a moment, a process that involved closing his eyes and scratching his rear end.

'Hey, yeah,' he said, having taxed his memory to the maximum, 'it was weird; I remember now.'

'What was weird?'

'Well – like – this customer comes in, and it's like real cold, you know, so he's like all bundled up with a scarf over his mouth – but he's wearing – like – a skirt.'

'A skirt!' Kozetsky exclaimed.

'Not exactly a skirt, I guess. More like – you know – what those Scotch guys wear when they're tossin' hammers at the Highland Games in Fergus.'

'You mean kilts?' Stan said and waited till the boy nodded assent. 'I'm surprised you've been to the Highland Games in Fergus.'

'Haven't, man. Caught a bit on TV once. Switched it off.'

'You're sure it was a guy?'

The young man scratched and pondered again. 'Not a hundred percent, man. But I didn't get the vibes – you know – the vibes you get from a chick.'

Stan sighed. 'What about the voice? Did it sound male or female?'

'Didn't hear it. These bashful ones, you know, man – they just fill out their slips and hand them over.'

Kozetsky pondered the kilt. There had been two other sightings of a figure in a kilt. One by Mrs Napoleon, and the other by Shana Pilton.

'Listen, friend,' he said grimly, 'you're going to have to lock up shop for a while. You and me are going to have a little session with the police artist.'

'So you found another piece of that print,' said Matthew. He was in the incident room, chewing on an almond croissant and drinking a can of Mountain Dew. Bain was watching him with a mixture of curiosity and revulsion.

'Yes, we did. Propped up in the soap-dish above the sink.'

He pushed the fragment of print in its transparent envelope across the desk to Matthew who swallowed the remainder of the croissant, wiped his fingers on a paper napkin and carefully picked up the envelope by a corner. Shana was almost unrecognisable with long, straight hair and no makeup. Above her on the wall was a thin sliver of the letter 'I', the tip of the curved left-hand edge of another letter, a 'C' or an 'O', and between them, clear and complete, the letter 'N'.

'No Police Court. No Annabel Lee College,' said Bain somewhat smugly. 'It's L, I, N, C, O, or L, I, N, O, C, O.'

'It sounds like some kind of manufacturer,' Matthew said. 'Linco Industries, or Linoco Inc. or something of the sort.'

'We've already checked with all the local boards of trade, the Canadian Manufacturers' Association, and all the other industrial and commercial federations. There's no Linco or Linoco anywhere in the area.'

'What about Winnipeg?'

Bain raised his eyebrows. 'Shrewd,' he said. 'Because of the postmark on the letter to Mr Knox. No, we already checked. No Lincos or Linocos there either.'

Matthew brought the fragment closer. 'It *looks* like the wall of a factory – but then it's an unusual public building that doesn't look like a factory these days.'

'Oh, I didn't say it wasn't a factory. When you put all the bits of the picture together, it seems pretty clear that we've got almost all of it. That would put the Kirkwood boy at the far left-hand edge of the picture and Knox at the far right. The letter "O" on the bit with Knox's face would therefore be at the far right-hand edge of the picture. That means it may not be the last letter of the word. And as it happens there are a fair number of factories in the area with the word "Lincoln" in their names: Lincoln Electrical and Lincoln Lubricating Equipment, for instance. There's also Lincoln National Life Insurance. I've got men out now photographing the signs.'

Matthew put the envelope back on the desk. It was easy to read the dissatisfaction on his face.

'Seems unlikely to me,' he said, 'that someone would photograph a bunch of theatre students outside a factory or a life insurance building.'

'Summer jobs,' said Bain airily. 'One or more of them may have been working there and maybe they decided to get together for lunch or a drink after work – and someone took a picture.'

'Possibly,' said Matthew, 'but why should the picture be so important to the murderer?'

'If we knew that, Mr Prior, we might have the answer to the whole thing.'

Matthew swigged back the dregs of the soft-drink can and threw it into Bain's waste basket.

'You know, Inspector,' he said as he got up, 'I think there's one person around who knows more than they're telling.'

'Who?'

'Ursula Hooper.'

'Doesn't that make two persons? Her and the murderer?'

'Not,' said Matthew, 'if Ursula Hooper *is* the murderer. It's odd, you know, that she's the only one who survived an attack by this very efficient killer. Could she have invented that little scene in the dressing-room to throw us off the track? After all, the only one who could have confirmed it is Cubby. *Was* Cubby, I should say.'

'The naked whacko with no hair – all made up? Could be, Mr Prior. But frankly I think she's telling the truth. To my mind, she's more likely to be the next victim.'

# Chapter Eighteen

With Shana's murder, the case began to make headlines not just in the national press but internationally. The fact that all the victims were working on the same production and that the play in question was by a fairly well-known British playwright produced a whole spate of sensational reports. *The New York Post* proclaimed: 'Private Eye's Play Makes Deadly Debut'; the English *Daily Express* trumpeted: 'Crime Playwright's Brother in Real-Life Death Drama' (which prompted Matthew to reflect bitterly that as usual Paul got top billing); in Paris, *Le Soir* commented: 'Un Roman Policier Est Realisé En Vie'. The result of all this attention was that the campus was crawling with newspaper reporters, TV camera crews and ordinary common-or-garden ghouls of the sort who stop and stare greedily at spectacular car-wrecks.

One consequence was that security became harder and harder to ensure. Apart from the nuisance of souvenir hunters who stole everything from Wacousta ashtrays to posters for Matthew's play, there was the danger that the next murder might be made easier by the number of strangers on campus. This worried Inspector Bain so much that he decided to assign a permanent bodyguard to Ursula Hooper. Two policewomen were chosen, one for day duty and one for night. The sight of these stern-faced women clumping around after Ursula during rehearsals brought Matthew almost to the point of hysteria.

Ursula herself was exercising such tight self-control that her performance became rigid and mechanical. Nor had she been able to identify the locale of the photograph. When shown the composite and asked about the sign on the wall, she claimed that she had no memory of the occasion, but there was something so flat about her denial that Matthew suspected she was lying. As for Joe Innocenti, his behaviour and his temper were becoming more and more unpredictable. He quarrelled violently with other members of the cast, argued with Matthew about stage business, arrived late for rehearsals, and several times walked off stage in the middle of a scene. The other cast members fought back against Joe, but Ursula seemed to shrink from him, taking his abuse silently and avoiding him whenever she could.

After one particularly noisy and chaotic rehearsal, Matthew decided to enlist the help of some of the more stable members of the company and asked Wayne Goffman and Rezi Yanouf to stay behind and talk. Rezi, he knew, was probably closer to Ursula than anyone else in the theatre department, and Wayne seemed to be one of the few cast-members who could deflect Joe's anger. Matthew sat down with them both near the back of the auditorium, out of earshot of the stage crew who were re-assembling some set pieces on stage. Against a background noise of hammering and shouting, he tried to steer the conversation towards the problems of the production.

'No big deal,' said Rezi. 'Every production I've been in here has been like this. Temper-tantrums, ego-trips – total chaos! Then the curtain goes up on opening night and somehow it all comes together.'

'Very comforting,' said Matthew. 'But somehow I think we're facing something worse than the usual theatrical madness.'

'Obviously,' said Wayne satirically. 'Like, not every

production I've been in has featured a real-life mad killer.'

Matthew granted him that. 'On the other hand,' he went on, 'most of you are dealing with that surprisingly well. Lulie and Duncan and Alan seem to be on a pretty even keel. You two are getting on with the job. The big spanners in the works are Ursula and Joe. Do you have any tips about how to deal with them?'

Rezi and Wayne looked at one another; Rezi's dark Eastern Mediterranean features and Wayne's chubby Northern European face both clouded with similar expressions of concern.

'It's not easy,' said Rezi after a pause 'Ursula's terrified of Joe. She thinks he's the one who jumped her in the dressing-room. Joe's mad at the whole world – his best friend, and the girl he was crazy about, both dead. Who can blame him?'

'Do you think it was Joe who scared Ursula that night?'

There was a longer pause, then Wayne said: 'It could have been. Joe has this weird exhibitionist streak. But it doesn't mean he was trying to kill her.'

Matthew looked thoughtful. 'It was certainly an odd way to approach a girl,' he said.

'The only reason Ursula thinks it was Joe is because of the ski-mask,' Rezi argued. 'You remember – we told her about Joe wearing the ski-mask when he streaked the dance concert.'

Matthew's eyes suddenly lit up. 'I know one way you two can help prove whether it was Joe or not. You all shower together after rehearsal, right?'

'Most times,' agreed Rezi.

'And Ursula told the police that the intruder had one unusual feature. He had practically no body hair.'

Wayne whooped. 'That lets Joe out,' he said. 'He's as hairy as a baboon.'

'He could have shaved or used a depilatory,' Matthew suggested.

A sceptical snort greeted that remark. 'That would have been one fast shave, man – to do it between the time he showed his ass to Calvin and when the naked guy appeared in the girls' dressing-room.'

'He'd have had to grow it back pretty fast, too,' Wayne pointed out. 'He was just as hairy as ever when I saw him in the shower the next day.'

That seemed conclusive. Matthew could think of no way, short of some skilful work with false hair, that Joe could have been hairless one day and hairy the next.

'Thanks for clearing that up,' he said. 'One more thing, though: was Joe jealous of Cubby?'

'Yes, he was,' said Wayne. 'He always wanted what Cubby had. He wanted Shana and he wanted the lead in the play. But he and Cubby were tight buddies. He wouldn't ever have killed him.'

The lines from *The Ballad of Reading Gaol* that he had quoted to Calvin drifted unbidden into Matthew's head. Maybe there was a great deal more to the 'tight buddy' relationship than anyone had guessed.

'All right, Rezi . . . Wayne . . . You've both been a big help. Maybe you could help Ursula too. Put her mind at ease about Joe. And I'll see you at tomorrow's rehearsal.'

The identikit picture that the police artist provided with help from the assistant at Valu-Video showed a face of indeterminate age with lightly arched eyebrows and high cheekbones with a sprinkling of freckles.

'I don't place much credence in this,' the police artist said as he handed it over. 'I've seldom had to deal with a less observant, more inarticulate fathead since I started this job. The only thing he seemed sure about were the eyebrows and the freckles; the hair and the lower part of the face were hidden.'

'Eyebrows!' said Stan Kozetsky despairingly. 'About as useful as earlobes.'

'And easier to disguise,' Bain replied. 'You can shave them – or add to them with a bit of false hair and spirit gum – or dye them.'

'Right,' Kozetsky said. 'So where does that leave us?'

'Up the creek. Still, there's the kilt and the freckles.'

Kozetsky groaned. 'Freckles aren't hard to fake. And as for the kilt, given this guy's powers of observation, it could as easily have been an extra large pair of Madras Bermuda shorts.'

'In this weather? You must be kidding.'

'So? Would you wear a kilt in this weather, sir?'

'I wouldn't wear a kilt at all, Stan. I don't have the knees for it.'

'All right, what else have we got?'

Together they reviewed the most recent evidence. Dodie Goldberg had come back from New York a changed girl. The group photograph had been taken outside a building on which, according to the best expert opinion, the letters L, I, N, C, O appeared. None of the possible buildings, either in Southern Ontario or in the Winnipeg area, had a sign whose letters matched those in the photograph. Calvin's letter had been postmarked 'Winnipeg', but no one involved with the play appeared to have any association with Winnipeg. Fraser McCullough had Winnipeg connections, but he seemed an unlikely suspect. A girl in a plaid skirt had twice been seen near a place where a murder had later been committed. A man in a kilt had rented a pornographic videotape which had later been found in the Morpheus Arms.

'I suppose,' said Bain wearily, 'the girl in the skirt and

the man in the kilt could be one and the same. After all, with all the kinkiness in this case, what's a little harmless transvestism?'

'What really beats me, sir, is the motive. They look like thrill killings, but they're not random enough. A small group of people is being targeted. But why? What could a bunch of college kids have done that would make someone want to kill them?'

'Maybe they didn't do anything. Maybe it's what the killer thought they did that matters.'

At that moment, their conversation was interrupted by a knock at the door.

'Who is it?' Bain yelled.

'Matthew Prior.'

'Come in. Make yourself at home,' said Bain resignedly, then, as Matthew dropped his lean frame into an empty chair, he added: 'Here he is, the headline grabber. You wouldn't think we'd done a stroke of work on the case according to the papers.'

'Come now, Inspector,' said Matthew. 'It was you, after all, who practically shanghaied me into this.'

'No unfounded allegations of police brutality, please. You'll have the Citizens' Review Board down on us like a ton of bricks . . . Well, what nuggets of information do you have for us today, Mr Prior?'

'I think you can strike Joe off your list of suspects,' he said. 'Like Esau, he's a hairy man. He couldn't have been Ursula's attacker.'

'We weren't seriously considering him anyway. At least not after Shana Pilton's murder.'

Matthew raised his eyebrows. 'Oh, why's that?'

'Because he doesn't look anything like this sketch, for one thing.'

Bain pushed the identikit picture across the desk. Matthew glanced at it, and then looked again.

'It's not much of a picture,' Kozetsky said. 'And according to the police artist, the guy who gave the description wouldn't have won any prizes for observation.'

Matthew picked up the picture and examined it closely. 'The eyebrows,' he said.

'That's one of the few things the guy seemed sure about.'

Bain waved his hand dismissively. 'If you'd seen as many of these things as I have, you wouldn't get excited about that. When we finally catch them they bear about as much resemblance to their identikit pictures as I do to Burt Reynolds.'

Consideringly, Matthew chewed his lip. Then he put his hand over the lower part of the picture and stared again.

'I don't know, Inspector. I can hear a little bell ringing somewhere at the back of my head . . . a regular tintinnabulation. But you're right, it doesn't look like Joe.'

'No, it doesn't. And, for that matter, I've never known Italians to go around wearing kilts.'

'Kilts! Oh, my Lord!' Matthew dropped the picture as if it had burned his fingers.

'Certainly not ideal wear in this brass-monkey weather,' Bain went on, 'but that and the freckles are the only other reasonably certain bits of identification we got from this joker at Valu-Video. I just hope our friend had his fur-lined jockstrap on underneath.'

Fine arched eyebrows and a kilt. To Matthew, the connection was all too obvious now and, coupled with the Winnipeg postmark, it seemed to point unrelentingly towards Fraser. Something, however, perhaps his tenderness for Bonny, made him hesitate to say anything to Bain and Kozetsky. Instead he changed the subject.

'So Joe seems to be out of it,' he said. 'Any other news I haven't heard?'

Kozetsky pushed the complete composite of the group photograph towards him. 'This seems to be the whole picture,' he said. 'Five people in the group: Hooper, Kirkwood, Goldberg, Pilton and Knox. No lead on the sign, though.'

'Odd,' said Matthew.

'More little bells going off?' asked Bain.

'Carillons – but I'm not sure why. Now that I see the sign all linked together, there's something vaguely familiar about it.'

'Sleep on it,' Bain suggested. 'Maybe it'll all come clear in the morning.'

'Oh, by the way,' Kozetsky said before Matthew could get out of the door, 'one thing we forgot to mention: I tracked down a friend of the Goldberg girl. She told me that she went off to New York at the end of her first year and came back depressed and moody.'

'New York'll do that to you,' said Matthew.

'It's a hell of a town,' Bain sighed.

'If you can make it there, you'll make it anywhere,' crooned Kozetsky.

'I'll take Manhattan,' concluded Matthew, and slipped quickly away before they all burst into a chorus of 'Give My Regards to Broadway'.

The next morning, Matthew was called in by Dean Ripper, ostensibly to discuss the progress of *The Armageddon Excuse-Me Fox-Trot*, but in fact to be bullied about the slow progress of the investigation. The Dean hinted to Matthew that he could stand some good publicity after the flop of *The Harmonious Blacksmith* on Broadway, and that a successful solution to the case would help sell tickets for his new play. He even implied that if Matthew cleared up the mess, he might be able to raise financing for a full-scale production at one of Toronto's experimental theatres. And who knows? From there it might find Broadway backers. Dean Ripper flashed a ferocious white smile. He did, after

187

all, he informed Matthew, have an 'in' with Joe Papp.

Matthew had dealt with more accomplished humbugs in his time and so, after duelling briefly over the coffee and prune Danishes provided by the Dean's secretary, Matthew was able to escape. Before he left, however, he couldn't resist giving the Dean a brief demonstration of his investigative technique.

'Tell me, Vern,' he said, 'did you see *The Harmonious Blacksmith* in New York?'

Ripper grinned again. 'Sure did. Just made it before it closed.'

'In that case it must have been the second night of the run. April the 6th.'

'Yes. I remember reading the reviews in the morning paper before I went to the show that night. It's the only time I've seen reviews on the obituary page.'

Matthew ignored that. 'Were you alone, or did you go with a group?'

The Dean scratched his tanned chin thoughtfully. 'If you really need to know, it was a group. A group from Wacousta, in fact. The annual New York trip. One of our Board of Governors was a backer of your show. He arranged a discount for us.'

'Fraser McCullough?'

'Yes, as a matter of fact.'

'Was he in town for the show?'

The Dean looked puzzled. 'He was, yes. I met him in the lobby at intermission.'

Matthew took a deep breath and came at last to the point. 'Did anything odd happen on that trip?'

The question made the Dean visibly uncomfortable. He squirmed in his chair, drummed his fingers on the desk-top, and cleared his throat.

'Er . . . ,' he said evasively. 'Odd? Hmmm . . .'

'Anything even slightly peculiar?'

The Dean's face darkened to a richer mahogany. 'Slightly peculiar! It was *damned* peculiar! One of our students disappeared from her hotel. It created a very sticky situation, considering who she was.'

'Oh, who was she?'

'Fraser McCullough's daughter.'

Matthew blinked. His line of questioning had led him further than he expected.

'Did they ever find her?' he asked.

'No,' said the Dean. 'They did everything they could. Pictures in the papers. Posters. Photographs on the side of milk cartons. Fraser even had a private detective. But it happens all the time, you know. Kids disappear. The police in the States didn't have any central registry of missing persons at that time. There have been cases where parents have ruined themselves financially trying to find missing children. Fraser's rich – and he must have spent tens of thousands looking for her – but it was no good. The police closed their books – missing, presumed dead.'

'Good Lord!' said Matthew. 'What about the other students? When did they see her last?'

'There was a party after the show in one of the hotel rooms. She walked out of the party and was never seen again.'

Matthew stood up to go, reaching for the last prune Danish on the plate. 'Thank you, Vern,' he said. 'You've been very helpful.' Then, just as he was about to open the door, he turned. 'One last thing. Do you know whose room the party was given in?'

The Dean was no longer smiling. In fact, his face wore an expression of downright misery.

'Does this have anything to do with anything? You're not supposed to be investigating Heather McCullough's disappearance.'

Matthew pulled something out of his pocket and held it towards Dean Ripper. 'Do you recognise this?'

'It's a ticket stub.'

'Yes, it's a ticket stub for *The Harmonious Blacksmith* dated April the 6th. It was pushed under my door in an envelope the day after Dodie Goldberg died.'

The Dean sighed. 'So you think there might be a connection?'

'It's a strong possibility. Whose room was the party in?'

'Cubby Kirkwood's.'

There was no heartiness left in Dean Ripper. He slumped behind his desk, slack-mouthed. In Matthew's mind, a few little pieces of the puzzle fell neatly into place. 'You really *have* been helpful, Vern. You don't *know* how helpful.'

But the Dean didn't answer. He didn't even look up as Matthew made his well-timed exit; he was too busy staring desolately at his beautiful model of the fine arts complex extension.

# Chapter Nineteen

The opening of *The Armageddon Excuse-Me Fox-Trot* was less than a week away, and the familiar theatrical panic had set in, heightened in this case by the unusual aura of danger that surrounded the production. The costume shop was a small Bedlam of people, cutting, sewing, basting, screaming and swearing. Vera Campbell, like a demented behemoth, lumbered around bellowing: 'Keep those hems straight! Rip them out! Start again!' In the scene shop, Ted Campbell was yanking at his beard and howling in despair at the incompetence of some second-year students who were attempting to paint flats. In the theatre box office, Tiberio Turchino and Meriel Kitt were trying to deal with a flash-flood of telephone calls and mail orders on a scale unmatched since the department – in the radical sixties – had mounted an all-nude production of *Ubu Roi*. It seemed clear that, if the show opened at all, the department would make a handsome profit.

Much, of course, depended on the cast. They had been under more than normal strain and several of them had come down with flu. As a result, rehearsals became more and more ragged. Joe and Ursula, however, seemed to have reached some kind of reconciliation and the tension between them was no longer affecting their fellow-players. But the presence of one or another of the two police-women was a perpetual reminder that things were far from normal.

In the early evening of the Monday before the opening, Matthew and Marie-Ange were working on the closing scene of the first act. It involved a troupe of seventeenth-century actors who were interrupted by a troupe of Cromwell's soldiers while presenting an illicit performance of the assassination scene from *Julius Caesar*. The soldiers arrest the actors, march them up the aisle and out of the theatre, and – after the theatre doors close behind them – the audience hear the sound of shots and the screams of dying performers. It made an effective first-act curtain, calculated to keep the audience in suspense through the intermission.

The rehearsal was going well. Joe, as the actor playing Brutus, had spoken the lines:

> 'Stoop, Romans, stoop
> And let us bathe our hands in Caesar's blood
> Up to the elbows, and besmear our swords,'

and Duncan Hogg had entered, leading the Roundheads, who aimed their muskets at the actors and herded them off the stage. Matthew watched with approval as the sombre procession moved past him towards the back of the auditorium. The doors closed behind the actors and there was the sound of a fusillade of shots, just as he expected. The screams that followed were spine-tingling, and Matthew had just turned to Marie-Ange to comment on the realism of the effect, when the doors burst open again and someone yelled:

'Get help, for Chrissake! Joe's been shot!'

'The bullet absolutely didn't come from one of the muskets,' Ted Campbell insisted. 'The damn things don't work. They're just props.'

'All the same,' Inspector Bain said, 'we'll have to take them all and examine them. Mind you – judging by the

angle of the wound and the bullet we found in the wall –
you're probably right.'

'Thank God it was just a flesh wound,' said Ted. 'Poor
kid. It's enough to make him give up acting for something
safer – like sky-diving.'

'He'll be OK. I doubt if he'll even need to miss a
rehearsal.'

They were standing in the lobby of the theatre, roughly
where the murder attempt had been made. The policewoman who was guarding Ursula had been standing with
her back to the door of the women's washroom. She had
seen Joe move in front of Ursula just before the muskets
were fired. In the circumstances, it was not surprising that
she believed at first that Joe had been wounded by one of
the muskets – and that the shot had really been intended
for Ursula. Since then, the area had been cleared and a
police team were going over it inch by inch, paying particular attention to the carpet near the door of the women's
washroom, from which – it now appeared – the shot must
have been fired. The washroom itself had already been
searched, but as it had a second entrance leading from the
main hall of the Fine Arts Building, it was clear that anyone
concealed inside could have escaped without being seen.

Ted Campbell lumbered away to collect the muskets
and hand them over to the ballistics and fingerprint detail.
As he left, Matthew appeared and tugged Bain urgently
aside.

'The bells finally chimed the right tune,' he said.

'Eh?' said Bain, backing away slightly.

'The carillon in my head.'

'Oh, yes . . .' Bain still looked nervous.

'It started playing "New York, New York". Listen: Dodie
Goldberg went to New York and came back a changed
person – a year and a half ago, wasn't it?'

Bain nodded. 'According to our informant.'

'That would have been the time of the theatre department trip to New York. They all went to see my play, *The Harmonious Blacksmith*.'

'Had a powerful effect on Dodie, did it?' Bain asked cautiously.

Matthew waved the question aside with an impatient gesture.

'After Dodie's murder, someone slipped a ticket stub under my door. It was for that particular performance.'

'Interesting,' said Bain.

'That evening, after the play, a party was held in Cubby Kirkwood's hotel room. One of the guests left that party and was never seen again.'

Bain lost his look of tolerant boredom and began to pay close attention. 'A Wacousta student?' he asked.

'Yes – a theatre department student – Heather McCullough. She was . . .'

'Fraser McCullough's daughter!' Bain exclaimed.

'Right! Now, the photograph – the composite – remember, I said something about it looked familiar. Well, it should have. When I was in New York that year, I went up to Broadway and 64th to look at the Lincoln Center for the Performing Arts. Oddly enough, I discovered that there's only one place on the outside of the complex where that name appears and that's at the back on the West End Avenue side. It's at the entrance to a kind of delivery bay. That's the sign in the photograph.'

'And you think the group in the photograph were at the party where the McCullough girl was last seen?'

'I'd bet my life on it.'

They stared silently at one another for a moment and then Bain said: 'Why isn't the McCullough girl *in* the photograph?'

'My guess is she was holding the camera.'

194

Bain took a deep breath. 'And her father,' he said, 'would have been given all her effects – the camera included. He could have had the film developed and put two and two together.'

'And decided that they should all pay for what happened to his daughter. You probably remember the case, Inspector: the New York police closed the file on it – "missing presumed dead".'

Bain frowned. 'There'd be no official presumption of death,' he said. 'But unofficially they may have suggested as much to McCullough. Still, it's far-fetched, isn't it, Mr Prior? And you're making too many assumptions. That she held the camera. That the group in the picture were the group at the party. That Mr McCullough somehow came by the picture.'

A vision of Bonny flashed through Matthew's head, and a doubt followed it. Was he building a case against Fraser because he was jealous? Was he betraying Bonny's confidence? Her safety, though, was more important than the risk that she might hate him. Summoning Dorothy's cool image, he silently appealed for help. She appeared to him, sitting behind her desk in New Scotland Yard, tastefully dressed in a tea-coloured shantung shirt and a cream linen suit. Propping her splendid chin on one hand, she said: 'Concealing evidence is a crime. Besides what happens to Ursula if you don't tell?' 'Good old, common-sense Dorothy,' he thought as she faded away.

The Inspector was still waiting, his eyes fixed quizzically on Matthew's face.

'No,' said Matthew slowly, 'the photograph mightn't be enough by itself – but a postmark might.'

'A postmark?'

'The envelope that arrived after Calvin was already dead. It was dated January the 15th, and postmarked Winnipeg.'

'I don't remember giving you that information.'

'Bonny told me. She saw it before she handed the envelope to you.'

'So, where does McCullough come in?'

'He was in Winnipeg that day – visiting his ex-wife – Heather's mother.'

The policewoman who was guarding Ursula's door nodded expressionlessly at Matthew and allowed him to pass on into the room. It was tidier than it had been on his last visit, and Ursula, looking shaken, was stretched out on the daybed under a pink blanket.

'Look, I don't want to worry you,' said Matthew, 'but there's one thing you could help us with . . .'

Ursula gestured weakly towards a chair.

'Would you like some tea?' she said. 'Gloria can put the kettle on.'

'Gloria?' he thought. The policewoman's name is Gloria. Good Lord!

'No, thanks,' he said aloud. 'I really won't be here more than a minute. It's about the photograph. I think it was taken outside the Lincoln Center in New York. Am I right?'

Ursula closed her eyes. 'New York?' she said faintly.

'Didn't you stay there – at the Hotel Empire – near the Lincoln Center about two years ago?'

'We stayed in some hotel. I don't remember the trip very well.'

'Your first trip to New York?'

'Yes.'

'Your only trip to New York?'

'Yes.'

'And you don't remember it very well?'

'No.'

'Do you remember anything?'

'I remember I got sick after I went to a Chinese restaurant. I'm allergic to monosodium glutamate.'

196

Matthew gave a snort of exasperation, and Gloria the policewoman threw him a warning glance.

'Please, Ursula, try to remember. It's important. Did someone take a photograph of you, Cubby, Shana, Dodie and Calvin anywhere in the city?'

Ursula turned her head restlessly on the pillow. 'I told you before. We were all taking photographs and making sketches all the time for our performance journals. It would be hard to remember one single time when it happened.'

'Ursula, it's your safety we're talking about here. If you know anything at all, you must tell me.'

He waited, but her face was deliberately blank.

'I think you'd better let her rest,' said Gloria the police-woman. 'She's had quite a shock, you know.'

Matthew left, half-hoping that Ursula would call him back and tell him what she knew about the New York trip. No matter what she had said, he was convinced that she was concealing something. But the door closed behind him and no repentant summons came from inside the room.

In downtown Toronto at the administrative offices of the airline, Sergeant Kozetsky was interviewing the records clerk. She was a tall, flamboyant woman whose smile, makeup and hairstyle suggested that she had fallen under the influence of Ann Miller at an early age. The computer in front of her emitted a series of curious bleeps and clicks as she tapped at the keyboard.

'Here it is,' she said at last. 'Passenger manifest for January 13th – Toronto to Winnipeg – 18.42 hours. Now what names did you want to check?'

Kozetsky read off the list of those who might possibly have been away from Wacousta at the relevant time and could have posted the letter to Calvin. As he recited the names, she shook her magnificent mane dismissively until he reached the Ms.

'How about McCullough?' asked Stan.

'What initials?'

'F.A. Fraser Archibald.'

'You got it. He was on the flight all right.'

Stan beamed. 'And do you have a record of the return flight?'

The computer clicked and bleeped again. 'January 15th – Winnipeg to Toronto – 16.10 hours.'

'You're a jewel,' said Stan.

'Listen, it's all in the family,' she grinned. 'I'm married to a Metro traffic cop.'

'Ah, too bad,' said Stan. 'I was thinking of asking you out to a movie.'

'I've got a sister who's looking.'

'Great, we'll keep in touch. Oh, by the way, could you get me a print-out of those manifests?'

'No problem – and I'll get you my sister's telephone number at the same time.'

Stan smiled bravely. 'All in the line of duty,' he thought as he headed for the door.

# Chapter Twenty

Bonny was scared. Fraser was behaving most peculiarly. He had asked her to meet him at his club in Toronto, the ancient and prestigious Cambrian Club, whose members included such notables as Hugh Kirkwood and St David Denby. There, he had hurried her into the visitors' lounge, which at that early hour of the evening was empty and ill-lit. When they had settled down in a sofa by the window, Fraser produced an envelope of colour photographs and spread them out on the table in front of her. All the photographs were of the same girl: she was fair-skinned and freckled with long, sandy-blonde hair and a wide smile. One was a high-school graduation picture; one showed her in a lakeside setting, wearing a swimsuit and leaning over a barbecue grill; another had obviously been taken when she was all dressed up for a formal party; the last one showed her in riding kit, patting the neck of a golden palomino, whose coat was almost the colour of her hair.

'Who is it? Is it . . .?'

'Heather, yes,' said Fraser heavily.

Bonny was at a loss. He had scarcely ever talked to her about his missing daughter and, indeed, when she had tried to ask sympathetic questions, he had usually cut her off – as he did at the book launch.

'She's very pretty,' was all she could think of to say.

'Oh, hardly that,' said Fraser. 'A nice-looking girl. And

a nice girl. A happy person to be around, too. She made you feel that the world was a new place – full of fresh chances . . .'

'Fraser . . .' Bonny put out her hand and gripped his which was trembling.

'No,' he said. 'I don't deserve any sympathy. I'd given her up, you see.'

'But you tried to find her. You *and* the police *and* private detectives. You tried very hard.'

'It doesn't matter, now. I think she's found *me*.'

Bonny's spine felt as if small cold paws were walking up it. 'What on earth are you talking about?'

'Have *you* seen her, Bonny? Have you? Anywhere around the campus?'

He picked up the photographs and thrust them at her. 'Look! Take a good look – and try to remember!'

Bonny looked hard. The lost face smiled back at her, eagerly, hopefully. Wasn't there something about it that seemed somehow familiar? But at last she shook her head. There was a resemblance to Fraser, and that was all.

'I'm sorry, Fraser, but I really don't think I've ever seen her.'

'Then I'm going mad,' Fraser said flatly.

Bonny studied his face anxiously. He looked desperately tired and the lines around his mouth seemed deeper – but what worried her most were his eyes. They were grey puddles of misery, sunk deep under his fine arched eyebrows.

'Of course you're not,' she began, but her voice was shaking too much to be truly reassuring. He interrupted her impatiently.

'I keep seeing her,' he said. 'Not directly. Never standing right in front of me so I could look and be sure she was real and not a ghost or some insane delusion. No,

I only see her out of the corner of my eye – just slipping round a corner – or disappearing through a door. Over and over again – the same image – a girl with long fair hair wearing a plaid skirt. And if I follow, she's gone.'

'It's this awful murder case,' said Bonny quickly. 'You heard the appeals for that girl to come forward. The one they saw near the ... Anyway, you heard them and your imagination did the rest. It couldn't be Heather, Fraser.'

'Then it's something worse.'

He scooped up the photographs, returned them to the envelope and put it back in his pocket.

'Something worse?'

But the impulse to confide seemed somehow to have left him. With a strained, unconvincing smile, he stood up.

'Come on, my dear,' he said. 'Let's have some dinner.'

'It was terrifying, Matthew,' Bonny said in her office the next day. 'He didn't seem at all like the old Fraser. Across the dinner-table it was like ... Well, I don't know exactly what it was like. But I felt as if somebody I didn't know was inside him looking out at me through his eyes.'

Matthew was munching a large chocolate doughnut and washing it down with a can of Coca-Cola Classic.

'It's possible, you know,' he mumbled through a mouthful of doughnut crumbs.

'What is?'

'That Heather McCullough is still alive – and – for some reason – has come back here without letting anyone know. Living in hiding, stealing food from the kitchens.'

'Why on earth should she? What would be the point?'

'Because she may not be the same happy, nice, life-loving girl who disappeared nearly two years ago. A great deal could have happened to her in that time.'

Bonny shuddered. 'Oh, Matthew, that's horrible. Sometimes I wish you'd keep your theatrical imagination to yourself.'

'Many a critic has felt the same way. Anyway, it's *your* imagination that's filling in the details.'

With an exasperated sniff, Bonny swivelled her desk chair and sat with her back to him, staring out of the window. The sky was heavy with ashen clouds, and the snow on the pathways had been churned by innumerable feet into a grubby sludge. She saw two or three theatre department students, wrapped to the chin in bulky anoraks, slipping and sliding towards the Fine Arts Building with expressions of intense disgust on their faces.

'Listen,' said Matthew contritely, 'let's put this in perspective. First of all, Heather goes to New York with a crowd from the theatre department. Sometime that weekend she takes a snapshot of Ursula, Cubby, Dodie, Shana and Calvin outside the Lincoln Center. On the night of April the 6th, she goes to see my play. After the play, her little gang decides to have a party in Cubby's room. She leaves the party and disappears into the night. Fraser turns Canada and the USA upside down looking for her – with absolutely no success. This year – somebody begins quite systematically to murder all the kids in the snapshot. One of the cleaners sees a tall girl in a plaid skirt enter the tunnels after Dodie Goldberg. Shana sees a similar girl peering out of the ladies' room in the theatre lobby just after she's left Cubby in the lighting booth. Fraser thinks he's also seen a girl like that – and believes it's his daughter.'

'Plaid skirts aren't that uncommon,' said Bonny.

'Kilts,' said Matthew thoughtfully. 'Which reminds me of the customer in the kilt who rented the porn videotape. Bonny, can you get me a copy of Heather McCullough's picture?'

'We should have one on file. It was before my time – but I can check.'

'One other thing,' said Matthew. 'What was Calvin doing in that picture? As I understood it, he only came here for graduate work last year.'

Bonny went to the file cabinet and began to riffle through the folders of student records. 'The graduate secretary would have Calvin's file. Here we have blue files for first years, red for second, yellow for third and green for fourth. Withdrawn or suspended students are brown. So Heather should be in among the browns.'

'Is she?'

'No.'

Bonny pondered for a moment. 'That's funny,' she said. 'She ought to be here if she was registered at all.'

'What about the beige files?' asked Matthew.

'Those are transfer students. Students who started their degree-work at other universities.'

'She wouldn't be in there?'

'No ... I don't think so. We don't have many of them. Let's see: there's Ann Armstrong, Lulie Burns, Mark Dickinson, Jules Hirschorn, Imogen Loach, Ken Meldrum, Sylvia Potter, Marie-Ange Sabatier, and Rob Wallace.'

'No Heather!'

'No Heather. I could try to get hold of one of Fraser's snapshots or ... Wait a minute! The Registrar's Office should have a duplicate of the file – if it existed.'

'Would you check, Bonny? Oh, Lord, I'm late for class. Check, and I'll talk to you when I get back.'

He strode down the corridor, conscious of one image that kept forcing itself to the forefront of his mind: the identikit picture of the indeterminate face with the freckles and the fine arched eyebrows. He tried to put together a composite in his mind: Fraser, in a kilt, with his face partly concealed. He shivered and hurried on.

In the windowless basement room where he met his playwriting class, he found a much-depleted group.

'Where the devil is everybody?' he demanded.

There were only half a dozen students sitting around the table: Alithea Trudy Birnbaum, Walt Dunn, Celia Isaacs, Meriel Kitt, and a couple of others. Among the missing were Tiberio Turchino and Ken Meldrum.

'Flu,' said Meriel. 'A whole bunch in my residence have it.'

'It happens every year about this time,' offered Walt. 'This is the flu capital of North America.'

'Oh, well,' grumbled Matthew, 'I suppose we can carry on without them. Just don't breathe on me any of you. I have a show to get on in a couple of days.'

The class limped along for about two hours until it was clear that nobody had anything more to contribute. Matthew suggested that they break early and use the extra time for polishing their manuscripts. On his way back to Bonny's office, he ran into Lulie Burns who was dashing towards the campus bookshop.

'I'm going to see if they have a copy of your play,' she told him.

'Very sycophantic,' he said. 'And what do you mean my *play*? Which one? I've written almost a dozen.'

'The one that was on Broadway,' she said.

'For five thrilling minutes. You mean *The Harmonious Blacksmith*.'

'Yeah, the one about Handel.'

'Did you see it? Were you on the Wacousta New York trip?'

'Unfortunately no. I wasn't here then.'

Matthew snapped his fingers. 'Of course, you're a transfer student, aren't you? Bonny told me. Which university?'

'U. of M.'

Matthew looked blank. 'U. of What?'

'University of Manitoba. I transferred last September. Me and Ken transferred at the same time.'

'I hope it's a change for the better.'

'Well, I can't say it's been dull. Anyway, I've got to run. See you in rehearsal.'

She sailed sedately on her matronly way, and Matthew continued, with pensive steps, towards the Fine Arts Building. So none of the transfer students, he reflected, would have been on that ill-fated trip to New York. And of those involved in the current production that meant Lulie Burns and Marie-Ange Sabatier. Where did that get him? Nowhere, he concluded, and climbed the stairs towards Bonny's office.

'Ballistics report's in, sir,' said Stan Kozetsky.

Bain stretched and yawned. He hadn't been getting much sleep lately and Olive was complaining about how little time he was spending at home. It would be a real relief when this case was over and life got back to normal again. Thugs carving each other up in beer parlours were more his speed. These complicated clever-dick killings gave him heartburn.

'I said "The ballistics report's in, sir".'

'I heard you the first time. I may be old but I'm not deaf.'

'Sorry, sir.' Kozetsky's voice was stiff with resentment.

The inspector looked up at him and forced a smile.

'Come on, Stan. You know me – all bark and no bite. Didn't mean to snarl at you. So what do the ballistics boys say?'

'Just what we expected, sir,' Kozetsky answered, still with a touch of frost in his tone. 'The muskets were all inoperable. The shotgun sounds came from the sound effects tape and the noise must have covered the sound of the real shot – which incidentally came from a .32 Browning automatic.'

'How's the patient?'

'Innocenti? Oh, he's all right. He lost very little blood. The bullet went through the fleshy part of his upper arm, missed the major artery and the bone. They've patched him up and discharged him from hospital.'

'He's a lucky lad,' said Bain, 'and that Hooper girl is an even luckier lass. That's twice the murderer has tried to get her – and failed.'

Kozetsky brooded for a moment. 'It's weird, you know, sir,' he said at last. 'The killer's been so efficient – except with this one victim. And there's something else that bothers me. The pattern.'

'The pattern?' echoed Bain.

'Yes. In every other case, the weapon had some sexual significance – the elephant penis, the tights, the ben-wa balls, the TV set with the porn video. But the two attempts on Ursula Hooper didn't involve any weapon of that sort.'

'A naked man in a ski-mask,' suggested Bain, 'is fairly sexy.'

'Yes, but on that occasion he had no weapon at all – only his bare hands. A gun – unless you take a Freudian point of view and call it a phallic symbol – is not exactly kinky in the way the other things were.'

Bain yawned again and slumped further down in his chair.

'Roll on retirement,' he groaned. 'This case is ruining my health and my marriage. Anyway, if you want my opinion, the bozo in the ski-mask has nothing to do with it. He was just some stray loony.'

They both lapsed into silence. The only sound in the incident room was the wind outside buffeting the walls and Bain's fingertips drumming on the desk.

'What's the word on McCullough?' he asked after a moment.

'He was in Winnipeg on January the 14th all right, so he could have sent the letter to Knox.'

'How long was he there?'

'He flew in on the 13th and out again on the 15th, according to the CP Air passenger lists.'

'And the Goldberg girl's murder was on the night of the 12th. So he could have done it, but, damn me, Stan, I can't see it – a member of the Board of Governors of the University, a prominent Bay Street businessman, a member of the Cambrian Club – running around in drag, bumping off students just because they *might* have had something to do with his daughter's disappearance.'

'Unless he's mad, of course,' said Kozetsky.

'Well, if he is we'd better make sure he gets nowhere near the Hooper girl. Get a couple more policewomen on the job, Stan, would you? As for me I'm going home to make peace with Olive and have a nap.'

'I think we should cancel the opening,' Roger said.

Reason, it would seem, was on Roger's side. The leading man, the assistant director, the lighting director and one of the dressers had been murdered, the new leading man had been shot at and altogether the morale of the entire company was in shreds. The cue-to-cue run-through had been disastrous; the dress rehearsal had reached a point of calamitous confusion that made the stateroom scene in the Marx Brothers' *A Night at the Opera* seem like a well-planned lifeboat drill. In short,

207

the indicators all pointed to a dignified admission of defeat.

But Matthew disagreed. 'Remember the Alamo,' he said.

Or rather that is what Roger understood him to say, which is why he turned on Matthew a look of blank incomprehension. 'John Wayne?' he asked in a tone of affronted bafflement.

'John Wayne?' repeated Matthew. 'What about him? Though, come to think of it, he might have been a big help right now. Oh! – I see! – you thought I said "Remember the Alamo"!'

'Didn't you?'

'No, I said "Remember the LMO".'

'Ah,' said Roger.

And indeed he did remember. The LMO was a rival of the ADC, Cambridge's chief dramatic club. Its standing was sometimes above that of the Marlowe Society and the Cambridge Mummers and sometimes below, depending on who headed the organisation and which of the many talented undergraduates had been persuaded to lend it their energies. The acronym, LMO, stood for Literary, Musical and Operatic, and the club had been founded in the early eighteenth century chiefly to allow the young gentlemen of the university to try their fledgling vocal skills on the operas of Lully, Purcell and Scarlatti. By the end of the nineteenth century, they were staging endless revivals of *The Mikado* and *HMS Pinafore*, and by the mid-twentieth, though they included an annual revue or musical comedy in their season, they mainly subsisted on a diet of Pirandello, Chekhov and the lesser Elizabethans. Roger and Matthew, at one time the president and secretary respectively of the ancient institution, had been responsible for dragging an impossibly complicated production of *Every Man out of his Humour* to the Edinburgh Festival. On the way to Edinburgh, the leading lady came down with whooping

cough, and the hampers containing the costumes somehow ended up in the lost luggage office at Aberystwyth
railway station. On opening night one of the stage-hands
got hopelessly drunk at the North British Hotel on Princes
Street and the principal comic actor lost his girlfriend to
an officer in the Royal Scots Guards. The next morning,
the *Sunday Times* critic announced that the LMO's modern-
dress production of a tedious Jacobean comedy had soared
to unexpected comic heights due to risk-taking directing,
extraordinary vocal effects, and surrealistic set changes.

'We have plucked defeat out of victory before,' said
Matthew.

Roger blinked. 'Surely you mean . . .?'

'Whatever!' Matthew went on impatiently. 'This is no
time to quibble over syntax. I say we go for it.'

'You're a tremendously silly man, and I hate you,'
sighed Roger, 'but I suppose we might as well.'

On the afternoon before the opening, Matthew called the
cast together in the theatre. They sat in the vast empty
auditorium, subdued and attentive, as Matthew addressed
them from the stage. Ursula, now with a policewoman on
either side of her, sat apart from the others.

'What I want you all to remember,' Matthew said, 'is that
when you leave the University, you will be professionals.
Being a professional means hanging on to your main
objective even if the theatre is falling down around your
ears. You have to be able to cope with distractions, with
terrible miseries in your private life, with indifference from
the public and treachery from your employers, with insen-
sitive critics, hyper-sensitive playwrights, and egomaniacal
directors, with low pay and wretched working conditions –
and still go on stage and give the best performance you are
capable of. This has been an ordeal for all of you, I know.
But I want you to do something for me – not because it's

my play we're doing, not because I'm directing it – but for your own sake. I want you to come out on this stage tonight – and *be* professionals. And for Dodie, Cubby, Calvin and Shana – give it your best shot.'

For a moment, he had a glimpse of Nell Finnigan, smiling ironically, but applauding him. Then he realised that the entire cast had stood up and begun clapping and whistling and cheering. It was the best response he'd ever had from an audience. Marie-Ange who was standing near him hugged him briefly, with tears streaming down her cheeks.

Beaming at the re-animated cast, he whispered to Marie-Ange, 'Lord, I wish I could write speeches like that for my characters.' She laughed and hugged him again, and then turned to the auditorium.

'All right,' she said, 'I think we all got the message. Now, you'd better go and rest up – and I want everybody signed in on the call-board by seven o'clock. See you later!'

The cast dispersed, talking together more cheerfully than they had in days. Only Ursula, pale between the two stern policewomen, still seemed downcast. Matthew conferred for a moment with Marie-Ange about some last-minute prop problems and then hurried off to Bonny's office.

'I've got it,' she said as he entered.

'Got what?'

'Heather's picture. They had one on file in the Registrar's office. And by the way, the grad secretary said that Calvin did his undergraduate work at Columbia. He was living in New York when Heather disappeared.'

She handed him a brown manila envelope and Matthew slid the picture out.

'It's all starting to fit,' he said, gazing at the photograph. 'And Heather certainly does have a look of Fraser about her, if you take off all that hair and age her about twenty-five years. Still, no matter how good Fraser looked in drag, he'd never pass for Heather. Except at a great distance.'

'In drag!' Bonny exclaimed.

'Latest theory from your investigating team. Fraser in a kilt and a long straight wig becomes the mysterious girl in the plaid skirt.'

'Matthew, I don't think that's funny!'

Bonny was furious. Her colour had risen and her eyes were blazing.

'Neither do I,' said Matthew thoughtfully, 'and I'm worried about you. Things look bad for Fraser. This obsession with his daughter. His fantasies about seeing her around campus. I'm very much afraid his mental balance may be a bit off . . . And by the way, the CP passenger lists showed him flying to Winnipeg on the 13th and back on the 15th.'

'I knew he was in Winnipeg.'

'And you knew the letter to Calvin was postmarked the 14th. But had you thought that Dodie's body was discovered early on the morning of the 13th?'

Bonny lifted her chin defiantly, but her eyes were troubled. 'Hundreds of people must have flown from Toronto to Winnipeg on the 13th and back on the 15th.'

'Nobody connected to the play could have. They were all involved in rehearsals and technical work. Ursula couldn't have, for instance. She was rehearsing the opening of the second act on the afternoon of the 14th.'

'I don't care. I just don't believe Fraser could have anything to do with it. He's a gentle man. Oh, Matthew, he couldn't have, could he?'

Snatching a wad of Kleenex tissue from the box on her desk, she pressed it to her eyes. 'I'm so scared for him, Matthew,' she said between gulps and sniffles. 'I know there's something wrong – but I don't believe he would kill anyone.'

Matthew covered her hand with his. 'My dear, I hope not. But I'd certainly be very careful. Don't forget the tear-gas attack. I don't believe he would want to harm you – at least the sane part of him wouldn't. But you might just somehow get in the way.'

He studied the photograph again, and then, picking up some sheets of typing paper, he used them to mask the picture at the sides and the top, covering the hair. Heather's face gazed back at him, bright, alert, expectant. A look of Fraser, surely, but also a look of someone else – someone who lurked in the shadowy corners of his consciousness. But who?

Matthew sighed and stood up. 'You'll be at the opening, I hope?'

Still mopping at her eyes, she nodded.

'So will Bain and Kozetsky. Stick close to them if you can. And for heaven's sake, don't let yourself be alone with Fraser.'

He left and closed the door gently behind him. For a moment, he paused, listening. Then he heard the reassuring clack of Bonny's typewriter. 'She'll survive,' he thought, 'whatever happens. I'll see that she does.'

# Chapter Twenty-One

Ordinarily the opening of a play at the Charles Heavysege Theatre – even one by a not totally unknown British playwright who was also directing it – would not have been one of the main cultural events of the season. Wacousta University was far enough away from Toronto, and bleakly unattractive enough in the winter, to discourage all but the most determined of theatre-goers. The notoriety surrounding this production, however, had created an atmosphere of expectancy and *The Armageddon Excuse-Me Fox-Trot* was sold out for the entire run. Sensation seekers, crime reporters from all the news media, the entire membership of the Toronto Drama Bench, the artistic directors of the Stratford and Shaw Festivals, the theatre officers of the Ontario Arts Council and the Canada Council, several bank presidents, the entire Board of Governors of the University, and, of course, the President of Wacousta were all converging on the campus for the first night.

Inspector Bain and his wife Olive were dressing for the occasion in the bedroom of their ranch-style bungalow in Mapleville. Olive was resplendent in a bottle-green evening gown with dramatic inserts of ecru lace. Bain was struggling with a black tie and wing collar. Wing collars, Olive had insisted, were 'in' again.

Patting a judicious layer of powder onto her pleasant face, Olive said:

'It's a pity it's taken a whole string of murders to get

you back into a theatre. But at least this time there's no danger of you nodding off in the middle of the play and drowning out the dialogue with your snoring.'

Bain grunted, cursed and yanked at his bow. 'Tie this damn thing for me, will you, Olive? When I do it, it looks like hell.'

With an indulgent smile, Olive deftly retied it for him, and then picking up a clothes-brush began to attack his dinner-jacket.

'Go easy with that thing,' muttered Bain. 'You'd think you were beating a carpet.'

'I've got a theory about these murders,' said Olive.

'You and a dozen others. What's your theory?'

'Well, it's always the least likely person isn't it, dear? Like in *The Mousetrap*.'

'Did I see that?'

'Well, I wouldn't say "see it", exactly. You were present in the theatre when it was being performed.'

'Well, what about *The Mousetrap*?'

'The policeman did it, dear.'

'Eh?'

'That's my theory. You're the murderer. You're doing it to sabotage the entire theatrical profession.'

Bain looked at Olive blankly. She returned his gaze with total unconcern.

'Olive, are you trying to make a joke?'

'Yes, dear.'

'Well, don't.'

'No, dear,' said Olive and began to drub him about the shoulders with the clothes-brush more energetically than ever.


Roger and Alison Mold were giving a small pre-show party, mostly for faculty members and their wives. Ted Campbell, trumpeting and guffawing and waggling his great brown beard, dominated the occasion while Vera, magnificent in a huge scarlet kaftan, struggled valiantly for at least visual primacy. Occasionally, as the Campbell brass section paused for breath, the mellow woodwind of Bob Pfaff could be heard, recounting tales of his days at the Bristol Old Vic. Alison, scurrying around with plates of canapés, was giving her usual impression of Mrs Tiggywinkle on a benzedrine high.

Matthew had dropped in to gulp a few Harvey Wallbangers – a devastatingly sweet cocktail made with Galliano that he had bullied Roger into providing. He was drinking fast because he wanted to be back in the theatre before the cast began to sign in. As he began to consume a plate of cheese fingers that he had wrested away from Alison, a frightening-looking woman with iron-grey hair and a face carved out of teak accosted him.

'You're the *Amadeus* feller, aren't you? And your brother wrote *Sleuth*?'

'Sorry – no – you're thinking of the Shaffers. I'm the *Harmonious Blacksmith* feller, and my brother, Paul, wrote *Cadaver*.'

'Oh,' she said, visibly losing interest, 'well, I dare say we'll be hearing great things about you one day.'

'Hello, Ramona,' squeaked Roger, appearing suddenly at Matthew's elbow. 'Matthew, this is Ramona Leman, she's the gossip columnist for the *Mapleville Courier*.'

'Society columnist, please,' said Ramona with hauteur. 'Now, Roger, where are all the bigwigs? I don't see a single name I can use.'

'I can think of a name you can use . . .' Matthew began, but Roger hustled Ramona out of earshot before he could say it.

Matthew finished the cheese fingers, glanced at his watch and began to push his way towards the door. Alison intercepted him. She was holding firmly onto the arm of a toothy, red-haired man in a corduroy suit. 'Matthew, I want you to meet Howard Flagg. He's writing a book on the British post-Pinter playwrights.'

'Writing a book, or making a book?'

Alison kicked him lightly on the ankle and raised her voice a couple of decibels. 'Howard's in the English department at the University of Manitoba.'

'University of Manitoba, eh?' said Matthew absently and then was disturbed by a sense of 'déjà vu' or perhaps more accurately 'déjà dit'. His own voice came back to him saying exactly those words on some other occasion. When? Ah, yes – when Lulie Burns had told him that she and Ken Meldrum had transferred from the University of Manitoba.

Matthew refocused on the rabbity academic in front of him. 'Where exactly *is* the University of Manitoba?' he asked.

Alison laughed. 'Oh, Matthew,' she said. 'So English of you not to know the geography of the country you're visiting. The University of Manitoba is in Winnipeg.'

'Winnipeg!' Matthew shrieked, terrifying both of them. 'Why the bloody hell did nobody say so before?'

And with that he charged out of the room.

Howard Flagg gulped and turned towards Alison. 'Goodness,' he said, 'he's even angrier than John Osborne.'

'And madder than my Great-Aunt Sophie,' said Alison. 'Come on; I'll find you something to drink.'


Stan Kozetsky had stopped to pick up his new girlfriend at her apartment in West Darlington. She was a very new girlfriend: someone, in fact, he had met only a day or two before at his health club. Her name was Lesley and she was everything Stan had been looking for in a woman since he turned fourteen and began to see a world of possibilities beyond the hockey rink. She had a body like a girl in a Speedo swimsuit commercial, a face like Catherine Deneuve, and a mind like Simone de Beauvoir. Her great problem was that most men were thoroughly intimidated by her, but Stan proved to be the exception.

Stan got out of his Ford Tempo and opened the door for her as she came out of her apartment block. She paused by the open door and gave him a quizzical look.

'Oops, I forgot,' he said. 'I'm perpetuating a mindless sexual stereotype of the helpless female unable to cope with such technological problems as operating a door-handle.'

'You got it, buster,' she said sliding into the passenger seat, 'but I have hopes for you. Where are we going?'

'To the theatre,' said Stan.

'You said that on the phone. Which theatre?'

Stan released the handbrake, put the car into drive and manoeuvred his way out of the visitors' parking area.

'Which theatre?' he repeated. 'Well, to tell you the truth, I was going to take you to the Women's Collective production of *Castration Anxiety* but they're sold out – so we're going to Wacousta to see *The Armageddon Excuse-Me Fox-Trot*.'

'What you mean is you're unofficially on duty and you've got to be there to keep your eye on things. I read the papers, you know, Stan. I know what case you're working on.'

'Right. But I think the play may appeal to you anyway. From what I can gather from Matthew Prior – he's the playwright – it's about the constant struggle of the aggressive side of the male psyche to suppress its feminine side – leading eventually to the total destruction of the planet.'

'Ha,' said Lesley, 'feminine equals non-aggressive, does it?'

'I hope so,' said Stan, taking his eyes off the road for a moment to glance nervously at her.

'Look out,' said Lesley, 'you almost hit that cyclist.'

217

They drove on for some minutes in silence until Lesley gave a sudden sigh.

'I hope this works out, Stan,' she said. 'God knows I never thought I'd be dating a policeman. A policeman, for God's sake! The male power structure in all its naked brutality.'

Stan blushed. 'Oh, come on now, Lesley . . .' he said.

'No, it's true. "To serve and protect" and all that rubbish. "To suppress and coerce" is more like it.'

'Damn it, Lesley, that's not fair. We try to do an honest job. What d'you think the world would be like if people didn't have some kind of protection against thugs and crooks?'

'You sound like my brother,' she answered.

Stan seized gratefully on a way of directing the conversation away from treacherous ground. 'I didn't know you had a brother. What does he do?'

'He's a lawyer.'

'Are you very close?'

Lesley sighed again. 'We used to be – oh, up until I was in my mid-teens.'

'What went wrong?'

The shadow of a remembered sorrow passed across her face. 'He decided that he needed to serve and protect me. He threatened the boys who wanted to take me out. Once he followed me into a disco and beat up this perfectly nice guy I was dancing with.'

'Is he still around?' asked Stan with some alarm.

Lesley smiled at him. 'Relax, Stan. He's far away – back home where my parents live in BC. He's married now with a couple of kids. But I tell you, if I hadn't left home when I was eighteen to come east to university, my life would have been a misery.'

'I guess he was just overdoing the protective older brother bit.'

'He wasn't older. We were twins.'

218

'Twins?' said Stan. 'Did you look a lot alike?'

'Two peas in a pod,' said Lesley. 'In fact, when we were much younger – before all this "serve and protect" mess – we would sometimes swap clothes for a joke. We could really fool people.'

Strong headlights swept across the windscreen from a truck going in the opposite direction, and simultaneously a bright light seemed to be switched on in Stan's head.

'Oh, shit!' he said, stepping hard on the accelerator. 'We've got to get to that theatre *fast*! I've got to see Bain!'

# Chapter Twenty-Two

Fraser saw her again. Just a glimpse, just an uncertain enough, tantalising enough glimpse to make him wonder if he was hallucinating. He had been having a sherry with the President and various other dignitaries in the presidential suite in the Central Administration Building, when he felt the beginning of a severe headache. Even though it was an icy cold night, he had slid back the glass door in the President's lounge and stepped out onto the little concrete balcony overlooking the campus. The sky was clear of cloud and brilliant with stars, and a white moon shone down on the monumental ugliness of the University buildings. He could see the theatre parking lot filling up as the audience began to arrive for the show – and outside the main entrance of the theatre were the bright floodlights of the TV camera crews, giving the occasion the air of a Hollywood première.

He took two or three deep breaths of chilly air and swivelled his body round to look in the other direction. It was then that he saw her, passing briefly through the halo of light from a lamppost on the path that led to the rear of the theatre. The long hair, the plaid skirt, the unmistakable configuration of the body, the characteristic coltishness of its motion, all belonged to his lost daughter. Either that or ... Hurriedly, he stepped back through the sliding door, excused himself to the President, and hurried towards the nearest elevator. One more to go! There was still time. If only he could get to the girl before . . .

The elevators all seemed to be grounded and rather than wait for one to make up its cranky mechanical mind to start upward, he decided to head for the stairs. The President's lounge was on the seventh floor and there were two flights of stairs between each floor. Hurtling down those fourteen flights, Fraser was grateful for his half-an-hour of aerobics every day. He reached the ground floor in two minutes, dashed across the lobby and out through the main door. The sweat cooled on his skin as he hit the freezing air outside. A hundred yards away down an icy pathway lay the stage-door of the theatre. How he kept his footing as he ran, he never knew, but it was almost as if he were lifted and propelled by an otherworldly force.

The stage-door loomed ahead of him, spilling light onto the snowbanks and the frozen path. Somewhere on the other side of that door, he would come face to face finally with that elusive figure that had bedevilled him for days. He slowed down as he reached the circle of light and took a deep breath to steady himself before plunging on into the darkness.

Someone *had* found a way in. But not through the stage-door as Fraser had imagined. Any fool could have guessed that the stage-door would be well guarded. Forethought and all that experience at the armoury had made it easy to prepare another means of entering the theatre unseen. Sleight of hand, practised over and over again, had made it possible to misdirect attention so that a key could be palmed, a wax impression made, and the key returned, all without arousing the suspicion of the key's custodian. It had worked at the armoury, making the abstraction of a Browning automatic and a tear-gas canister quite simple operations; it had worked on that fool of a motel manager; now it had worked on the technical director of the Heavysege Theatre, Ted Campbell. All it took was hanging around his office and asking naive questions about the lay-out of the theatre and how it would be incorporated into Dean Ripper's extension. That little piece of acting accomplished two things: it revealed the existence of a little-used door into the scene dock and, while Ted had his back turned and was rambling on lengthily facing the framed ground-plan of the future construction, it had made it possible to take a wax impression of the master key. Now, no door in the theatre would be impenetrable.

Only one thing was still troubling: Ursula herself. She was so quiet, so kind, in some ways so like that lost one who would not be forgotten. Could she possibly share in the blame? Did she really deserve to die like all the others? Twice, some doubt had forced itself forward at the critical time. That moment of hesitation in the dressing-room; that wavering of the hand that held the automatic. But she had been there. There in that hotel room. And all five of them *were* guilty – if not of the actual crime, then of not preventing it.

Crouched in the darkness of the lumber storage room, beneath the backstage area, someone brooded and slowly came to a decision. A regretful decision. Celestial Seasonings it would be. How celestial, Ursula would soon find out. Meanwhile, there was something else to attend to: a noise outside; footsteps approaching the door.

'Oh, Lord, damn and blast!' said Matthew to himself as he tried for the fifteenth time to get the engine to turn over.

Halfway between the Molds' house and the campus, he had slowed at an intersection to make a turn and the engine had died on him. It was a trick that was peculiar to

222

his Dodge Aries when the weather was particularly cold. Usually, it started again with a little coaxing, but this time it sat there stubbornly refusing to give the remotest sign of life. Worse still, it had stranded him on a remarkably untravelled stretch of road. Not a single car had gone by since the Aries had stalled. The only thing to do, he concluded, was to start walking and pray that he would make it to the theatre in time to warn Bain and Kozetsky. Grabbing his navy-issue duffel coat from the back seat, he put it on, locked the car and set off down the road as fast as his long legs would carry him. All around, the acres of snow-bound fields were phosphorescent under the cold shimmer of starlight. The sense of space and emptiness chilled him, and in all the enormous silence there was no sound except the crunch of his footsteps on the frosty road.

He had walked for five minutes before he heard the thrumming of a car engine behind him. Pulling his white handkerchief out of his breast pocket, he signalled frantically and to his great relief the car slowed and stopped.

'Excuse me,' he babbled as he reached the driver's window, 'I wonder if you can help me out . . .'

'Hop in, Mr Prior. I think we're heading in the same direction.'

It was Stan Kozetsky.

Matthew scrambled into the backseat, acknowledged an introduction to Lesley, and urged Kozetsky to drive on. Lesley sat there, bewildered as Matthew and Kozetsky tried to talk at the same time. Out of the confused hubbub of parallel monologues, she was aware of three words that occurred again and again: 'Winnipeg', 'airline' and 'McCullough'.

Bain was in the theatre lobby with Olive when he saw Stan, Prior and an unknown girl pushing their way through the crowd around the door, stepping over television cables, and avoiding microphones that were thrust at them.

'Stan!' he yelled, waving his programme. 'Over here!'

'We've got to secure the backstage area,' Kozetsky blurted out as soon as he reached Bain.

'Done,' said Bain. 'What d'you think I am, lad? An amateur? I had the whole theatre searched at five o'clock this evening as soon as the actors and stage-hands cleared out for dinner. And I've had someone posted at the stage-door and any other door that anybody could slip through since we finished the search. I don't think we've much to worry about.'

'Has McCullough arrived yet?' Kozetsky asked.

'No, he must still be at the President's cocktail party – but the boys are all alerted to be on the lookout for him.'

Ted Campbell and Vera came lumbering up at that moment and Matthew put his hand out to stop them. 'Ted,' he said, 'how many entrances are there to the theatre?'

Ted pulled at his beard, frowned and pondered. 'Well,' he said at last, 'counting the access doors to the scene dock and the pass-doors between the theatre building and the classroom building – eleven.'

Matthew turned to Bain. 'Are they all guarded?'

'No need,' said Bain.

'No,' agreed Ted, 'that's right. Everything's been locked up since five this afternoon, except the stage-door and the lobby doors.'

'And they've been guarded?'

'Yes,' said Bain impatiently, 'and I've told you there's no problem.'

Matthew turned back to Ted. 'Who would have keys to the other doors?'

'Various folks would have various keys. Marie-Ange has keys to the stage-door and the pass-doors. The head of the set-crew has a key to the loading-bay doors. The wardrobe mistress has keys to the stage-door and the costume shop. But nobody has keys to *all* the doors except me. I hold all of them, the master key as well.'

'Would any of the crew have loaned their keys to someone – or let someone in?'

Ted shook his shaggy head. 'No. They've been under orders not to all year. Ever since that outbreak of pilfering last semester.'

The clock in the lobby showed twenty minutes to curtain time. Matthew looked up at it, then at Bain, then at Ted.

'I'd like to make another search – even if we have to hold the curtain. And I'd like to make absolutely sure no one gets at Ursula. Can we get her a dressing-room to herself where those two policewomen can keep her in view all the time?'

'Number One,' said Ted. 'The star dressing-room.'

The star dressing-room of the Charles Heavysege Theatre was seldom used. Most of the time, to discourage any inflation of the ego, the student actors were housed in two large communal dressing-rooms – one for the males and one for the females. But the star dressing-room had been incorporated into the original building plans because occasionally the theatre hosted professional performers. They came either to give solo shows or to play major roles in fourth-year productions to give the students the experience of working with someone of established stature and skill. Gielgud had used the star dressing-room when he came to perform *The Ages of Man*; Alec McCowen had occupied it on his *St Mark's Gospel* tour; it had housed Kate Reid during the run of a one-woman show based on the career of Sarah Siddons; and on one occasion, much to the delight of the students, its tenant had been Quentin Crisp who had come to deliver one of his extraordinary harangues on 'style'. For Ursula, no less impressive was the dressing-room's association with such first-rank Canadian actors as William Hutt and Claire Coulter, who had used it while adding their lustre to student productions.

The famous occupants of the room had not, of course, been expected to get ready for a performance with two uniformed policewomen watching every dab of grease paint and every stroke of liner. The tension of worrying about her own safety and the consciousness of being so closely observed made Ursula's hand shake so badly that she smeared the mascara on her lower lid.

'Damn,' she said, grabbing for some cold cream to repair the damage.

'It's all a bit heavy, dear, isn't it?' said Gloria. 'You're not playing a tart, are you?'

Ursula explained that her makeup had to be heavy to 'read' to the audience.

'Read?' Gloria sounded baffled.

'If I wore regular street makeup, the stage lights would wash it out,' Ursula explained. 'Wait till you see me on stage. It'll look all right – honestly!'

'If you say so, dear,' said Gloria. 'At least it's nice to see you with a bit of colour in your face. You've been looking very pale and peaky.'

There was a sudden banging on the door and Ursula leapt in her seat.

'Half-hour call!' a voice yelled outside.

Trembling, Ursula laid down her mascara brush and buried her face in her hands.

'I'm so scared,' she whimpered.

The second policewoman, whose name was Irene, came over to her and put her arm round her shoulders.

'You're safe. It's all right,' she said. 'Nobody's going to get at you. We'll be here with you, and we're going to be standing in the wings – one at each side. And we'll lock the dressing-room when we leave so nobody can get in.'

'I'm sorry,' said Ursula, lifting her head. 'And thanks. I feel much better with you around.'

'That's right,' said Irene. 'What you need is a nice hot drink. Would you like some coffee?'

'No, thanks. I'm allergic to that too.'

'Oh, I'm sorry, dear. I should have remembered. You only drink that funny tea. What is it again?'

Ursula picked the box up and waved it. 'Celestial Seasonings.'

Gloria took the box from her and went over to fill the kettle.

'That's right,' she said. 'I can never remember that name. Herbal, isn't it?'

'Yes, but listen – I don't think I'll have any just now. I'll wait till intermission. I don't want to get the urge to pee half-way through the first act.'

The policewomen raised their eyebrows silently at one another. Really, these stage people and their language! Irene sat down again. 'All right, dear,' she said, 'but just stay calm. Everything's going to be all right.'

Meanwhile the theatre had been searched again from the catwalks above the stage to the scene dock and storage room below. The search was difficult because the scene shop, the props room and the wardrobe were so cluttered. There were racks of clothes, piles of flats, tottering mounds of furniture, and crates of odds and ends heaped one on top of the other. Many places to hide, in fact, but no one, it seemed, hiding anywhere.

Matthew paused as they entered the lumber storage room. 'That's odd,' he said. 'Why the large sinks and steam pipes in here?'

'What? Oh, yes,' said Ted. 'I remember. This was originally supposed to be a kitchen. We had big plans before the budget cuts started. There was going to be a restaurant built onto the theatre upstairs. Anyway the cuts came, but we'd already started to put in the kitchen. The restaurant never got built so we turned this into storage space.'

'Anyway,' Kozetsky said, 'there's no one in here either.'

'That's it, then. There's nowhere else except the furnace room.'

'Let's not overlook any possibility,' said Matthew. 'We'd better check that out too.'

They left, turning out the lights as they went – and someone began to breathe again. They hadn't noticed the unused dumb-waiter hidden in a corner where the service tables would have been. In the darkness, a hand raised the hatch and a slender body eased its way out into the room. Another hour and it would all be over.

# Chapter Twenty-Three

The auditorium was full, a phenomenon unmatched since the notorious all-nude production of *Ubu Roi* in 1969. Roger Mold and Alison were sitting in the front row with the President and his party. Bonny saw them as she came down the aisle to take her seat. She looked around to see if she could spot Fraser but he was nowhere to be seen. He had promised to meet her in the lobby, but when the warning bell rang she decided to take her seat and let him join her there. Matthew was nowhere to be seen either. Had she known him better she would have realised that he never watched any of his plays from the auditorium. He either stayed in the lighting booth, swearing and groaning and upsetting the lighting crew, or paced up and down in the lobby, listening for audience reaction and chewing his nails.

At this moment, however, he was still with Bain and Kozetsky organising the last details of security. The pass-doors from the auditorium to backstage were locked; the stage-door and all other means of access to the dressing-rooms were secured. Ursula's dressing-room was to be kept locked at all times, and when she was on stage the two policewomen would be watching her from the wings. Towards the end of the first act, when the entire cast was on stage and the dressing-room area was cleared, one policeman would be posted at the door from the back-stage area to the dressing-rooms, and the rest would be in the auditorium and the lobby to cover the risky moment when the Roundheads marched the troupe of players up the aisle and shot them outside the auditorium doors. It was unlikely, of course, that even an insane killer would risk shooting Ursula in a crowded theatre. The three of them agreed, however, that even the unlikely must be prepared for.

At last – fifteen minutes late – the house-lights went down and the murmur of the audience subsided. Settling back in their seats, they waited for the usual pre-show music or for the lights to go up on the stage. Instead, in the unrelieved darkness, they heard over the sound system an eerily echoing voice begin to recite Jaques's famous speech from *As You Like It*:

> 'All the world's a stage,
> And all the men and women merely players:
> They have their exits and their entrances;
> And one man in his time plays many parts . . .'

The first few lines were delivered at normal speed but as the speech continued, the voice began to speed up. Faster and faster it went until it disintegrated into a high-pitched unintelligible gibbering, as in a tape-recorder out of control. The gabble ended abruptly and simultaneously the lights hit the orchestra pit to reveal a group of writhing bodies in a Dionysiac frenzy. Out of this laocoön came gradually the low ululation of a ritual chant that grew in volume and intensity until – as it climaxed – Joe Innocenti broke away from the entangling limbs, leapt onto the stage and proclaimed: 'I can take *any* empty space . . .'

From that point the first act proceeded with only minor hitches: a forgotten light cue here, a fumbled line there, a late entrance, a misplaced prop. They were the kind of minor mishaps which plague any opening night and which most audiences are prepared to indulge. An hour went by and, at last, Cromwell's soldiers entered and herded the players up the aisle and into the lobby. A fusillade of shots rang out, followed by the screams of the dying actors. The audience was suitably startled and as the lights went up, they left their seats chattering and exclaiming, and began moving towards the lobby. As Bonny walked anxiously up the aisle, she looked from side to side, hoping that Fraser, having arrived late, had taken a seat near the back so as not to disturb the performance. But there was still no sign of him.

The cast meanwhile had made their way back to the dressing-rooms. Ursula and the two policewomen went first so that no unexpected move could come from within the jostling crowd of actors. Safely inside the Number One dressing-room, they locked the door behind them.

'Phew!' said Ursula. 'I could use a cup of tea now.'

Irene filled the kettle and plugged it in.

'Help yourselves if you want some. There's a stack of paper cups over there,' Ursula said.

'Is it just that funny tea?' asked Gloria.

'Sorry,' said Ursula. 'No Red Rose, I'm afraid. Oh, wait. There's some instant coffee somebody left behind.'

'I'll have that then. I don't like scenty teas or herbal teas. I tried some Earl Grey once. Very delicate in flavour, if you know what I mean – but no real guts to it.'

'You're not allergic like me. I have to be very careful what I eat and drink.'

The kettle boiled. Ursula took a tea-bag out of her box of Celestial Seasonings and dropped it into a paper cup. Irene poured boiling water on it.

'Thanks,' said Ursula and began to sip.

'No milk or sugar, dear?'

'No, it's really quite sweet on its own. Sometimes I add a bit of honey.'

She sipped again. 'This seems even sweeter than usual.'

There was a sudden commotion in the corridor: voices were raised, doors banged. The three women in the dressing-room froze.

'I'll go and see,' said Gloria. 'You both stay here.'

The corridor was jammed with half-dressed young men, talking and shouting. A couple of policemen came running from the backstage area followed by Matthew, Bain and Kozetsky.

'The mirror in the dressing-room,' Wayne Goffman shouted as they approached. 'It's smashed and there's a big hole in the wall.'

Matthew was first into the men's dressing-room. Shards of glass lay scattered on the makeup table and the floor. Behind the mirror-frame was a square opening in the wall, the top of a shaft that led down to the lower level of the building.

'Damn!' said Matthew. 'Why didn't we check all the walls in the storage area? A kitchen that was below a restaurant would have to have a dumb-waiter!'

Bain groaned. 'Stan, get down there fast. Take one of the men with you. Is someone still guarding the stage entrance?'

'I came running when I heard the yells,' said one of the policemen. 'Sorry, sir.'

'Ursula's safe anyway,' said Matthew. 'Gloria and Irene are with her.'

'No, I'm here,' said Gloria.

'What the hell—' began Bain, but he was interrupted by a loud cry from Ursula's dressing-room.

The door of Number One burst open and Irene shot out.

'Quick!' she said. 'We need an ambulance. She's been poisoned.'

At the same moment, Kozetsky and a younger officer named Judd were hurtling through the below-stage area towards the lumber room. Passing the props room and the loading bay, they came to the open door leading into what had been intended as the restaurant kitchen. It was dark and shadowy inside, and utterly silent. Kozetsky clicked on the light, and the room sprang into view: piles of two by fours, sheets of plywood, vices, tools, work-benches, but not a sign of a human figure.

'Over there,' said Kozetsky. 'The far wall. That would be directly under the dressing-room.'

The wall was partly obscured by abandoned flats that had been leant against it out of the way of the work area. The smell of glue and turpentine and wood-shavings was strong. Coughing as the dust filled their lungs, they began to lug the flats away from the wall.

'Did you hear something, sergeant?' said Judd.

'Hear something? What?'

'It sounded like a groan.'

Redoubling their efforts, they succeeded in moving the last flat and saw a large square panel in the wall, a sliding door.

'Careful,' said Kozetsky. 'This lunatic could be armed.'

Judd drew his Smith and Wesson and aimed. Kozetsky stood to the side of the sliding panel, and, after taking a deep breath, jerked it upwards. No one sprang at them from the interior. There was no motion at all from inside. Judd lowered his gun.

'He won't be any trouble, sergeant.'

Stan stepped away from the wall and looked inside the dumb-waiter. Slumped there unconscious, blood trickling from a scalp wound, lay Fraser McCullough.

After the emergency team had taken Ursula to hospital and Bain had accompanied Fraser to the emergency room under police guard, Matthew and Kozetsky returned together to Number One dressing-room.

233

'The musket shots must have covered the sound of breaking glass,' said Matthew.

'But how could anyone have had time to get into the dressing-room *and* doctor the tea-bags?' asked Kozetsky.

'I don't think the tea-bags Ursula brought in *were* doctored. It was no secret that Ursula drank only Celestial Seasonings. What could be easier than to buy an identical box, doctor the bags and substitute the doctored box for hers?'

'But when?'

'Clearly between the time the muskets went off and when the cast arrived backstage again. Six minutes at the very most. But this one loves to cut it fine.'

'So someone must have gotten hold of a master key to all the locks in the theatre building. And it looks as if that someone might have been McCullough. That kind of puts paid to the theory we came up with in the car.'

Matthew rubbed his forehead wearily. 'I don't know, Stan. There's something about this that still bothers me. Something about that Winnipeg trip. Did you get a copy of the passenger manifest?'

'It's in the incident room.'

'I think we ought to take a careful look at it.'

'Stay here. It'll take me five minutes.'

Stan left and Matthew sat and brooded at the dressing-table. Supposing it really wasn't Fraser. What would happen next? The killer's task was presumably over now that the last person on the photograph had been dealt with. But was it? Could the final victim be, in fact, the killer?

Someone tapped at the door and then opened it. It was Bonny.

'Matthew, I thought I might find you here,' she said, looking palely determined. 'I've got to know what's happened to Fraser. He was supposed to meet me at the theatre and—'

234

Matthew pushed a chair towards her. 'Sit down,' he said. 'This won't be pleasant, I'm afraid.'

She crumpled into the chair and put her hand over her eyes. 'They've arrested him, haven't they?'

Matthew frowned. 'I'm sorry. It looks pretty black for him. Ursula's been poisoned, and Fraser was found unconscious in the dumb-waiter the killer must have used to get up to the dressing-rooms.'

Bonny took her hand away from her eyes and looked up at Matthew. 'You don't believe he did it, do you?'

'I'm not sure, but maybe you can help.'

'How?'

'By remembering some things. For instance, how did Fraser behave after Heather's disappearance?'

'I didn't know him then. I only met him after I joined the theatre department eight months ago. All I know is what he told me. He spent thousands looking for her, but it was hopeless. His wife, Meg, and Heather's brother, Hamish, felt he hadn't done enough. It broke up the family. Meg got a divorce and went off to live in Winnipeg with Hamish. Fraser kept in touch, and visited them occasionally.'

'Did Fraser believe Heather was dead?'

'He seemed to at first – but lately, as I told you, he began to think that he'd seen her around campus.'

The door opened again and Kozetsky came into the room. Seeing Bonny, he paused awkwardly. 'Miss Dundee!' he said. 'I'm sorry, I had no idea you were still in the theatre.'

'Bonny may be able to help us, Stan. She knew Fraser better than anyone else around here.'

Stan managed a faint smile and then passed over to Matthew what he held in his hand.

'Ah, the passenger manifest. Let's see . . .'

Matthew scanned it closely, running his finger down the page, and then his face lit up.

'You've spotted it too, have you?' said Stan. 'Two of them. F.A. and H.K.M.'

Matthew nodded. 'Now, Bonny, you can really help us. Do you remember that day we had lunch at the Dodge City Steak House? You told me on the way back to campus that the last place Fraser and his family were all together and happy before Heather disappeared was his cottage on the lake.'

'Yes, I remember. It was their summer cottage at Illyria.'

There was a moment's silence and then Matthew broke it with a half-suppressed groan.

'Illyria! If only I'd known the name of the place. If only I'd known the University of Manitoba was in Winnipeg!'

Kozetsky and Bonny stared at him incredulously.

'What on earth are you talking about?' asked Stan.

'No time for long explanations. But we've got to get there fast. I've a feeling that if we hurry we may be in time to prevent a suicide. Bonny, you've been there . . . You can show us the way?'

'I – I think so.'

'We'll take my car,' said Stan. 'It's faster.'

They all crowded into Kozetsky's black Ford Tempo and set off. Across to Highway 400 and then north through the starlit night, the car sped with no regard to the posted speed limit. Unassuming as the Ford looked, it had a turn of speed that put Matthew's Aries to shame and it held the road like dental adhesive. About forty miles north of Mapleville, Bonny directed them to pull off onto a side-road, and – a few hundred yards further along – onto a track that wound through a densely wooded area. There was almost no sound but the humming of the engine and the creaking of branches in the wind. Kozetsky cut the engine at the top of a small slope and they coasted silently down to a clearing at the edge of the lake. It was a large open space with a dock and two cottages, though hardly cottages in the English sense, Matthew thought. They were handsome stone structures, one of them almost as large as the dower house at his country home, Down Hall.

The smaller of the houses was lit up, every window pouring light into the surrounding blackness.

'That's the children's cottage,' said Bonny. 'This is the place they loved so much in the summer.'

'And it looks like someone's at home,' said Kozetsky.

They left the car and made their way as quietly as they could over the frost-encrusted snow. The front door was unlocked and they entered the dazzling brightness of the interior. It was handsomely furnished with antique Canadian pine and carpeted with hand-woven rugs. A wood fire crackled in the fireplace and the remains of a solitary supper lay abandoned on a tray. From some other room in the house came the faint sound of a flute playing the *Pavane for a Dead Infanta*.

They followed the sound down a passage and stopped before a painted door – yellow with a decoration of forget-me-nots. In the centre panel was a small porcelain plaque with the word 'Heather' inscribed on it. Matthew turned the handle gently and pushed open the door.

Standing on the threshold, Bonny and the two men saw a bedroom that seemed full of sunlight even on that winter night. The pale yellow walls, the drapes patterned with spring flowers, the carpets the colour of blue lakewater seemed to have preserved for ever a gentler season than the one that gripped the night outside. On the bed in the centre of the room sat a cross-legged figure, a figure with long straight hair hiding the face, flute still held to the lips. It was dressed in a blouse and plaid skirt and the legs that emerged from beneath the skirt were pale and hairless.

# Chapter Twenty-Four

'You'll be glad to hear that Ursula survived again,' Matthew told Roger in his office the next day. 'Any girl who can live through three murder attempts is going to go far in the theatre. Not even one of John Simon's more poisonous asides will affect her.'

'What *was* in the tea-bags?'

'Cantharidine.'

'Can-what?' said Roger.

'I should have known the next murder would have something to do with *The Spanish Tragedy*.'

'*The Spanish Tragedy*? Thomas Kyd, you mean? What on earth are you babbling about?'

'Parallels,' Matthew said smugly. 'I wondered at the time if we were dealing with a revenge tragedy – and we were. Ken Meldrum was working on an updated version of *The Spanish Tragedy* in my play-writing class. I don't have to remind you, I'm sure, that Kyd's bit of bombast is about a father revenging his son's death by killing the actors during the production of a play. And cantharidine, by the way, is the medical name for Spanish fly – a drug with a largely undeserved reputation as an aphrodisiac.'

'But aphrodisiacs aren't poisonous, surely?'

Matthew grinned. 'In my experience they aren't even aphrodisiac. But cantharidine is a particularly treacherous substance. It's a preparation of powdered blister beetles. A small amount – a very small amount – irritates the urethra enough to produce feelings of sexual excitement. But as little as ten milligrams can be fatal. Don't you remember that amorous chemist in Cambridge twenty years ago who accidentally killed his girlfriend with it?'

Roger stared at him. 'Good God, I believe I do,' he said. 'It made headlines in the *News of the World*.'

'Right,' said Matthew. 'And Ursula was the perfect subject for it. That health food mania of hers wasn't just a whim. As a lot of the students knew, she suffered from various food allergies – which made her extremely susceptible to any chemical irritant.'

'Poor mousy Ursula. I'm glad they got her to the hospital in time.'

'She's not quite out of the woods yet. You can die up to a week after taking the stuff, but the hospital seems confident she'll make it. Anyway, if Ken had managed to murder her that way, it would have completed the pattern. All the murder weapons had some sexual connotation.'

Roger frowned and chewed his lower lip dubiously. 'But what about the other two attempts? There wasn't anything sexual about them, was there?'

'Depends how you look at them. But it seems that he was reluctant to kill Ursula at all. That's why his early efforts were so half-hearted. He couldn't quite believe – until the very last – that she was as guilty as the others.'

Roger held up his hand. 'Whoa!' he said. 'Let's go back a bit. *The Spanish Tragedy*. That has to do with a *father* revenging a *son's* death during the performance of a play. This wasn't happening here.'

Matthew stood up. 'I refuse to talk any more until I've had my mid-morning snack. I want a Dr Pepper and a big sticky Chelsea bun.'

In exasperation, Roger pressed the buzzer on the intercom. The communicating door between his office and

Bonny's opened and she appeared on the threshold looking still somewhat wan.

'Bonny,' Roger said, 'this man is being particularly difficult this morning. He is practising one of the cheapest techniques for creating suspense. Even his brother – in his most unscrupulous moments of theatricality – wouldn't stoop to such hoary devices. Would you mind getting him some of that filthy junk food he ruins his constitution with?'

Ten minutes later, when Bonny returned with a tray from the cafeteria, Matthew resumed.

'Would you like to hear this, Bonny? You needn't if you don't want to.'

Bonny gave a pale smile. 'I'll stay,' she said.

Roger took a chocolate milk off the tray and Matthew crammed a large segment of Chelsea bun into his mouth. 'Now,' he mumbled through a mouthful of crumbs, 'Ken, poor boy, was quite mad. Losing his sister, to whom he was perhaps unhealthily attached, and losing her in such a way, sent him off balance. He also began to hate Fraser, and Meg probably did her bit to fuel that hatred. Fraser, of course, eventually got all of Heather's effects back from the police, and Ken extracted some of them from his father's study before he and his mother left for Winnipeg. Among them were two important clues: the ticket stub for *The Harmonious Blacksmith* and the roll of film. Ken was also one of those serial killers – well known to criminologists – who delight in toying with their pursuers. Jack the Ripper was fond of sending little messages to the police, for instance. Anyway, that's why the ticket stub was pushed under my door; that's why the scraps of photographic print were left so conveniently about. He also suffered from another famous syndrome – the "stop-me-before-I-kill-again" bit. He half wanted to be caught – that's why he took such tremendous risks. Several of the things he did were attempts to implicate Fraser: the disguises, the

241

*Spanish Tragedy* clue, and finally when Fraser followed him into the lumber room, knocking him out and leaving him in the dumb-waiter. He was also confused about his own identity. I should have realised that earlier when he was working on that updated version of *Twelfth Night*.'

Matthew paused for a gulp of Dr Pepper and another chunk of bun.

'Ah!' said Roger. 'That famous transvestite, Viola.'

'Not only that – but, as I'm sure you remember, Olivia falls in love with Viola masquerading as Cesario, then later mistakes Viola's brother, Sebastian, for her.'

Bonny reached for her coffee cup and turned to Matthew. 'Are you saying that Ken not only disguised himself as Heather, but began to believe he *was* Heather?'

'I'm not sure,' said Matthew, 'but I believe so. Kozetsky's girlfriend gave him a lead when she talked about her and her twin brother swapping clothes to fool people when they were young. Fraser says that his kids did the same thing. Anyway, if Ken thought he *was* Heather, then who was "missing presumed dead"? Ken or Heather? Whatever he thought, he believed his father should have acted like Hieronimo in Kyd's play and avenged the death of his offspring, whether it was his son or his daughter.'

'But what about Fraser? He must have known that Ken was on campus, and that Ken was really Hamish. Why didn't he suspect him?'

'He knew, and I think he did suspect him. But he didn't want to admit it to himself. His conscious mind would rather believe that Heather had indeed come back – or that he was hallucinating. Lord knows, no father wants to believe that his son has homicidal tendencies. But that last murder attempt was too much for him. He had seen Ken go towards the theatre – or rather he had seen Heather, as he preferred to believe. When he was attacked in the lumber room, he was in shock for a while. He didn't really see

242

his attacker, so he still wasn't sure whether it was Ken or Heather.'

'Were they identical twins?' Roger asked.

'No, you dolt. How can children of different sexes be identical? But there was still sufficient resemblance to confuse people, especially from a distance.'

'And the letter from Winnipeg?'

'Kozetsky checked the passenger lists. There was no Ken Meldrum on the flight to or from Winnipeg. But as we found out later there were two McCulloughs. F.A. and H.K.M. Fraser's wife's maiden name was Meldrum. Ken's real name was Hamish Kenneth Meldrum McCullough. Ken posted that letter to Calvin.'

Bonny shook her head in disbelief. 'But why wouldn't Fraser have suspected that?'

'Because he didn't know about the letter till last night. Bain asked him about it when he came round from his concussion.'

Bonny sighed. 'What a horror for Fraser! First his daughter . . . then his son . . . I suppose Ken transferred here deliberately to find out what had become of his sister?'

'Yes,' said Matthew. 'All he had to do was track down the people in the photograph and get them to talk about it. Apparently, he was lucky first go. Calvin developed a thing for him and Ken was willing to sleep with Calvin to find out what he wanted to know. So it was Calvin who confirmed that the five in the photograph were the only other guests at the party Heather disappeared from. And Calvin also told him that he was almost certain that Cubby was chiefly responsible.'

'Politician's sons!' groaned Roger.

'I wonder what Cubby did?' said Bonny.

Matthew shrugged. 'That's one thing that Ken couldn't get out of Calvin,' he said. 'But there's one person who still might be able to answer that question. Ursula.'

243

# Chapter Twenty-Five

Unexpectedly, Dean Ripper's boast about having an 'in' with Joe Papp turned out to be legitimate. Mr Papp, lean and grizzled in an army surplus shirt and a Giorgio Armani suit, appeared at the theatre on the last-but-one night of the run. Matthew was standing in the lobby at intermission talking to Roger, Alison and Bonny, when the Dean led the famous producer of the New York Public Theatre across to them. Matthew had, in fact, met him briefly several years before at a Manhattan gathering in honour of Nell Finnigan, who was then appearing with the National Theatre of Great Britain at the Brooklyn Academy of Music in a production of *A Woman Killed with Kindness*. He did not expect to be remembered, and wasn't. His Broadway failure, *The Harmonious Blacksmith*, was. But the New York producer was generous enough to say that New York audiences didn't understand its 'charm', and that he would like to look at the script of *The Armageddon Excuse-Me Fox-Trot*. 'It's like *Marat-Sade* rewritten by Monty Python,' he said. 'It might just go.'

It was, in fact, produced in New York the following year as a musical with a score by Henry Krieger and sets by Ming Cho Lee. It closed during previews.

Meanwhile, untroubled by any premonition of this, Matthew was feeling euphoric. The cast, after a slow start, had suddenly found the life of the play and had presented it to the audience with a 'smack-them-between-the-eyes' energy that disguised some of the longueurs of the action and much of the inadequacy of several key performers. Joe Innocenti, however, transcended his own limitations to such a degree that at times he seemed to have tapped a direct power-line to the god Dionysus. His climactic battle with Rezi in a post-nuclear Samuel Beckett bunker had the audience within an inch or two of the edge of their seats, and when the last echo of his final line ('Any space? Hell, I can take *all* space!') had died away, the cast came out for their curtain call to what Matthew later described as a 'crouching ovation'.

The cast party was held that night to allow the stage crew to get democratically drunk with everyone else, since after the final night they would be too busy striking the set. Everyone gathered in the basement recreation room of Ted and Vera Campbell's converted schoolhouse, which had been riot-proofed for just such occasions several years ago.

'The walls are covered with foam rubber,' said Ted. 'And the whole place is flame-resistant. Our injury statistics are at the low end of the scale.'

By midnight, a deep pungent smog of marijuana fumes blanketed the room. Matthew, who was dancing with Bonny, got a contact high and began to improvise a break-dance routine which left him breathless and with a suspected sprain of the upper left dorsal. But, happy though the occasion seemed, it gradually succumbed to a blight as more and more of the revellers were jarred by unbidden reminders of those who were missing. 'About this time,' thought Joe, 'Cubby would start doing his Elvis Costello imitation.' Vera noticed a sagging hem on someone's skirt and thought 'That looks like Dodie's work.' Someone put a Carol Pope record on the turntable and Lulie thought, 'Shana must have been her biggest fan in the whole world.' Gradually, as the gloom spread, people began to leave in ones and twos. They even forgot to present Matthew with their thank-you gift – a two-gallon jar of maple syrup – and Ted and Vera found it in the basement, behind a sofa, three months later.

Matthew drove Bonny home and sat with her for a moment in front of her house, uncertain about what move he was expected to make. He half hoped she would invite him in for a nightcap, but at the same time, he wasn't sure he would accept. Bonny stared ahead through the wind-shield, smoking a Virginia Slim and letting the white clouds escape from her mouth in wavering arabesques. Mike Hammer would take her inside and throw her into bed. Lord Peter Wimsey would offer some quaint pleasantry and drive off like a perfect gent. What would Matthew do?

Almost immediately, the question became academic as Bonny turned to him and said with manifest seriousness: 'Matthew, there's one thing I'm very grateful for.'

'Hm?' he murmured.

'You've never made a crude physical pass.'

'Or a crude verbal one, I hope?' he said nervously.

She shook her head. 'No – and you've never played any of those other games: 'little boy lost', 'weary swinger' and so on. I get so tired of that. And I'm grateful to you for reassuring me that a man and a woman can have a real friendship without a lot of other stuff getting in the way.'

Matthew grinned self-consciously.

'I'm marrying Fraser, you know,' she went on. 'It's not that I'm hung up on older men generally, but over the last few months I've seen him go through some really bad patches and he's never really dumped his misery on me, or used me as a kind of pacifier. He's always been tender. And I want to help him get his life going again. I want to give him a new family. The truth is, Matthew: I love him.'

246

Matthew said the only possible thing. 'I hope you'll both be very happy.'

Bonny kissed him on the cheek and got out of the car.

'Goodbye, Matthew. Go back to Henrietta and Nell and Dorothy. Someday maybe you'll decide which one you belong with – before it's too late.' And with that, she ran up the path and into the house.

Matthew was chagrined and relieved. He started the car and drove slowly away whistling 'My Bonny Lies Over the Ocean'.

The next evening was the closing night of the show. Some of the energy of Friday's performance was missing, but all in all the players acquitted themselves with credit. Matthew thanked them afterwards and said a not-too-regretful good-bye. The following day, Sunday, he paid a visit to the West Darlington General Hospital. Ursula was lying in her hospital bed, attached to the IV machine, looking pale and somewhat puffy. It was still a little difficult for her to talk because of some residual blistering in the mouth, but she was sitting propped up by pillows and her eyes had lost the dull glaze they had had when he saw her last. He handed her a bag of grapes and a paperback copy of Nell Finnigan's autobiography, *An Actress Despairs*. She thanked him and asked about the show. Finally Matthew came to the real point of his visit.

'You were very lucky, Ursula,' he said. 'You survived this mess. Tell me: what really went on that weekend in New York?'

Ursula smiled wanly. 'You mean you haven't worked it out for yourselves – you and Inspector Bain and the sergeant? What a team!'

'We've worked out the motive. We know that Ken believed you were all responsible for what happened to his sister. We're just not sure how much you *were* responsible.'

Ursula turned her head on the pillow and gazed out of the window at the cold, blue sky. 'I'm not sure either,' she said. 'It was two years ago almost, and I'm not sure I can remember who I was then.'

Matthew waited.

'We were first-year students,' she went on after a moment. 'At the end of our first year. We had finally adjusted, I guess, to being away from home, to the pressures of being at university . . . You know how it is. We were the big stars at our high schools and here we were starting at the bottom again, realising that we weren't as smart and as talented as we thought we were. Then, by April, things were coming into focus; some of our confidence was coming back. The New York trip came along and we were thrilled and excited. None of us had been there before – except Cubby. We were looking forward to staying in a hotel, seeing 42nd Street, going to some shows. They'd arranged tickets for us for *The Pirates of Penzance* with Linda Ronstadt on the Friday, and your show on the Saturday.'

'Bless them,' said Matthew.

'Anyway, we were all pretty high on the whole experience. Manhattan! Fifth Avenue! Broadway! Greenwich Village! I mean – here we were, kids from places like Kapuskasing and Cobalt and Gravenhurst. Toronto was the most glamorous city we'd ever seen – and suddenly we were in the Big Apple. We went kind of wild for a couple of days. We were hungry for some excitement after all those dreary winter days on campus. It was as if we were trying to devour the whole city stone by stone.'

'The monsters who ate New York,' Matthew offered.

Ursula giggled, looking suddenly younger and rekindling a spark of that impishness which hid behind the mousy façade.

248

'Something like that,' she said. 'Anyway, for some reason there were six of us who started hanging out together – a sort of unlikely group in a way. Of course, Dodie was different then. She was more outgoing and she had a funny sledge-hammer sense of humour. Shana was in her pre-punk phase and she was all fizzy and bubbly. Cubby wasn't much different. He always seemed s-o-o-o-o sophisticated to us hicks. It was Cubby who introduced us to Calvin. He'd met Cal some other time when he was in New York – and Cal was, like, this incredible, amazing, *real* New Yorker who knew everything about everything. He was in his final year at Columbia. And, of course, there was Heather McCullough. She was pretty and rich and really very, very nice. The other girls in the group – me included – envied her, I guess – but we also liked her. We figured that both Cubby and Cal would be hot for her, but somehow they weren't. We didn't figure out why until later.'

'Because they were wrapped up in each other?' asked Matthew.

Ursula made a sour grimace. 'Not exactly. Calvin was wrapped up in Cubby – and Cubby was wrapped up in himself. Anyway, we were all enjoying the weekend together – listening to the musicians in Washington Square, going up the Empire State Building, taking the circle tour of the island by ferry, eating cream cheese and walnut sandwiches at Choc Full O' Nuts. Then came the last night of the trip, your play at the Aldridge Theatre and after that, the little party in Cubby's room. All six of us were there – and we were all smashed on wine. A few joints were passed around and eventually Calvin produced some special stuff. I don't think he really wanted to, but Cubby made him . . .'

She paused and a spasm of something like pain passed across her face.

'Is anything wrong?' Matthew said quickly. 'Shall I call a nurse?'

Ursula shook her head. 'No, I was just thinking: they could all be alive now if Cubby hadn't . . . Oh, that's stupid – if, if, if . . . If my grandma had wheels she'd be a streetcar.'

'Go on,' said Matthew.

'Cubby and Cal and Shana dropped some acid. I pretended to, but actually spat up the tab into my handkerchief, and I'm pretty sure Dodie did the same. But Heather made a big production out of not taking any. She had a tendency to be a bit self-righteous, and when Cubby tried to insist she take one, she grabbed it and flushed it down the john. Cubby was furious but he acted like he was amused. Anyway at some point we decided we needed food and we ordered corned-beef sandwiches and coffee from room service. The waiter brought the stuff up and we helped ourselves. The whole acid thing seemed to have blown over, except that Cubby and Cal and Shana were acting peculiarly: not quite in 'synch' with the rest of us, going 'Wow' a lot and laughing quietly. I guess they were seeing rainbows and having mystic communion with the furniture. Heather had left her coffee cup half-full when she went to the john. Cubby went over and dropped something into it. I saw him do it, but I somehow couldn't believe that he was stupid enough to give anybody acid against their will. Anyway, as it turned out it wasn't acid.'

'It wasn't?'

Ursula paused again. Her eyes were full of misery and her voice shook as she resumed.

'I know I should have warned her – but there wasn't time. She grabbed the coffee cup and drained it, before I could say anything. Nothing happened right away so I felt relieved. But within half an hour, Heather was freaking out. She couldn't possibly have known what was happening to her: I guess she thought she was going crazy – or had stepped through a door right into hell. Dodie thought

250

she was just being hysterical. The others were looped. I was rigid with shock. I tried to stop her when she ran out of the room, but I wasn't strong enough. When I followed the elevator doors were already closing, and by the time I got down to the ground floor, she had disappeared. We never saw her again.'

Ursula's voice broke completely at this point and she covered her eyes with one hand. Matthew began to worry that his questioning had brought on a relapse and reached for the nurse's bell.

'No, don't ring,' said Ursula. 'I feel better getting it all out.'

'What was it Cubby gave to Heather?'

Ursula gulped, controlled her voice and went on with the story. 'I finally got the truth out of Cal. It was something he'd bought on the street as "angel dust". I don't know if you know much about street drugs. A lot of them are made in home labs by amateurs. This was some type of PCP but probably combined with something else. Drugs like that are called "designer drugs" and some of them are lethal. I did a lot of reading about it afterwards, and some of these concoctions can cause amnesia and psychosis.'

Matthew's face was grim.

'I know I should have reported it right away,' said Ursula as she saw his expression. 'But I was scared. I kept telling myself that she would turn up in a day or so. Then, if I'd told, I would have gotten into terrible trouble. I'd lose my scholarship. I'd have to go home to Wiarton and bang would go all my dreams of being the famous Ursula Hooper. We all talked it over and we agreed we'd never mention the drug trip. But it changed everything. Dodie was so horrified by the whole thing that she kept away from all of us after that. The rest of us felt that something ugly had come into our lives and it would never go away again. Except Cubby, I guess. Cubby never thought about much but Cubby.'

251

Matthew reached out and grasped Ursula's hand. 'It's been a long nightmare, but it's over now. You've faced up to it – and I'm afraid you're going to have to accept a lot of guilt and maybe a lot more pain – but at least it's not hidden away inside poisoning you bit by bit.'

She took her hand out of his and looked straight at him with those large, incongruously beautiful, brown eyes. 'And what about Heather's nightmare?' she asked. 'Is that over?'

Matthew thought for a moment about all the things that might have happened to Heather after she left Cubby's hotel room. 'I don't know,' he confessed, 'but whatever happened to her, I don't think she would have wanted to destroy all of you.'

A nurse came bustling in carrying a tray of medication. 'Time's up,' she said. 'I have to see that this young lady gets some rest.'

'Goodbye, Mr Prior,' said Ursula, 'and thank you.'

Matthew's plane landed at Heathrow at seven-fifteen in the morning. By the time he had disembarked, passed through the passport check, collected his luggage and cleared customs, it was past eight o'clock. He had sent telegrams the night before to Henrietta, Nell and Dorothy to let them know his arrival time. Whichever one came to meet him would be the one who cared most, he told himself, and he would deposit the tired remains of his life in her keeping. What would happen if all three turned up he refused to consider, but probably it would be nothing worse than a tense communal breakfast in the airport cafeteria.

He came out into the arrivals area and looked around. There were large groups of Japanese following leaders with tiny flags; there were African tribesmen with C&A overcoats over their robes; there were Arabs, Scandinavians, Mediterraneans, and a few tired British businessmen in

252

drip-dry suits, but there were no welcoming arms for him. He walked over to the message centre and there – under the 'P' – were three notes for him. One said Mrs Prior welcomed him back but one of the children had mumps and she couldn't meet him. He had an immediate qualm about the effect of mumps on male testicles and hoped it was Sofia who had them and not Bryn. The second note said that it was about time he got back but sorry, darling, Nell was on location for a film. The third said how were the Reichenbach Falls and too bad but Dorothy had to be at a police conference in Birmingham.

Feeling bereft and unwanted, he began to lug his bags towards the entrance to the Piccadilly underground line. Then he heard hurrying footsteps behind him.

'Hold on, Dad. I'll take one of those.'

He stopped and turned. It was Bryn: fifteen years old, floppy-haired, smiling and totally mump-free. Oh, Lord, now he felt guilty about wishing them on Sofia.

Bryn came up, hugged him and grabbed the largest bag, hefting it easily. 'Have a good trip?'

'Like the curate's egg.'

Bryn laughed. 'Well, I hope the bad parts weren't too bad.'

As he turned his head, he caught a glimpse of something flashing on Bryn's ear.

'Bryn, is that a— Is that a—?'

'What?'

'Earring?'

Bryn fingered it offhandedly.

'What, this? Yeah.'

'What the hell for?'

Bryn grinned. 'Oh, this is just the beginning. Tomorrow I'm getting the makeup and the dress.'

'Bryn!'

'Oh, come on, Dad. All the blokes are wearing them.

253

In the left ear, notice – just in case you think I've turned queer.'

'Ha, ha,' said Matthew mirthlessly.

They made it down to the underground platform and caught a train just as the doors were about to close. The few green belts of Middlesex that were still left slid past the dusty windows while Bryn and Matthew sat and contemplated one another with curiosity and affection. Matthew lit a cigarette and then put it out again with a curse when Bryn jerked his thumb towards the 'No Smoking' sign.

'You coming back to stay with us?' Bryn asked.

Matthew wished even more that he had a cigarette so he could hide behind a cloud of smoke.

'No fear,' he joked weakly. 'Mumps are a serious matter to a man of my age.'

Bryn sighed.

'Tell me, Bryn: how is Sofia?'

'Oh, she's getting over them, but she won't look in a mirror yet. Getting vain, that girl.'

'Bryn, if someone did something really bad to Sofia, what would you do?'

'Something bad like what?'

'Oh, like turning her on to drugs . . . or . . . or . . .'

'Or getting her pregnant and running off?'

'That kind of thing.'

'I'd probably kill the bastard.'

'Oh, Lord,' said Matthew. 'Maybe I'd better come home for a while.'


Two months later, after Henrietta had thrown him out again, Matthew got a letter in the mail postmarked 'Mapleville, Ont.' Inside was a handsome engraved invitation to the wedding of Mr Fraser Archibald McCullough and Miss Flora Catriona Dundee at St Andrew's Presbyterian Church in Toronto. With it was a note:

Dear Matthew,

Fraser and I think about you a lot and hope you're happily settled with H., N. or D. Roger and Alison send their regards and say they will see you in London on R.'s next sabbatical. The best news of all comes last! Heather is back! She turned up in a psychiatric hospital in New Mexico; she had been in some kind of mental fugue ever since that horrible New York weekend, and has only recently begun to recover her memory. Fraser, of course, is overjoyed and though Heather isn't quite well yet, at least she's home. So far, we haven't dared tell her about Ken; we've said he's in Europe for a year. How dreadful, Matthew, that it was all for nothing – all those poor souls.

Bless you, and let's keep in touch,

Bonny

(Fiona Catriona Dundee)

P.S. Guess who the happiest man in the world is now – apart from Fraser, of course. It's Dean Ripper. The government got booted out at the last election and Hugh Kirkwood lost his seat. The new Minister of Colleges and Universities – who just happens to be an old buddy of the Dean's from his sixties radical period – has just announced a special physical plant appropriation for Wacousta. They start building the new fine arts complex extension this summer.